MAMEY

MAMEY

a Spanglish novel

ANNY CABA

Para mi mamá Yomaris,
Abuela Pura y Tía Seneida

For all the Dominicans who are
siempre speaking Spanglish

Published by Anny Caba, Rahway, New Jersey, 07065
Printed in the USA

Names: Caba, Anny, author
Title: Mamey: a Spanglish novel
Description: First Edition
Library of Congress Control Number: 2025910347
ISBN: 9798992796902 (hardcover) | 9798992796919 (paperback)
        9798992796933 (ebook)
Subjects: Novel

Cover art: Pegge Hopper, *Okapaka*. 1989, Hawai'i.
Cover design and typeset by Anny Caba | AnnyCaba.com
This book was typeset in Lato, Times New Roman, & Signatra by Fontdation

"Here I am chewing English and spitting Spanish."

-Josefina Báez

Vega Family Tree

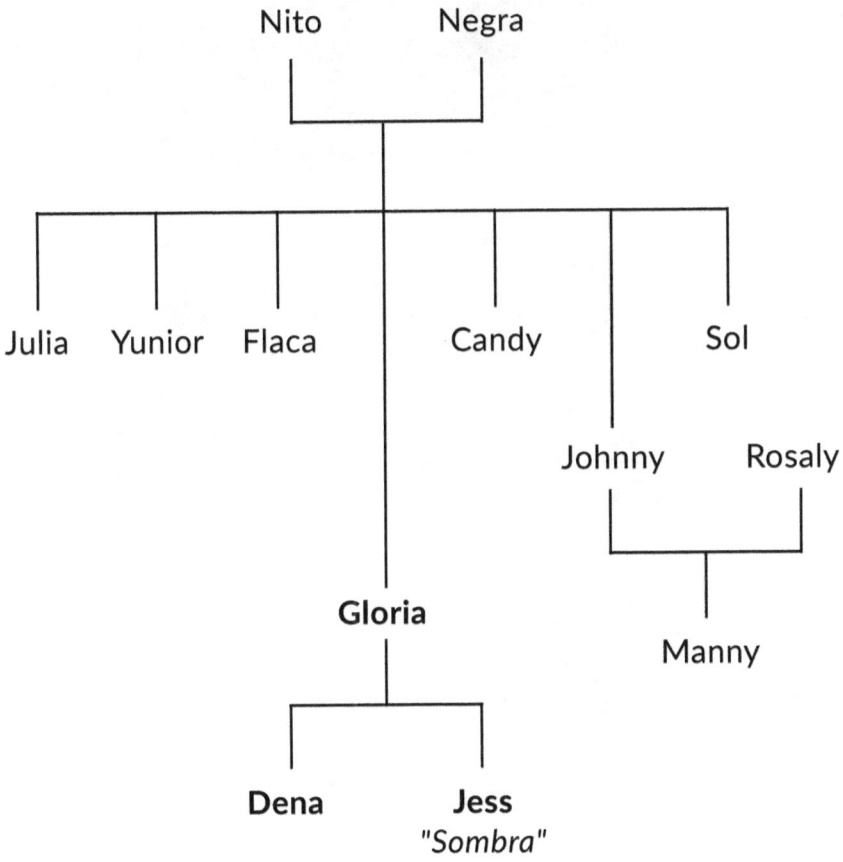

One Week Before

Dena

"Dos pastelitos y un café." Dena reached into the bottom of her bag for her wallet. One look inside y no había nada ahí. She looked up at Berto weakly.

"Está bien mija, pa la próxima," he winked.

Gracia' a dio', she thought. Between prepping her presentation for work and rushing to go see her mother, she had forgotten to withdraw cash at an ATM.

"Un día de e'to, debes comprar una máquina y cobrar con tarjeta," she suggested to the older street vendor.

"¿Y yo voy a saber usar una de esa' máquina'? Yo no sé na de eso. Mira, ya tá tu café con un chín de leche y una cuchara de azúcar." He passed her the cup with his brown speckled hand. "Y los pastelitos," he handed her one in a brown paper bag and the other wrapped in a greasy napkin. After thirty years in this country and befriending everyone on the block, Berto supo con una mirada when someone needed a pastelito to go and when they needed one inmediatamente. Dena took a bite of the crispy pastelito. El queso amarillo y el queso de freír had melted together. The cool afternoon air congealed them as one. Every bite contained the perfect combination of both.

"Gracias." Dena had known Berto since she was a little girl tagging along on her mother's diligencias. Every morning, except on Sundays, Berto woke up at 5 a.m. to drop pastelitos into a three-inch pool of canola oil one by one and watch as they floated up and browned like girls en la playa en RD.

"Y tu mamá, ¿como tá?"

Her mother, Gloria, would always stop by, place one hand on her hip and the other on his stand, and burst out with "¿Y tú?" She liked to start conversations with an "and," as if to pick back up where she left off. "Aquí, pero siempre e'toy aquí. Ere' tú la que tá perdida," he would tease. "¿Y la hija? ¿La mujer? ¿La finca?" Gloria always asked. He would respond casually at first. But after another round of questioning, he'd spill his problems out like melted cheese stretching on and on. Gloria loved it. She was the type to tell you with one bellowing "¡Oye!" exactly what you were doing wrong and how to fix it. It was never easy. She didn't care. She would tuck a loose strand of hair behind her ear, smile, and wave goodbye victoriously.

"¿Está tranquila?" Berto asked Dena again. He spoke gently as everyone in the neighborhood did when talking to a child about a dying parent.

"Sí, más o menos. Hablando mucho con los enfermeros. Tú sabes." Dena was sure every nurse her mother ever had was frightened of her.

"Que bueno. Me alegro. Mándale saludos a la vieja." He immediately regretted his last word. "¡Ay! No le digas que la llamé vieja," he laughed nervously while patting Dena's arm. She nodded, knowing her mother would have smacked his shoulder and snapped back with a "¡¿A quién tú ta llamando vieja?! Yo soy más joven que tú, ¡gordo!" Adding an insult just to spite him.

"Sí, se lo digo. Bueno, me tengo que ir. ¡Muchas gracias!" She power walked down the street, taking bites of her pastelito along the way.

Dena was tall and curvy, and as much as she tried, she could never quite tiptoe into a room. By her third step into her childhood home, she saw her mother glaring at her from across the room. Her ankle boots clacked a little too loudly on the linoleum floor, announcing her arrival. Meanwhile, Gloria remained as vigilant as possible despite the morphine dripping down, flowing through her bloodstream.

Dena approached slowly, refusing to touch anything. Even the furniture seemed fragile beneath the eerie lull of the heart monitor. The worn bedsheets were thin enough to expose Gloria's bony limbs underneath. The fabric pilled along the edges from overwashing. Permanent stains painted them abstractly. She could vaguely make out folds of surplus skin where there used to be harmonious curves and caramel creases. But the vacant figure, full of chemicals, wasn't her mother—it was a hollowed-out version of her.

"¡Ay, mija!" Tía Candy came in from the kitchen, startled by her niece's presence. Her arms stretched out wide for a hug. Wobbly fat hung from her wingspan.

"Cion, Tía," Dena said faintly. She had overheard her aunt on the phone in the kitchen a second ago saying "Sí, grave. Muy grave…"

"Dios te bendiga," replied Tía Candy, kissing her cheek and leaving half an orange lip print on her foundation. Despite the dire circumstances, Tía Candy always wore a full face. Tending to her appearance kept her grounded.

"Hey." Jess came in behind their tía and nodded in her sister's direction. As the first official New Yorker in the Vega family, Jess typically avoided hugs and kisses. She settled in a dark corner across the room and started scrolling on her phone. Although her face was tilted down towards the screen, her body was always facing their mother in constant anticipation.

Two months prior, Gloria had been hooked up to machines at the Columbia University Irving Medical Center uptown. It was the riverside view she always wanted, along with never-ending staff. "Viviendo como una rica," she announced when she first arrived. Later on, she fought with every ounce of energy she had left—which wasn't much—to return home. The hospital was too sterile. They spent too much time telling her what to eat and when. She missed the cracked crown moldings, the loud city streets, and the footsteps of la vecina upstairs, which used to drive her crazy but now comforted her like pattering rain on a thin tin roof.

"She so better now, pero esta mañana 'taba bien mala, mija. No good." Tía Candy shook her head, though her short, Kool-Aid red hair remained perfectly still from all the hairspray. "Ven a hablar con ella. She miss you too much." Candy sometimes spoke English when she was in distress, as if a shared language was the missing link that bridged their pain.

"Tía, pero estuve aquí antes de ayer."

"Yo sé y yo sé que tú ta busy." Candy's overly blushed cheeks turned a deeper shade of red. She hated being pushy. "Vete. Ella quiere hablar contigo. Quien sabe cuanto tiempo le queda," she nearly whispered, hoping Gloria wouldn't hear her and wilt away right before their eyes.

Tía Candy's fake designer bag sat slumped on the couch, overflowing with old lotto tickets, miscellaneous receipts, a pill bottle stuffed with twelve kinds of over-the-counter medications, three lipsticks, two shirts, and zero pants. She simultaneously over and under packed for her overnight stay. Dena could tell her aunt was more anxious than usual, as she mumbled to herself, "Tanta cosa que hacer," over and over again. Dena knew better than to tell her tía to relax. It would only make her hands twitch and her feet pace, eagerly looking for something to do.

"Hi, Mami." Dena spoke to her mother now, half expecting another *"Ay, mija,"* only this time in Gloria's loud, croaking voice. But her eyes, glazed over and empty, stared back vacantly. They had sunken into her face months ago, deepening the dark circles around them. Today, they were even more distant than usual.

Gloria's face had aged about twenty years in the last two. It had been so full and round before. Now it was covered in fine lines. Her thick brown hair—which she used to blow dry straight every week for thirty years—grew in scraggly patches. Its texture had evolved to that of a broom in the campo made from dried fallen twigs. Her hands quivered at her sides. In stark contrast, her nails were coated in cobalt blue. Tía Candy painted them in an effort to keep her mind distracted from looming death. She was convinced that color and small acts of kindness could keep her sister conscious.

"They put her on extra painkillers today," Jess said, as if she knew what her sister was thinking. Dena was slightly upset that she left work early for zero response, though she would never say it. She worked as a data analyst at a marketing agency downtown. Her boss loved having important, unannounced meetings at the end of the day. Dena always felt she had to work twice as hard to be taken seriously in corporate. The memory of getting made fun of for having a thick Spanish accent as a child still haunted her. It pushed her to perfect her speech, to fight for the highest grades in every class, and, eventually, change the pronunciation of her name to "Dina" in English. Not that her family cared. They all refused to wrap their tongues around her new identity. To them, she would forever be "Deh-na."

"They said you're doing better now than this morning," Dena said, extending her hand to touch her mother's arm. She knew the basics at this point, the dos and don'ts of dealing with a sick Gloria. She was too prideful to be babied and too social for distance. They could ask about her day, but not how she felt directly. Otherwise, she would respond, *"¿Como me veo?"* It was a mix of playful banter and bits of rage flushing out of her system. She could tolerate a hand placed onto her arm or leg, but not for long, or she would spit out an *"Ustede' si joden."* Two years of doctor's visits, X-rays, CT scans, bloodwork, enemas, two juicers (the result of a video online that convinced Candy natural remedies would provide the cure), good news, bad news, and worse news. And Gloria was still saying, *"Todavía no me he muerto,"* as if she was winning, as if her sinking chest, fallen hair, and weakening grip were merely battle scars.

"¿Quieres beber algo?" Dena scanned her mother's face for an unspoken answer. Gloria slightly squinted, deepening the creases around her eyes. "Está lejo'," tío Yunior liked to say, as if she were exploring some other world because this one was too painful.

"¿Quieres algo?" Once more, Dena was met with silence. At this point, Gloria would have made a rude comment about her chosen shade of lipstick. *"Eeeese te pusiste, ¿cuando tienes taaantos?"* Dragging her vowels, mockingly. Dena could always tell how well or poorly Gloria was doing based on which body part she picked apart. Her weight was always an easy target, especially since she had put on a few pounds recently. Noticing lipstick, however, took energy and focus. The same was true of food: if Gloria ate, it was a good day. If she complained about the seasoning, it was an even better one.

"She's been refusing to eat." Jess had been watching the interaction from across the room, half expecting Dena's arrival to stir their mother up despite the painkillers.

"So she hasn't eaten at all today? It's 3 p.m." Dena had almost forgotten her sister was there, curled up in a dark corner. Jess's childhood nickname in DR was "Sombra," resulting from her shy disposition and habit of lurking in the shadows. Although it had been years since Dena had heard the name spoken out loud, she remembered it now as her sister looked up from her phone.

"We tried, but she wouldn't even open her mouth. She hasn't eaten in almost three days," Jess said before returning to her screen. Dena knew this disease would steal her mother's energy, time, and patience, but the saddest thing to watch was the deterioration of her once full body. She lost nearly half of her weight and all of it from her favorite places. Now, her appetite was gone too. The woman who once picked things off of other people's plates while they were still eating was swatting food away before she even knew the menu.

"Well, has she at least had water today?"

"She just kept mumbling 'desabrido'." Now, *that* sounded like their mother. She didn't want water, only jugo, refresco, una fría—hasta Brugal. ¿Pero agua? No. Dena smiled slightly, imagining her mother scowling at a nurse trying to convince her to hydrate. She recalled watching a home aid change an IV from blood to saline, and Gloria turning to her just to say, *"Coño, me quitan una y me ponen otra. ¿Cuanta' cosa' que me tienen que dar?"* She used her limited energy para darle un boche a la enfermera, quejándose de the people and modern medicine keeping her alive.

"How are you?" Dena asked her sister, whose eyes were also prone to wandering these days.

"I'm okay. I'm just tired." Jess sat hunched over in her chair, waiting for their mother to make a move, a request, or any sound requiring her immediate attention.

"Have you eaten?"

"Yeah, I had some bread this morning." Jess was swimming in an oversized black hoodie and dark gray sweatpants. Of the three—mother and daughters—Jess was the skinniest. Though not at the same rate as their mother, she was declining alongside her: her limbs slimmed down, her black hair looked less full, her cuticles bled more frequently as she constantly picked at them. Secondhand symptoms.

Suddenly, the door buzzer rang. El padre from the church down the street was patiently waiting outside. Candy invited him over earlier in the day.

"Vamos a rezar," Candy announced when he came in, motioning everyone to Gloria's bedside. The only thing that could actually calm Candy was standing still in prayer. They all closed their eyes except for Dena, who wasn't in the mood to participate in pseudo-Catholicism today. As the group echoed el padre's words, she stared at her mother. Gloria turned her eyes up to meet hers. Dena imagined her voice beneath the silent stare. *"Cierra tus ojos para rezar, muchacha 'el diablo."* She obliged.

As soon as she did, however, she heard Gloria's breathing turn into gurgling. The home aid rushed in, the electronics beeped loudly, and everyone's heartbeats quickened except for the one that slowed down. A wave of chaos, noise, and panic swept through the room. They managed to return Gloria's heart rate to normal, but it left everyone else uneasy. Dena stayed for another half an hour before politely excusing herself from all the frenzy.

Outside, Dena slid her sunglasses on and pushed her earbuds into her ears. Only viejitas wouldn't notice them and consider talking to her. Fortunately, they were never out in the afternoon entre todo ese rebolu. They were home in their batas watching las noticias de la tarde.

She watched her hood in slow motion. A pack of teenagers gathered on a nearby stoop, avoiding going home the way she used to years earlier. Street vendors packed up their carts and tables. Dudes lingered outside barbershops. Women picked up groceries. Girls giggled in packs. As she stood on a corner waiting for the light to turn, a kid swerved his BMX bike around her. It was far too small for him, but essential for the wheelie he popped afterward. No matter how terrible her day was, The Heights always reminded her that there were a million other stories at play, distracting her, if only momentarily. For this reason, she never left, even after moving out of her mother's home years ago, working downtown, and earning enough to live elsewhere.

The street sounds were muffled within the thick walls of her apartment. She set her bag down, changed into her fluffy house slippers, and reheated old takeout from the fridge. Outside her window, she could see bright green sprouting on the trees and in the cracks in the sidewalk. Although summer was not yet in full swing, she was hot and sticky like a half melted popsicle from the bodega. She took a long shower to wash off the stress of the day and followed it with her five-step skincare routine.

As she rubbed overpriced serums on her soft skin, across her round cheeks, and into her dark circles, she saw fragments of her mother—the old Gloria—staring back. It was in her arched eyebrows, espresso-colored eyes, and full lips. She had the same café con leche complexion that made her glow even in the depths of winter. And the same baby hairs that framed her face in a heart shape. Gloria passed along the habit of straightening her hair and keeping it in a tight bun when it was dirty. She taught her to always carry lipstick in her bag and how to apply it without a mirror. She reminded her that there was beauty in her marks and curves. But Gloria's once full face had sunken in, her features exaggerated by deep shadows. Her skin had ashy blue undertones instead of the long-held golden hues.

The problem wasn't that her mother was going to die. No, that was inevitable. She knew Gloria was sick, the unmanageable weight of it, the coughing heartbeat she visited four times a week just to make sure it was still there thumping. It was the drama she couldn't handle. The "come or else" sense of impending doom. But that's just the way la familia Vega was. Even if it had been the flu and not the poison that is cancer, they would have called daily to recap every moment in explicit detail: the rise and fall of her temperature like a stock tracked hourly, the color and volume of her released bodily fluids, the age and race of every nurse who went into the room. A whole novela.

A stream of sunlight poured in through Dena's window. The sun was receding across the Hudson, turning the river a deep orange color. It reminded her of the last summer she spent with her parents in DR together, thirteen years ago. She and Jess begged them to go to the beach every day of their month-long trip. But they claimed there were too many diligencias que hacer, which they believed was code for not wanting to do anything, thereby pretending there was too much that needed to be done.

Finally, the day before returning home, Gloria gave in. A few tíos, tías, primos y la familia de un amigo joined them. Coolers, thick plastic totes, and car trunks were packed as tightly as possible. Dena was ecstatic until she was sandwiched in a narrow back seat with four other people. Her parents wouldn't let her sit in Tío Johnny's pickup bed because they claimed the ride was too bumpy. They wouldn't open the windows because her mother refused to sit *"en un carro sin aire."* She spent the ride trapped and angry, imagining she could feel the breeze outside.

At the beach, she ran in first. Slowly, or maybe all at once, sand found its way into all her crevices, pouring out every time she scratched her head. Salt water burned her eyes. The sun branded her skin. The only time she got out was to eat tostones y pescado frito, then wait the obligatory 30 minutes before Gloria gave a nod of approval for reentry. In the afternoon, after hours of sunbathing and salt water rinses, her mother announced it was time to go home with the threat of "Que se muevan rápido o no regresaremos." But the sun was setting, and Dena was upset they would leave before the best part.

"Quédate a vivir aquí si quieres, pero yo me voy," shouted Gloria loudly enough that Dena could hear from inside the water, thirty feet away. If it wasn't for Dena's father, Gloria would have driven off and made her think she wasn't coming back just to teach her quién mandaba.

Dena wished she could have stayed beneath the orange-colored sky that swept through just before nightfall. In the car, she commented, "Que lindo está el cielo así de naranja."

"¿Pero quién dice 'naranja'?" Her mother scoffed back. "Eso es *mamey*."

Dena couldn't tell the difference, but she knew better than to talk back.

She thought about her mother's living room now, full of miscellaneous afternoon guests from the neighborhood. She wondered if the same copper light in her apartment was pooling on the haystack of wires by Gloria's bed. Probably not. Gloria had probably asked them to pull down the shades. The setting sun was usually too bright for her. Even in a fully temperature-controlled room, she would say, *"Me estoy quemando con tanta luz."*

2023

Gloria

"Siete dólare'. ¿Tú puede' creer eso?" Gloria turned to Candy and frowned.

"Dios mío, un robo." Her younger sister nodded in agreement. They went back and forth about the cost of the mundane fruit as Gloria went into her knife drawer and pulled out the longest, sharpest knife, one that most people reserved for meat but she used to cut into her overpriced pineapples.

"Mami, claro que eso cuesta tanto. Eso no es de aquí. Tienen que pagar impuestos y… "

"¿Que impue'to' ni impue'to'? Eso e ahora que tá así. Yo compré una piña el otro día por la mitad de ese precio. Hummm." Gloria cut her daughter off and then into the fruit. Dena rolled her eyes. Of course, that was not true, but she didn't care to argue. Instead, she attempted to refocus the conversation on why they had come in the first place.

"Entonces, ¿que te dijo los doctores?" For weeks, Dena and Jess had been telling their mother to go to the doctor. It was not like her to avoid a professional opinion. In fact, she swore by them. More than once, Gloria called them while lying on a doctor's table, eager to share innocuous news. For the last few days, however, she had been strangely secretive about her latest appointment.

"Fuiste, ¿verdad?" Jess asked, leaning against the door frame. There was not enough space in the kitchen for all four women. Dena and Candy sat on the only two chairs that fit inside, while Gloria maneuvered around them. Their placements were second nature after nearly thirty years of shuffling around in the same home.

Three decades saw a lot of change inside their apartment but none in its dimensions: the paint layers on the walls had thickened and bubbled like overcooked farina, the floor tiles grayed over time, and the curtains became more whimsical as Gloria went through longer bouts of boredom. The one kitchen window faced the back of another brick building and rarely let light into the room, though that didn't stop Gloria from growing a few unruly plants on the ledge. The straggly malamadre plant grew especially long. It had over a hundred babies dangling off its thin, green branches. Every time a visitor came over, she insisted they take one home. Taking one was like accepting her advice: a tedious task.

"Esa piña no sirve pa na." Candy shot Gloria a sour look as she peeked into the fruit. The girls watched a piece of skin fall sideways from the blade, revealing a brown, mushy interior. Jess sucked her teeth in disappointment. She was hoping this would be her dinner.

"Maldita fruta vieja. No se preocupen; corto la cáscara y hago un té," Gloria said proudly, waving her knife in the air as she spoke. "¡Nada se gasta aquí!" It was true. Nothing in her household was wasted: old banana peels were placed on foreheads to cure headaches, coffee grounds into potted plants for added nutrients, even old milk could be revived into an arroz con dulce with enough sugar and heat. Conquering spoiled milk is a true talent of the poor.

"The doctor?" Dena tried to get her mother to concentrate

as she finished slicing around the fruit and threw the peels into a large metal pot.

"Entonces, fui al doctor. Hablé con ellos. Ustedes saben que yo he tenido un dolor aquí." She pointed to her lower abdomen. The women nodded in unison. "Me hicieron varios estudios. Tú sabe'…" She paused as Candy gave her another sour look. "Diablo, tres semanas duré en eso. Fui pa'ca, fui pa'lla." She began pouring a gallon of water into the pot. It was bottled spring water, as she refused to drink what she considered the "nasty" New York tap

"Okay, ¿pero qué te dijeron?" Dena asked a little more impatiently.

"Cuantas cosas, Dios mío. Porque ellos querían revisar todo y asegurarse." Gloria finished chopping the rest of the fruit, attempting to salvage the sweet, saturated bits. She took a bite and tried to mask her disappointment as she passed a plate of the medio pudrido piña around.

"Mami, ¿que te dijeron?" Jess asked, now just as impatient as her sister. Gloria had a tendency to drag a story, usually for a punchline. This story didn't seem as funny.

"Bueno. Entonces…después de todo eso, parece que encontraron algo."

"Ay, ¿y que fue?" Asked Candy, gently pushing the plate of rotten fruit away.

"Dijeron que es cáncer."

"¿¡Que!? Pero, ¿¡cáncer cáncer!?" Candy didn't understand her sister's calm demeanor.

"¿Y qué otro tipo de 'cáncer' hay?" Gloria, annoyed, went back to her tea. She added cloves, anise, and a couple of cinnamon sticks that she broke down with the back of her knife.

"Cancer?! For how long? What else did they say? Why are you so calm right now?!" Jess, usually the quietest person in every room, was bursting with questions.

"Ajá, ¿y qué tú quieres? ¿Que me vuelva loca y me muera

temprano?" Gloria snapped back, before adding honey to the pot.

"Ya. No tanto," said Dena, watching her mother generously pour the honey.

"Tú sabe' que la miel de e'te país no sabe a na," she said, holding the bottle in a fully vertical position, squeezing it tightly. Gloria famously over-sweetened everything she touched.

"Okay…¿entonces ahora que tienes que hacer? Do you need surgery? Do you need to take something?" Dena, recovering from initial shock, looked up. Unlike Jess, who avoided eye contact, she stared directly at their mother. Gloria accepted the challenge.

"Dicen que yo puedo hacer quimioterapia, pero yo no quiero eso." She turned back to stir her tea and cover the pot.

In Dena's mind, the only reason her mother went to the doctor was because a few weeks earlier, she refused to dance at a baby shower due to a "stomachache." An obvious lie. There was no way that would slow down Gloria. Meanwhile, the said pain did not prevent her from consuming an entire plate of food and taking another one sealed with aluminum foil back home. They argued with her for weeks until she finally agreed to go.

"What? Mami, you don't know what you need. The doctor does." Dena stood up, frustrated.

"No me hables así en mi casa." Gloria swung a large metal spoon in her daughter's face. Candy, who didn't believe in violence, lifted her arms to separate them. It was a mild attempt to intervene in a house where she had little authority.

"Pero, claro que tienes que hacer lo que te piden." Candy avoided saying cáncer, as if the word itself would dispense toxins into her own body. She grabbed her niece's arm and pulled her back to her seat, then looked back at Gloria, anticipating a more reasonable response.

"No, yo no. Yo no soy tan estúpida, no. Yo sé lo que hace eso. Yo lo he visto en otra gente." She shook her head back and forth as she spoke. "¿Y de'pué' qué? Voy a tener que estar aco'tada en una cama el día entero, dependiente de otra gente. No. Mejor me muero." She turned her back on them and waited for her tea to boil.

Dena and Jess looked at each other in complete disbelief. It was out of character for their mother to argue with anyone in a white coat. When they were kids, a doctor told Gloria that apples and pears would give her children diarrhea, so she didn't let them have any for five years. Suddenly, she was declining medical advice—her holy gospel. It was the equivalent of her riding down Riverside Drive on a tiguerito's scooter without a helmet on.

"Entonces, si no vas a hacer el chemo, ¿qué vas a hacer?" Candy asked softly, knowing her sister never conceded when cornered.

Of course, Gloria knew for a while that something was wrong. The pain had been creeping into her abdomen for months, years. She had trained herself to tolerate pain, dance with it, suppress it, but never confess to it. The doctor's appointment was not just to appease her children. It was time to face the demon growing in the pit of her belly.

"Dicen que tal vez con una cirugía se puede sacar todo. Yo no sé muy bien cómo funciona eso, pero con eso ya tá. Voy en un día. Me lo sacan y se resuelve todo." She turned the tea down to a simmer. The rest of the women exhaled as hope filtered back into the room.

For the next twenty minutes, her daughters pried into the details trying to fill in the infinite blanks that Gloria carefully left out of the story. How many doctors had she seen? Were they sure? What was the scale and stage of the problem? They asked until their mother se cansó de eso.

"Dejen de hablar de eso ya." She swatted the air in front of them with her metal spoon and turned around to look inside the pot. The water had browned and thickened like tanning oil. She pulled a wire mesh strainer from one of the cabinets and poured everyone a mug full of tea. She took a sip, her lips unfazed by the scalding liquid.

"Está demasiado amargo." She stirred in another spoonful of honey.

Six Days Before

Dena

Around three in the morning, as uptown lulled to a hum, Dena's phone vibrated by her side.

"Hello?"

"Dena…She's gone…" Jess whispered over the line.

"¡Nooooo! ¡Mi hermana querida!" Tía Candy's jarring cry rang in the background of the call.

"Okay, I'll be there soon." Dena hung up and let out a short breath, fearing if she breathed too deeply her mouth would open wide and remain unhinged. Her shoulders fell back into her comforter, her chest began to tighten. She counted to three and forced herself up to turn on the lights. A checklist of things to do unfurl in her mind. She grabbed a manila folder filled with contacts and funeral info, then threw on a jacket, leggings, and sneakers. She paused to look at herself in the mirror.

"Yo no ando con gente fea," Gloria's voice reminded her. Her eyes began to swell. She wiped away the emerging tears before they flooded her apartment and carried her away.

Dena stood outside her mother's building and hesitated going in. The sky above was tar-black due to the new moon and air pollution. Her mother's living room light was the brightest thing in sight. A couple of silhouettes walked beyond the curtains so the windows had a faux flicker. Upstairs, she took one step into the doorway but couldn't get herself to move any closer.

"No seas cobarde." The lifeless body taunted.

Her eyes scanned the room. Tía Candy's head was down. Two neighbors were consoling her. Jess was calling Tío Yunior, the oldest Vega brother, who assured her he was on his way from New Jersey. Dena tiptoed towards her sister and hugged her tightly. Jess handed her a scribbled, tear-stained list that she managed to wring from Tía Candy's hands. It said who had been called and who was left. In the kitchen, Dena worked her way down the list. Most people picked up, assuring her they would relay the message to someone else, creating an endless phone chain. By dawn, everyone in the tri-state area and DR who knew Gloria would know what had happened through phone call or WhatsApp message. Within a week, even those who only knew her in passing would know, too.

For months, Dena had collected information: funeral homes, transportation services, and the names of important contacts. It was equal parts duty and guilt. She felt it was the best way she could contribute, considering she hated care-taking. The mere thought of wiping down her mother made her cringe, not to mention the sly remarks Gloria made every time she inevitably did something wrong. The truth was Tía Candy and Jess were better suited for those things: the intimate, insidiously dirty things. Candy had been a caretaker in New York for twenty years and Jess worked as a hairstylist, constantly tending to other people's needs. Dena was more akin to filing paperwork and making calls. Within an hour and a half, she sorted the funeral, flights, and finances.

Gloria was adamant that she be buried "en su propia tierra." The only reason she didn't die there too was because she didn't have any health insurance on the island. She wanted pills that made her float, not choke on water as she crossed the sacred river. Most Dominicans do a velorio in The Heights before sending their loved ones overseas. Not Gloria. She insisted que "No van a durar un mes en eso. Me entierren de una vez y salgan de eso." She was to be shipped home and buried as soon as the next flight would allow. Even after death, her rigid demands kept her family in line.

Once the body cleared customs, Tía Julia, the oldest Vega sibling, would have a velorio set up and waiting by Abuela's house. Candy, Jess, and Gloria would fly to Santiago in two days. The funeral home assured Dena the body would be embalmed and processed by then. After landing, Tío Johnny, the youngest Vega brother, would pick them up. Three days later, the funeral home on the island would provide a private car to transport the body. Dena would arrive on that day, just in time for the funeral.

She claimed that her boss wouldn't give her enough days off. He was a middle-aged, middle manager who's stomping loafers always shook the doorway before he came into view. He appeared intimidating, but he was as kind as he was loud, always giving her grace since he lost his mother to the same disease. The truth was, Dena wanted to evade distant relatives as long as possible. Burying her head in work was easier than handholding the grieving.

At the wake, Sol would have 60 plastic seats arranged out front. Sol was the Vega family's second cousin and adopted hermana de crianza. She moved into the Vega household when her biological parents were overburdened by her ten siblings. Although they didn't share blood, she was the most loyal of the bunch, handling everything on the island that the rest couldn't do from the States. Together with Julia and Johnny, Sol would sort the food, drinks, and bouquets.

"Cuídate, mija, y descansa," Sol urged Dena over the line just before hanging up.

When Dena stepped back into the living room, another dozen people were crowded in the apartment. A handful were curious neighbors from the building who heard Candy crying through the walls. A few were from around the neighborhood, including Berto, who would skip his morning shift in honor of his old friend. Tío Yunior had arrived with his wife, Tía Yoselin, and their two daughters. His son was away at college doing an engineering program. He sent his condolences. Candy's two teenage sons stood to the side, their father sandwiched between them, unsure how to console her. Yoselin went to Candy's side instead. After more than two decades of marriage, they were sisters too.

When the two morgue employees arrived, Jess realized first. She ran over and fell into her mother's lap, making muffled sounds through tears. Tía Candy ran to her side and held her. Their cries got louder as the morgue workers moved closer. Even though they were the two most petite women in the family, their cries filled the room. They wanted to expose their wounds until their throats scabbed over, a desahogarse de todo el dolor.

Dena tried to console them, holding one hand to each of their backs, but it only made them sob louder. She looked at Tía Yoselin and then back at them as if to say, *"Ayuda."* Yoselin whispered something in their ears that brought their wails down to a hum.

"Mi mamá" and "mi hermana" echoed in the small apartment, layered beneath the sound of chatter, footsteps, and moving wires.

Tío Yunior and his family were the last to leave. Dena closed the door behind them, careful not to let it slam. She walked around the living room and softly blew out all the candles the guests had brought. She pulled the stained sheets off the bed and threw them in a hamper. Finally, she looked around for Sombra and found her little sister sitting in a dark corner of her bedroom, just as her nickname suggested.

Years ago, when Dena moved out, Jess made it her own by replacing their two twin beds with a larger queen, hanging her artwork on the walls, and stringing fairy lights above her headboard. Lately, its charm had been erased by clothes thrown around, art supplies locked in their boxes, and blackout curtains that remained closed throughout the day. It looked unrecognizable to Dena now, nothing like their vibrant childhood bedroom full of CDs, posters, and shared sneakers they bought to match every outfit imaginable. It was as if the color and life had been sucked out of the apartment, out of their lives.

"Jess, where's your suitcase?" Dena asked softly while walking around piles of clothes. Jess pointed to the floor of her closet. Dena opened it up and started collecting whatever she thought Jess might need, smelling each item to ensure it was clean, and folding them into neat piles.

"Dena..." Jess sighed deeply, expanding her cheeks. Although Jess was thin with small features, all the recent crying made her perpetually puffy.

"Mhmmm." Dena continued to fill the suitcase, determined to finish before the sun rose and declared a new day.

"I can't..." she spoke quieter than before.

"You can," Dena responded.

"No, I can't..." She insisted. Dena sat beside her and held her little sister in her arms. Jess broke down crying and didn't say another word for a couple of minutes.

"It's okay. I know this sucks, but everything is taken care of," Dena rocked her gently. "We just have to go, do la novena, and everything will be okay...Okay?" She held her own tears back as Jess cried into her shoulder, soaking her tank top. "You used to love going to Abuela's house. Think about it that way:

23

a trip to Abuela's." Dena could feel her sister's lips curve into a tiny smile on her shoulder. Jess looked up at her, realizing she had yet to cry. Just as she was about to ask her how she was, Dena stood up and headed towards the kitchen. Jess shuffled behind, dragging her chancletas across the floor. Dena poured two bowls of cereal with almond milk and placed a banana between them.

"You need to eat something." She pointed to the open chair, commanding her to sit. They munched through their bowls slowly, avoidantly swirling pieces around. Halfway through, the cereal was too soggy to enjoy. Dena dumped the rest, washed the dishes, finished packing, and pulled the curtains shut in the time it took Jess to crawl back into bed.

"It's okay. Everything's going to be okay." Dena brushed her sister's hair away from her damp cheeks and waited for a reply. When she didn't hear one, she knew Jess's sleep deprivation had caught up to her. Although she was already asleep, Dena tucked the sheets around her little sister, as she used to do when they were kids. For years, it was part of her nighttime ritual: tuck Jess in, then rest.

" 'Sana sana culito de rana, si no se sana hoy se sana mañana,' " Dena whispered under her breath. At age six, she convinced Jess the phrase had magical healing powers. It was the only thing that kept her little sister from bursting into tears after a minor cut or running to Gloria, which resulted in double the punishment for both of them. If Jess was okay, then she would be okay too. As she watched her sister sleep, Dena's eyes swelled again.

Back home, without any calls to make or plans to configure, Dena lay down in bed. She wiped her tears away as flashing images filled her mind.

She thought about the impending novena, the nine days dedicated to honoring the deceased through hour-long prayer sessions. She remembered the hora santas vaguely from her father's passing. For nine consecutive afternoons, she repeated prayers solemnly amongst a room full of women. It was a dreadfully boring and dutiful task. But obligation was the rule of order en la familia Vega: everyone did what they must, lest they be known as malcriada or malagradecida.

Then, there was the fact that she had not been to DR in ten years. If her reputation was built on action, Dena's performance for the night could win her an award. If it was based on compartiendo con la familia, she knew before the trip even began that she would disappoint everyone. She didn't hate spending time with them necessarily—their energy overwhelmed her.

Inevitably, another to-do list started forming in her mind. Instead of resting, she pulled herself out of bed to make a double espresso and send emails. It would be another few hours before she lay back down. Then, she could blame the espresso shots for always winding her up and eventually sending her crashing down.

2016

Gloria

"¡Buenos dias!" Gloria nearly sang as she cranked the metal blinds on the windows open.

Dena's eyes stung from the glaring light. She touched her phone to read the time: 8:06 a.m. "¡Ma! ¡Es demasiado temprano!"

"¡Nunca es temprano para limpiar!" Gloria shouted excitedly.

"Ugh! ¡Quiero dormir!" Dena pulled the thin sheet over her face. A groggy Jess turned over in her bed, accepting defeat.

"'Dormir'. ¡Ja!" Gloria's laugh echoed in the small room. "Los oficios se hacen temprano—¡no se dejan para mañana!" It was only their second day of vacation, and their mother was already putting them to work.

"Papi nunca me hubiera hecho esto," Dena mumbled beneath her sheets.

"¿Qué te dije a ti? ¡Dejas de hablar de tu papá!" Her mother smacked the bed beside her face before leaving the room. Sombra trailed behind.

"¡Te espero afuera!" Gloria yelled from the living room. "¡¿Me oíste?!"

"¡Sí!" Dena responded instantly. With every passing year after Antonio's death, Gloria grew more impatient. Dena expected her mother to relax without a partner to argue with. Instead, she used all of her stored energy on her daughters.

It took one marriage, two kids, and three different jobs for Gloria to settle into the monotony of her American life. The years were long and life in New York was stressful. The weather fell into extremes: too cold, too hot, too humid, and too windy. By the time Antonio passed, she found herself slipping into daily tasks like rainwater into the city sewers. Everything went well unless there was a sudden downpour; then chaos ensued.

But in DR, the sun was brighter, the food was fresher, and her daughters were forced to obey her every command. En su isla, they had even more rules, including no motorcycle rides, no talking to desconocidos, and no sighing for any reason. She enforced most of these by giving them endless chores. If their eyes and hands were busy, they wouldn't wander onto any boys. They never went to a resort, the beach, or even a nice restaurant. Their activities were limited to an exact one-block radius where she could control their every move.

Dena stepped into the kitchen and went straight for the coffee.

"She's gonna get mad," Jess said without looking up. She was in an extra-long T-shirt, crouching down and scrubbing the inside of the fridge. Gloria, sensing movement, immediately came in to give her eldest daughter a glaring side-eye.

"¿Y tú?"

"Ya voy. Solo quería beber café." Dena held the mug in her hand out as proof.

"Más te vale que solo vas por eso porque yo te llamé hace media hora a venir a comer." Gloria never let the girls sleep in, especially when she was courteous enough to cook breakfast early. Dena turned her back to roll her eyes discreetly, but Gloria sensed it anyway.

"Mira muchacha, debes de estar feliz que tienes a tu mamá aquí contigo. Malagradecida."

"Sí, Mami. Gracias por el desayuno." Dena sipped her coffee as slowly as possible.

"Date rápido que quiero terminar de limpiar temprano." Gloria looked at her threateningly.

Every year, Gloria sought refuge in DR for at least two to three weeks. Julia and Candy, who lived nearby in New York, often joined with their kids in tow. Yunior traveled home less frequently, claiming he was still recovering from two decades of picking fruit under a scorching sol caribeño.

When Mamá Negra, the family matriarch, got ill, her heavy body, swollen ankles, and crippling foot pain prevented her from working. Four of her kids, off in America, paid for her retirement. Sol and Flaca, the remaining sisters, became her full-time caretakers. After Negra passed, Flaca moved to Florida, leaving Johnny and Sol as the only siblings left en Campesito. On this day, three of Gloria's sisters and their kids were landing. She wanted to guarantee a clean house full of food for their arrival. When Gloria returned from buying groceries, she found her daughters sitting on the couch texting. "Ya, ¿terminaron?" She asked, suspicious of their speed.

"Sí, Mamí." Jess helped her mother carry the grocery bags inside. In the kitchen, Gloria pulled a worn cutting board from under the sink and placed the peppers on top.

"Vete a cortar." Gloria pointed her chin towards the board. "Y tú, ven a pelar estos guandules." She turned to Dena, who took the bowl begrudgingly, sensing that her mother had given her the most monotonous tasks on purpose. Gloria moved around them, collecting items from the grocery bags and pantry.

"Mira, tú ta lenta con eso." Gloria frowned at Dena's progress. Her daughter picked up her pace, hoping to rest sooner. "Ayuda a tu hermana," Gloria ordered Jess after she finished cutting the vegetables. She grabbed an olla from under the sink, placed it on the stove, turned the knob, and lit a match to start the fire. She began making white rice before taking out the meat she seasoned the previous day.

"Aprendan, mis hijas, para que consigan un marido."

"Ojalá él cocina y yo no," said Dena, who was daydreaming about hanging out with the kids from down the street. Gloria forbade them from going out, since most of the kids they grew up with every summer now had un marido o un hijo o "un actitud," according to her.

"¡Ja! Buena suerte con eso, mija. Hasta tu papá no pudo cocinar y duró quince año' viviendo conmigo," Gloria snapped back. "Espero que le' guste la comida," she said as if they had the freedom of opinions.

"Claro, Mami. Siempre está rico," Jess appeased Gloria's ego. When her daughters finished, Gloria placed the guandules in water to soak overnight.

"¿Ni son para hoy?" Dena asked, confused.

"Claro que no. Necesitan tiempo para ablandarse. Que tú crees, ¿qué es tan fácil?" Gloria was just as confused. Her daughters' ignorance never failed to surprise her. They reeked of unconscious privilege. She wished she could stick them on the island for a year para que aprendan lo que es pasar trabajo de verdad. Maybe then they might learn how to conjugate all their verbs correctly and the proper gender for every noun. Gloria learned basic English to navigate the U.S. but only spoke Spanish with the girls, hoping to raise them like true Dominicans. But it was never enough. No amount of sazón en polvo or rolling Rs could make them understand her childhood, her tierra, her life.

Julia, Flaca, Candy, and their kids spilled into the house as they finished cooking lunch. Tío Johnny, his wife , and their son Manny followed closely behind, as they all lived in town. The family ate chaotically: some people inside the house, some outside, and some standing waiting for a seat to open up. Gloria ordered her daughters to wait until everyone else served themselves to eat. Then, she ordered them to start cleaning before they were halfway through their plates. Usually, the tías helped out, but they were exhausted from traveling with kids and grateful for Gloria's girls que "siempre son tan obedientes."

"If we do everything she says, maybe we can convince her to let us out of the house later," Dena whispered to Jess as they washed dishes.

"Mira, puse el café. Cuando sube, sácalo y compártanlo. Después pongan otro. Y piquen lo' dulce' de coco que compré para que todo el mundo tenga un chín," Gloria instructed before returning to her sisters en la marquesina. She sat back and watched her sisters gab as they sipped their cafecitos.

"Entonces, ¿cómo está todo por allá?" Flaca asked her sisters, each rocking in a separate chair.

"Bien. Tú sabes." Julia gave a rundown of everything going on in New York, inserting the perfect amount of gossip for her sister to feel like she had been there herself.

"No me digas," Flaca gasped at each one of Julia's stories. She had refused to move north, claiming it was too cold for her thin bones. But she loved hearing the crazy chisme from the City, since most of the people who went from Campesito to America ended up there, including four of her siblings. She settled in Florida instead, where her husband's family had lived for years. There was always tension in her house in Florida, not unrelated to the fact that she missed her family deeply. But back home in DR, beside her sisters and best friends, Flaca was at ease.

La casa de la familia Vega had a gravity that pulled them all back no matter how far away they went. It had been twenty years since they all lived there together. In that time, the walls, furniture, and screaming children running around had changed, but the scent was permanent—irreplaceable. It was the smell of black dirt, soggy wood, bursting fruit, and blooming flowers. The sounds were the same too: shouting neighbors, revved up motors, and toads calling for each other at night.

"Mami, ¿podemos salir un rato ahorita?" Jess asked sheepishly. Gloria knew Dena put her up to it. They had finished distributing the coffee and cleaning up, but that did not mean they were free to run wild.

"Mira muchacha, ¿tú tá loca? Tu' primo' llegaron casi ahora. Mejor juega' con ello'," Gloria said loudly enough for Dena to hear from across the room. Jess returned to Dena, head sunk low in defeat.

At eighteen, Dena was the oldest cousin in the family. Most of them were in elementary or middle school while she was starting college in the fall. They wanted to play with dolls and toy cars, but she wanted to go out like she did with her friends in New York or, at the very least, run and stretch her limbs. Although she ran track in high school, her mother forbade her from running in DR, claiming it was dangerous. All she could do was hide in her room and play downloaded games on her phone.

"Te vas a poner ciega. Deja eso y regresa afuera a estar con tu familia," Gloria found her lying in bed minutes later. Dena withheld a sigh and got up.

"Mejor, dámelo," Gloria said stiffly, holding out her hand. Dena passed her phone over wordlessly and walked out. Gloria looked at the lock screen. It was a family photo taken in New York just before Antonio passed. He had been the one to argue that Dena should get a phone at fifteen, though Gloria hated the idea. Dena had cropped her out of the frame. Gloria wondered if she would spend the rest of her life trying to get her face back onto the screen. Antonio would always be the "good" parent. She was evil Gloria with strict orders and high expectations. On second thought, they could hate her all they wanted, but she would ensure they never made the same mistakes she had.

One Day Before

Dena

A roaring applause erupted all around Dena as the wheels came to a screeching halt on the tarmac. Her melatonin pill wasn't strong enough to muffle the sounds of the joyous crowd.

"Por fin," the older woman next to her said loudly in her ear. There was a communal sigh of relief as the plane slowed down and turned towards the gate. People turned their phones off of airplane mode, a woman yelled at her hyperactive toddler, and several passengers unclipped their seatbelts to look for bags in the overhead compartments before the flight attendants could even reach for the intercom. Dena wished she could drift back to sleep.

The arrivals hall at Cibao International Airport had high ceilings and open doors. Only a few planes arrived daily, yet it felt crowded and stuffy to Dena. There was always chatter from visitors, residents, and airport staff members who looked like they were hanging out instead of working. Outside, the humid air surrounded her like a thick cloud. She understood why so many women left their tubis in place long after they landed. Her hair, by contrast, was expanding by the minute como un pan en el horno. She patiently waited on the sidewalk, avoiding eye contact with strangers which usually lingered too long.

"¡Prima! Pero tú sí tá buenamoza." Manny pulled up beside her.

"Manny, ¡cuanto tiempo!" She gave him a big hug. "Wow, pero, ¡mírate a ti!" She poked his biceps, impressed by their bulky size. He had grown an inch in height and gained ten pounds each year they spent apart. He had been a scrawny bobblehead kid with a big laugh and a body begging to be fed. Now, he was a man, undeniably, standing over six feet tall with a clean shape up and a cloud of cologne trailing behind him. He put her suitcase in the trunk as she hopped into the passenger seat. His jeepeta drove smoother than she expected. Manny was very excited about it. Then again, everything excited him. He was ten years older but just as energetic as before.

"Mira que suave maneja e'to. ¡Mira, mira!" He moved his palm across the front dashboard. "Casi nuevo. Solo tiene tres año'. Lo e'toy pagando de'pacito. Tú sabe'." He glanced over, waiting for her approval. She smiled uncontrollably. Manny's enthusiasm was always contagious.

"Y tú, ¿cómo te sientes? Sabes que yo quería a Tía mucho. Era como una madre pa mi." His voice cracked unexpectedly.

"Sí y ella te quería mucho a ti." She reached out and touched his shoulder. Gloria and Rosaly, Tío Johnny's wife, were pregnant at the same time. She had Manny shortly after Gloria had Jess. After he was born, Rosaly would call her sister-in-law multiple times a day asking for advice. Gloria loved playing the role of wise older sister. Eventually, she felt she had raised Manny too.

"Me dijeron que estaba bien mala. Tanta fuerza que tenía Tía. Una mujer así. Al final el cáncer acaba con to'," he said, attempting to pull wisdom from their tangled trauma. "Creo que es mejor que no la vi así," he reasoned. "¿Y tú? ¿Cómo tú tá?" He tried asking again.

What could she say? More importantly, what would she say as people asked this over and over again in the coming days? Was she okay? Could she tell it was coming when it did? How weak had cancer made her vibrant mother? Was it only a matter of time before it came for them too? The idea of talking to a flock of people and expressing her sadness sounded worse than the actual situation itself. Yes, her mother had died. Everyone's mother passes. Isn't that the preferred order? It had been coming for a long time. It wasn't a surprise. She didn't need the nine days of mourning, the boring prayers, the long stares from strangers that seemed more upset than her. She longed to fast-forward through the week like she did when streaming a show online, to click into the scenes that seemed essential and glide past the rest. She paused for a moment, gazing up at Manny. This scene was important. He was her favorite cousin, and his ceaseless joy made everything lighter.

"Estoy un poco estresada pero sigo aquí. Gracias por preguntar." She rolled out another closed smile. "¿Y tú, primo? ¿Cómo estás? ¿Sigues jugando pelota?"

"Sí, prima, claro. Eso se lleva en la sangre. Tú sabe'."

"Quiero ir a verte jugar si tienes un juego."

"E'ta semana no juego. Pero si quieres, podemo' jugar delante de la casa de Abuela como ante'," he joked, reminiscing when they were younger and the neighborhood kids would play together on the muddy street in front of Abuela's house.

"Mejor no." She remembered the cardboard bases and worn-down balls they used until the seams burst. Gloria let her play as long as she could see her from the window. But when she got older and curvier, her mother decided that was only for the boys. She began to play volleyball and run track in high school to avoid going home. Gloria allowed for sports, which required good grades and came with free adult supervision. Born an overachiever, Dena excelled immediately. She became captain of her volleyball team as a junior and won several medals in track. She fell in love with pushing her body and mind to their limit. The only thing she would miss on this trip to DR more than her bed was the gym.

"O podemos salir a beber una fría un día y te presento a mi novia." He raised both eyebrows. She looked at him sideways, raising one as well.

"¿'Novia'? Pero ¿'novia' como la última o una novia seria?" She joked.

"¡Diablo! ¿Y cuál fue esa?" He squinted his eyes, trying to recall which woman on his roster he had previously introduced her to. "No. No. Olvídate de eso. E'ta e mi novia de verdad. Ya no ando en la calle como antes." His cheeky grin said otherwise. "Y tú, prima. ¿Tienes a alguien por allá?"

"No, ¿con qué tiempo? Trabajo demasiado y ahora con…" They locked eyes, and she didn't have to finish her sentence. Manny understood her with only a few words. He was always there for her. Like years ago, when she kissed a boy during one of his baseball games, he was the one who took her home afterward so no one else found out. Unlike Jess, Manny could keep a secret.

As they drove, she stared out the window. The air smelled of smoky woods and deep-fried pork rinds. Manny went around a couple of trucks, one carrying cattle and another carrying a stack of plátanos higher than the length of the truck itself.

"¿Eso no es peligroso?" She pictured it falling over, creating an uncrossable mountain of green.

"Ah, ¿eso? No, eso no es na. La gente aquí lleva má a vece'," he said as she shook her head. DR was the most deadly country in the world in terms of road accidents. It was a fact she learned after her father's passing.

They drove another twenty minutes south towards La Vega Real, the great plain the Spanish christened accordingly because it stretched out flat and wide across the center of the island. Then, they cut left across the busy highway and slowed into her hometown. Campesito was tiny. The downtown center was half a mile long and wide. In the daytime, it was a sauna lit by the hot Caribbean sun. At night, a surge of mosquitoes came out to feast. Music could always be heard loudly nearby or faintly in the distance. Everyone spoke, drove, and danced fast, defying the pressure cooker heat that slowed other people down.

"Suena igualito." Even with the windows sealed, Dena could hear a group of guys blasting dembow outside of a colmado.

"Tú sabe' que la gente aquí toca música a todas hora'," he said, swerving around them and driving towards the main road bridge. Two bridges connected the East and West sides of town, which was divided in half by el Rio Camú. One bridge held the main road across town, along with a pedestrian sidewalk on each side. The other was a makeshift bridge made up of a five-foot-wide pipe surrounded by diagonal beams that kept it hovering above the water. It had been built a few years prior to streamline water transportation across town. The locals turned the bridge into an improvised crossing by walking along the precarious, rounded top.

"¿La gente usa eso para cruzar?" Dena watched in horror as a woman held her baby in one arm and casually walked across. One bad move could toss them downstream or worse if the tide was low. The pipe had been built in the time since she had last visited. But she could tell it had already been worn down from everyday use: the paint on it was chipped and a couple of the diagonal beams looked slightly out of place.

"Claro que sí. ¡Yo también! Ha'ta con bicicleta vi'to yo un tipo pasar por ahí. Es peligroso, sí. Pero la gente aquí no tiene paciencia. Todo el mundo anda corriendo de un lado pa otro," he said just as he cut off a motorcycle on the road.

As they got closer to the house, Manny pointed out all the new and remodeled houses they passed. The neighborhood was getting extreme makeovers—American visa edition. Todos los vecinos se fueron, or they had a primo or amiga or hija's babyfather's tía who left and, inevitably, their wooden shacks were torn down and remade as modern, concrete homes. The best ones had iron gates, washing machines, and Wi-Fi.

Driving down the road, they greeted four or five people, whom she could not remember nor name. She smiled and waved politely as they pointed out "la hija de Gloria y Antonio."

Dena stepped out of the car and into a soft pile of mud from recent rain. It was smeared across the road like creamy peanut butter on casabe, never quite soaking in.

The front of Abuela's house was filled with cars but no people. The velorio was held four houses down at a building Dena did not recognize. A few years prior, Gloria made her and Jess donate to build it. It was a place for funerals, birthdays, and any other large gatherings, since everyone's home was too small and the church was constantly falling apart. From Abuela's driveway, she could see nearly a hundred people huddled inside and around it.

The street was lined with dozens of plastic chairs on each side, filled with what felt like every person who ever met her mother, although it was not even close. Gloria's New York friends couldn't fly in on such short notice, not with their limited PTO and the high cost of flights. Eventually, Dena would have to set up an in memoriam mass for her mother back home. For now, she focused on the scene before her.

Los vecinos watched Dena intently as she walked down the street. A few brave ones went up to her weepy-eyed and asked, "¿Por qué Gloria? Tan joven. Le faltaba tanta vida."

She caught the light brown eyes of a moreno as she walked. He gently bowed his head, comforting her from afar amidst the chaos. She continued walking, looking for any immediate family members that might also distract her. It wasn't until she caught sight of Jess below the shade of a moringa tree that her stomach started to churn. Her face felt unbearably hot, the street too crowded, and the eyes directed at her too focused. She wanted them to look away, but she could feel them multiplying. Dena bent down and held Jess, who mustered enough energy to lift her arms halfway for a hug. Her sister's hands were ice cold against her back, and she was thinner than usual, more fragile.

"She's gone, Dena. She's really gone." Jess's scratchy vocal cords made her voice barely audible. Her eyes were redder than they were a week ago. She was always a heavy crier, even as a little girl Dena remembered her crying por cualquier cosa. But she hoped the heavier tears had passed by now.

"Have you eaten today?" Dena asked.

"A little. I had morir soñando with galletas earlier." Morir soñando sounded incredible: orange juice, carnation milk, ice, sugar. Any single one of those things would suffice for the long night she had ahead of her. Gloria used to make it for them on weekends if she managed to get home early from the salon. Dena could never get the recipe right; the milk was always slightly curdled. *"Por no tener paciencia,"* her mother would proclaim.

Dena scanned the area for food, but quickly gave up when she realized forcing Sombra to eat would turn the scene into an even bigger spectacle. She let her sister resume her position, slouched over in a plastic chair as she continued walking towards the hall. The eyes returned—or they never left. They were waiting to see how she would react. They were waiting to whisper and frown. They probably had a stack of cold, damp towels waiting by the sink. Maybe el padre will be there with a crucifix and a bible ready to throw holy water on her. They would watch to see if it calmed her or made her cry more.

As she entered the building, the air stilled, the voices quieted, and the center space cleared. She tried to focus on the white, chipped floor tiles. But someone had mopped the tiles so clean she could see everyone reflected in them, their limbs stretched out and exaggerated by the light. She turned her eyes up to stare at a corner of the ceiling. It was rotting brown, most likely a continuous leak compounded by rainy seasons. The stain stretched out like a banana leaf towards the ground. She followed the mold down until she saw two people hovering above the casket: Tía Candy and Tía Julia.

"Cion, Tía." She tried to hug Julia calmly, but her aunt pulled her in and wrapped both arms around her, squeezing tightly. Julia's glasses fogged up from hot tears. Her salt and pepper hair, which was always pulled back neatly, was sliding out of its bun.

"Ay, mi hija, ¿Cómo va ser? ¡Mi hermana tan fuerte y Dios nos la quitó! ¿Por qué? ¡Por qué! No, ¡Dios! ¡Noooo!" Tía Julia, Dena's calmest aunt, buckled in their embrace. Julia had never been one to show much emotion or fuss. She was usually clear-minded, organized, steady. Dena didn't know what to say to this version of her. Luckily, she didn't have to think for long. Sol and Tía Rosaly came over, pulled Julia away, and propped her up on a chair. They went to hug Dena before promptly returning to their sister's side. Sol rubbed Julia's head while Rosaly knelt and massaged her worn knees. They were kneading the grief and guilt out of her. Julia had retired early and moved back to DR a year before the diagnosis. Gloria assured her that she would be fine without the extra help. Even though Julia returned a couple of times, she was never around long enough to cure her younger sister. This silently gnawed at her like roaches in the night.

"Dios sabe lo que hace."

"Solo Dios manda."

They took turns negotiating with Julia's shame as she nodded silently. Her husband, Hernando, stood a few steps away, letting the women do the consoling. Candy joined the small group after hugging Dena. It was strange seeing all of her aunts, who always wore colorful prints, in somber shades from head to toe. Even stranger was seeing them—the strong, joyous women she grew up around—bend over in pain.

Gloria lay in an all-white casket with gold-painted legs, which Dena picked out earlier in the year. It wasn't ideal, but it was all they could afford with her mother's retirement plan: working until the day she died. For years, Gloria reported half of her income from hairstyling at the salon and pocketed the other half. Her savings were slim, and her retirement fund was nonexistent. No one said it aloud, but everyone knew donations were expected.

Gloria was made up in her usual bright colors: brown eyeliner, burgundy lips, coral blush, and a fresh coat of red nail polish. It looked like her mother, it even smelled like her—one of her aunts must have spritzed her favorite perfume—but it wasn't her. She was thin and withered. None of the firecracker attitude was there. The two-piece navy skirt suit sagged on her deflated body. It didn't show off her best features, something she would have hated. Even on her deathbed, her fingers trembled with anticipation. In the casket, Dena saw them motionless for the first time in her life.

Dena saw her mother fight cancer for two years, laughing at it. One time, high from pain medications and in a fit of rage, she even heard her mother mock it: "¡Ven! Estoy aquí, cáncer, coño. ¡Voy a seguir viviendo!" That was back when she was still eating regularly and dancing at parties. Before her internal organs felt like they had been wrung dry daily and left to rot in a dark, damp room.

Dena squinted at the stranger in the casket, attempting to identify features that reminded her of her mother. The longer she stared, the more distant this body felt to the memory she knew. She wondered how long she had to stand there for it to be considered acceptable. A minute? An hour? An eternity of haunted nights?

For two years, the last five days, all morning, and the ride into town, she had been preparing for this moment. She imagined that she would break down. It was clear that the whole town was expecting her to. To everyone's dismay, including her own, she was incredibly stoic, tightly wound like caña. Maybe if someone twisted and squeezed her hard enough, tears would pour out. But for now, no había nada. Nada de nada.

In the ten years since she was last in Campesito, Dena had gone to college, worked four different jobs, had two boyfriends, and managed—after a wretched uphill battle—to move out of her mother's apartment. Her entire life had changed, and Abuela's house still looked exactly the same: frozen in time.

The peach walls in the living room matched the faux-marble floor. The couches were covered in fat decorative pillows, its cushions were stiff and uncomfortable. The walls and shelves were full of photos of Abuela's seven kids and twelve grandchildren, at various stages of life, covered in everything from hospital blankets to graduation gowns. None of Dena's cousins could skip school or work to come. Only Manny, who already lived in Campesito, would be around for this arduous week.

The living room was for show, not practical use. Everyone spent their time in the marquesina—the extended garage where cars were meant to park, but none ever entered—instead. It was wrapped by vertical iron bars and swirly heart-shaped ones sandwiched in between. An 8-person dining table sat in the back, with a door leading to the living room. Six rocking chairs sat in the front of the room, facing the street. This was where her family ate, gossiped, and rested. It was the setting for most of her childhood summer memories.

Dena left thin drag marks of mud as she went down the narrow hallway into Gloria and Candy's old bedroom, now hers and Jess's. She made sure to turn on the air conditioner and spray herself with bug repellent before lying down. A few minutes later, her back spasmed at the sound of a piercing cry.

Tía Flaca had just arrived from Florida. Dena rushed to the living room window and looked down the street, contemplating if she should assist.

Tía Flaca was skinnier than Dena had ever seen her, worn down by a messy divorce and years spent apart from her siblings. Though her lifelong nickname rang true, Flaca was surprisingly strong. Dena saw her tall, thin aunt place both hands on the left side of the casket, and rock it backward. Four people had to restrain her. El padre, who was making his rounds, immediately started making crosses on her forehead. Dena watched for a few minutes, fixated on Flaca, who suddenly looked as if she was in a dull trance. The quiet, weeping Flaca was much more disturbing than the vulgar one she spent decades enduring. All the raw ferociousness was wiped away, leaving a murmuring shell struggling to understand why God took her little sister from her. Tía Flaca and Gloria lived a thousand miles apart but were forever bonded as "las del medio," sharing the middle child spirit and syndrome accordingly. Growing up, they shared friends, clothes, and chores. Flaca didn't just lose her sister, she lost her lifelong best friend.

As her cries subsided, Dena decided to return to the somber room.

Sorrow came in waves throughout the night, rolling in as new attendees arrived. The crowd fluctuated, the women took turns praying, and the men continued to sip. One by one, they walked over to hold Dena's hands, look into her eyes, and say "Ay, mija" or "Ay, prima" or "Ay, Dena," harmonizing their pain with her grief. She nodded respectfully, gently recovering her hands from their sweaty palms.

Dena had only attended three other wakes in her life. One was her boss's mother, whom she had never met. She had gone as a courtesy. It was a hushed affair. There was none of the screaming hysterics she saw at Dominican ones, none of the exposed agony. Everyone was contained, held together by a solemn understanding that anguish was meant to be hidden. The second was a while back in The Heights. One of Gloria's friends had passed away. She dragged Dena out of obligation. Jess, her usual plus one, was busy taking a final exam for one of her college courses. Dena was the one who encouraged her to go to college, and thus she couldn't guilt Jess into attending. The last, or rather the first, was her father's. She was only fifteen, and the memory became hazier as time passed. She remembered the itchy dress her mother made her wear, which was snug against her newly expanding curves. Jess refused to get up from a corner, so Dena had to keep bringing her food, water, and toys. Abuela, her father's mother, sobbed loudly the entire time, calling out to her son like an echo in an empty cave.

None of those funerals prepared her for this moment. Children and acquaintances can hide in the background. Here, she was expected to grieve out loud. She wanted to be like her sister, Sombra, and crawl into a dark corner away from the light.

Later in the night, Dena stepped outside in hopes that the cool air would awaken her senses. But the chirping grillos in the distance pacified her into a drowsy state.

"¿Cómo te sientes?" Tío Johnny placed a reassuring palm on her shoulder. In the same way that Gloria was Manny's second mother, Tío Johnny was her second father. She felt closer to him than Tío Yunior, who lived in the neighboring state but never came around, claiming he was always too busy.

"Bien, Tío. Váyase a dormir un rato. Nosotras seguimos aquí," she said, offering him a way out. He shook his head, dismissing her suggestion. Just like Manny, he was always looking for someone to help or something to fix.

"No, ta bien, me quedo un ratito más." Tío Johnny never moved to the U.S. He and Rosaly had Manny as teenagers. He couldn't imagine leaving them behind for a couple of years while he waited for the paperwork to go through. Instead, they decided to stay on their little island. He was happy with his ferretería, his friends, his freedom. At forty-two, he still had all his hair, a full belly, and glowing skin. Island life suited him.

"Okay, yeah. Gracias, Tío," she nodded, eyes barely open. Johnny headed back to his friends, all older men from town, who would stay as long as their wives told them to, and the rum kept flowing.

Dena looked for Jess, who was back in the same seat from hours earlier. "Jess, you should go shower. It's been a long day. You need to rest," Dena encouraged. Jess stared back weakly before looking around the room.

"They're going to be here all night. We can go shower then come back." Dena tugged her sister's arm gently. She had never seen her brown skin so swollen. She wanted to press the puffiness out of her face, to squeeze the pain out all at once. "Come on. We'll go together and set an alarm so you can come back before morning. We can go eat, too," she offered. Jess finally agreed and held out her hand, needing help getting up.

Dena liked to think Sombra was strong in her own way. Recently, her sadness seemed like gravity pulling her down. Everything from her eyelids to her shoulders drooped towards the ground. She put her arm around her little sister and lifted her. Manny came over to help, too. Slowly, they walked her to the house. Inside, Jess pressed her heels down firmly, fully supporting her own weight. Dena went to open her sister's suitcase and realized that, after three days, she had yet to unpack.

"You go first." She handed Jess fresh clothes to change into. As she waited to shower, Dena turned off the air conditioner, which had officially chilled the room, and turned on the fan. Its blades cast shadows that danced on the walls. She could hear a couple of mosquitoes buzzing around, but she was too tired to kill them. Even with the heat, the bugs, and all the babbling outside, she felt relieved. She dozed off counting the days she had left on the island like sheep.

2013

Gloria

As Gloria penciled in her eyebrows, she looked back at her daughters through the foggy, antique mirror.

"Mira, ¡ponte el vestido que tú no te gobiernas todavía!" She yelled at her oldest, who recently started complaining about her clothes.

"¿Pero por qué no me puedo poner pantalones? Todas las otras niñas tienen pantalones," Dena groaned. The statement reminded Gloria of her younger self, and she did not like it at all.

"No me hagas pasar vergüenza. Ya te dije una vez." Gloria secretly wished someone would give her a reason to burst. Jess, already in her black dress, walked in to try and alleviate the commotion, a tactic that never worked.

"Mira a tu hermana. Ella se porta bien. Deberías ser más como ella: una niña tranquila, respetuosa." Gloria preferred her quiet daughter, but she only said it through sly insults and backhanded compliments aimed at her eldest.

"Tranquila pero nunca habla."

"¡Mejor así! ¡Calladita te ves más bonita!" She said, swiping on brown lipstick. "Y no te me vayas levantando la voz delante de la gente. Más te vale que te portes bien." Gloria's index finger pointed directly at the center of her daughter's face. She felt like her father in all the worst ways. "¡Ahora mando yo!" She said coldly, implying what they already knew, though no one dared say out loud. The bratty child, hit with a wave of emotions, threw herself onto the bed. It was true: Gloria was the only boss now that her father had passed. Eventually, Dena got up to put the dress on. Jess helped zip her up.

Tía Candy quietly waited outside the bedroom to walk them to the church. She held an arm out for her sister, preempting a sudden collapse. Gloria waved it away, insisting she didn't need any help. As they walked to the front door, Gloria saw an old photo of her, Dena, and Antonio before they left for America. Before her ankles expanded from stomping across concrete, processed foods compounded in her body, and she started stabbing new holes into her old belts. She thought about how miserable she had been then and, ironically, how skinny she looked. If only she could feel and look her best all at once.

The street outside of the little house was filled with people who arrived by the carload, poured out quickly, and wept in unison.

"¡Ay, Gloria!" Antonio's eldest sister reached for her as they stepped out of the front gate. "¡Mi hermano! ¡Un hombre bueno y honesto!" She wept in Gloria's arms who, in turn, held herself upright with clenched fists. Tears streamed down her face, but nothing left her mouth. She was fighting a breakdown. She was fighting defeat.

Antonio was known in Campesito as "Antonio Gordo." Not because he was particularly big, but because there was a skinny Antonio. He was the "other" one. In the same vein, he was "el esposo de Gloria," "el hijo menor de Loro y Suzi" y "el hermano del doctor Nelson." He never managed to stand as his own man. His biggest dream was to marry Gloria and go to America. Once he did, there was not much left to accomplish. His legacy was now in the hands of his widow and two daughters. Gloria knew all of this. For fifteen years, she made visits back home and answered monotonous questions about her husband. They inquired but never dug deeply. They laughed at his jokes but never really cared.

As she walked down the street, more people approached her—some hesitantly, some forcefully—praying God would set their pain free, hoping Gloria's presence would make Antonio feel closer. She held the guests one by one as they presented themselves until she was standing in front of the church feeling ten years older and twenty pounds heavier.

She winced when she saw the casket from afar. The weight of tragedy laid itself upon her like the two-ton car that flattened her husband two nights prior. The casket was sealed shut so his family and friends could bear it. Since his broken body was concealed, Gloria couldn't figure out where to rest her eyes. On the grieving patrons? On the wooden box filled with remains? On the mistress he went to see that night? She chose the last.

Maribel de los Santos was four feet nine inches tall with heels on. She had pale skin and gaps in between all of her teeth. She was rumored to practice vudú, the kind that soaked rags in animal blood and pinned needles into cotton hearts. People said she learned it from her mother, and her mother from her mother. But Gloria believed a dark practice like that grew from an inner rage that no good mother would pass down to her child.

It had been over three years since Gloria found out about the affair. His bloodshot eyes and bad breath exposed him one night. She confronted him that very day by slapping him across the face. It was the first time in his life that Antonio defied his wholesome image. He was testing his limits, attempting to prove, perhaps to himself, that he wasn't just some cookie-cutter husband who did as he was told. But then, something switched: the sex was so intoxicating he couldn't stop even if he wanted to. He swore to Gloria that it was meaningless, that he would end it, that all men had to get it out of their systems at one point. But she knew better.

"Hola." Gloria approached Maribel, who had chosen to sit in the back row, a place her mother claimed was saved for sinners.

"Hola." Maribel stood up and wiped a tear, attempting to escape. Gloria leaned into the tiny woman's ear.

"Que Dios te perdone por lo que has hecho." She pulled back and looked Maribel in the eye. Her body stiffened beneath the cold stare.

"Y a ti," Maribel said under her breath before scurrying away. Gloria wanted to swing at her, but she was gone before she could lift a finger.

"¡Ay! ¡Maldita!" In the next instant, the widow's entire body collapsed to the ground. Maybe Maribel had put a curse on her. Maybe Antonio was laughing at her from his sad wooden box.

"¡¿Por qué?! Me...de...ja...ste...so...la!" She heaved between syllables. Antonio never really won Gloria over. Even as his wife, she was always just out of reach. But his lover dared to show her face and speak to her at the funeral. It felt like he was getting his revenge from beyond, as if he hadn't already gotten it when he was alive.

"Dios...mi...o...por...qué..." She thought about Antonio's body thrown over the side of a dark country road. Her sisters hurried to her side. Rosaly and Sol fanned her and whispered prayers into her ears. Flaca, who never particularly liked Antonio, or most people, remained calm at her feet. Candy went to check on the girls. Julia placed a damp towel on her head. Yoselin, who was still relatively new to the sisterhood, stood by, waiting to be tagged in. They were a loyal fleet awaiting their captain's command.

Gloria was always too proud to ask for help, this moment included. She didn't tell anyone about the affair, hoping it would fizzle out and the smoke would clear. She only told Yunior about the mountain of debt Antonio had left her from gambling, lotto tickets, and last-minute flights to DR. He was the financier of the family and the only sibling who wouldn't chismear. Like their mother, he swore by his duties, doing nothing more and nothing less. She didn't share her secrets, her traumas. This funeral was embarrassing. As she flailed her arms and tried recovering her breath, she couldn't help but feel ashamed. Now everyone would know that Gloria—la rebelde, la loca, la brava—cried fervent tears too.

To spite them, she wore a bright, guava-colored shirt that perfectly accentuated her figure. Even in her puddle of sorrow, they saw her defiance. Even as a grieving widow, she was the most radiant woman in the room. Her mother-in-law, who had been weeping in the front, looked at her from a distance with clear disgust. Slick comments could be heard throughout the room. "¿Rosado? ¿Pero por qué?" "¿Como se va a poner un color?" "Dios la perdone." They served as cold water to her hot face. Within a few minutes, she sobered up and got back on her feet.

"Cuidado," said a worried Julia.

"Estoy bien." Gloria wiped the dust off her pants and proceeded to the front of the church, where the casket sat on top of a wooden table covered with a thick ivory tablecloth. She looked at the smiling photo of Antonio, a couple of years before the crow's feet around his eyes had stretched and reached his hairline. They printed and laminated the same pocket-sized image for guests to carry in memoriam. The image showed Antonio at his best: young, vibrant, discovering another woman.

Gloria waved her daughters over to sit next to her during the procession. Instinctively, Gloria wrapped an arm around each of her girls and pulled them towards her. It was confusing to Dena, as an hour earlier her mother threatened to hurt her in public. Then again, nothing Gloria did made much sense to her, especially after her father started taking solo trips to DR and her mother became increasingly erratic and rude. She believed Gloria must have driven him away.

After la misa, the crowds filed out into the high noon sun. From the corner of her eye, Gloria spotted a tall, lanky moreno in a gray suit. She squinted and wiped her eyes to make sure he was real. He held up his hand, gently waving from a few feet away. She shivered in shock, her stomach clenched, her heartbeat quickened. She looked around to see if anyone else had spotted him. Could they see what she saw? Was this ghost from her past really here to haunt her? Did he want to talk? He walked towards her as she considered her options: stall, run, fall, cry. Nothing felt right.

"Mira, váyanse con Tía Candy y Tío Johnny. Yo voy ahora," Gloria ordered her girls away before they saw him. Weeping, Jess held onto Dena as they walked towards Tio Johnny's car up front. Gloria walked around the right side of the church. Marcelo followed her faithfully. She stopped walking when she was sure no one else could see them.

"Hola." His hands hung by his sides, too afraid to reach for her.

"¿Que haces aquí?" Gloria attempted to remain unflinching, arms crossed over her chest.

"Vine a ver si estabas bien." Yet the sound of his voice electrified every nerve ending in her body. The years of icy silence melted away.

"No, obviamente no lo estoy," she said dryly. He tried not to smile at her honest response. She was exactly how he remembered.

"Vine a dar el pésame," he said. She dug her heels in and brushed the tears away from her eyelashes. The pueblo's presence, hovering beyond the small building, clouded her vulnerability. They could not be seen together. Not today, not ever.

"No deberías estar aquí," she said, pronouncing every syllable carefully.

"Yo sé. Pero…" He was racking his brain for the perfect

words to string together. He looked into her eyes for guidance, but they were black and glazed over like overused car oil.

"No te preocupes por mí. Como decía papá, 'lo único seguro en la vida es la muerte'. Debes irte." She redirected her gaze to the tree behind him.

"Sí, claro." His head sank low, though his eyes were still glued to her. He breathed in as if to start another sentence but before he could get anything out, she was already walking away. He watched her leave yet again. She had the same switch to her hips, the same long, dark hair. But it wasn't his Gloria anymore. It wasn't even Antonio's Gloria. The young Gloria, who was once curious and free, was gone. Now, she was "la mamá de Dena y Jess," "una de las hermanas Vega" y "la señora del salón," her identity forever tied to motherhood, sisterhood, and work. She would never again be una amante.

Gloria's sisters stood behind her as they boarded up Antonio's mausoleum at the cemetery with the last brick. They waited with open arms to comfort the family he left behind. Despite the tight bra encircling Gloria's body, the new shoes blistering Dena's toes, and the wet hair sticking to Jess's face, they stood upright until it was over.

That night, one emotion kept dripping into Gloria's mind: shame. Shame that she was relieved Antonio's faucet of debt was finally turned off. Shame that her daughters saw her as a tyrant. Shame that even though no one said it to her face, there were rumors about the woman who sat in the back of the church and left once Gloria spoke to her. Shame that she sent Marcelo home without so much as a hug or kiss on the cheek. Shame that her marriage was a failure and that she was partially to blame.

She thought about her mother's words the day before her wedding: *"Vas a tener que escuchar a tu esposo y hacer lo que él dice."* Although her mother meant well, Gloria rejected her advice almost immediately. She thought about their last annual summer trip when she confronted Antonio. She knew he had returned to his old mistress after a year apart. Gloria looked him directly in the eye and said, "Antonio, no vayas a ver a esa a mujer. Dios me perdona, pero algo malo te puede pasar. Ella está metida en cosas malas." She hoped her betrayed ego could be disguised as genuine care. Seven months later, he died on the side of the road on his way to see her. She didn't have proof, since no one dared tell her where he was headed that night, only her intuition.

When she got the call, it felt as if someone had sucked the marrow out of her bones and spit them onto the road beside him. She was weak, angry, paranoid. But for all the fights and disagreements they had, she never wanted him dead. If God was into punishing, and she knew that He was, this was a step too far.

Later at night, Gloria stepped into the backyard to breathe in the cool, crisp air. Luckily, un vecino was blasting merengue from his patio. She walked through the garden, bent over a bush, and cried, grateful her family couldn't hear her inside.

"Dios mío. ¿Quién me va a ayudar a cuidar a mis hijas?" She thought but didn't dare say out loud. She never voiced her sorrows in case someone somewhere might hear. After a few minutes, she brushed her tears away and tiptoed to the back concrete wall.

Her tree was empty, except for one fruit dangling above her. It was still early in the season. She contemplated her next move, weary of her own desires. It wasn't right, but the day had been too hard, her sorrows ran too deep. She swallowed her pride and yanked the fuzzy, brown ball off its thin branch. She sunk her teeth into its delicate skin and pulled it off. She looked around, in case someone was lingering in the dark, and when she knew only the insects were watching, she traced her tongue along the ripened flesh. Instantly, she was pressed against his chest, and surrounded by his scent. She took a large bite and felt his hands tracing the dimples in her lower back. Another bite, and his nose grazed her spine. Another, and his fingers spread her legs apart. Another and another until she sat on the dirt as comfortably as if she was back in his arms. She scraped the pit clean and tossed it in the grass.

As she caught her breath, she thought about how good he looked in his slim suit, his features sharpened over time. It irked her that he had somehow become more handsome while she, after childbirth and constant exposure to pollution, had become more bloated and gray—another one of God's injustices.

"No importa," she thought, staring back at her tree. It didn't matter what he looked like or said or did. She decided long ago that only one thing mattered to her: her daughters. As the last fading memory washed over her, she clasped her hands in prayer and vowed to never lay with another man again. She had heard too many horror stories to let a man into her home with two young girls around. From now on, she would devote all of her love to them.

"Dios, te pido que hagas lo que quieras conmigo pero que deja mis hijas que vivan sus vidas. No necesito a ningún hombre. No te pido amor ni dinero ni nada más. Solo quiero que ellas puedan lograr todo lo que quieran, que tengan una vida mejor."

Day One

Dena

Los gallos de la vecina declared madrugada, commanding Dena awake. A motorista zoomed past her window, cranking the engine as he rode. Two street dogs barked as they chased him away. She could hear rumbles from the velorio down the road. Whether she liked it or not, it was time to get up.

As Dena slowly uncoiled from the sheets, she realized Jess wasn't in the bed beside her. She went to the bathroom to shower. Random tiles had been replaced along the walls sporadically: a mosaic of half-done handyman jobs. The shower head was broken. Ice-cold water spewed sideways from the bottom faucet. She splashed some up at herself with a large, recycled butter container. After a few miserable minutes, she attempted to close the faucet, but it spun endlessly around, never fully closing.

The kitchen was completely vacío, a drastic change from the previous day when an assembly line of women made mini sandwiches to serve at the velorio. In the empty room, she noticed that the countertop was peeling and that a couple of the cabinet doors couldn't fully close, their hinges slightly askew.

Her family always avoided things until they were in a state of disrepair.

She made herself a sandwich and swallowed it quickly, fearing someone else might expect her to make more. She set up la greca with as many coffee grinds as possible and a dash of nutmeg. As she waited for it to percolate, she went to the living room, pressed her fingers into the metal slots in the window, and leaned in to check out the velorio. A moderate crowd lingered in the distance. She returned to the kitchen for her cafecito with a small spoonful of sugar. As she sipped, she felt immediately relieved. Coffee soothed her nervous system.

Outside, hibiscus pink bloomed from the eastern part of the sky, marking the center of the sunrise. Dena thought back to all the trips she took as a child. Her mother never unlocked Abuela's doors before sunrise. A few times, she tried catching glimpses of it through the window's iron bars, but if her mother ever caught her, she would give her morning chores.

At the velorio, Dena spotted Jess, eyes fully closed, in a seat by the casket.

"Did you sleep?" Dena asked, nudging her shoulder. Did her sister make it to bed at all?

"You didn't feel me?"

"No, I was exhausted last night." Dena sat down next to her, hoping it would ward off other people.

"Yeah, me too. I slept next to you for a couple of hours, then I came out here not that long ago," Jess said, though her ojeras said otherwise.

"Well, go back in and try again. I can sit out here and talk to the guests." Dena rubbed her little sister's back.

"Yeah...okay." Jess massaged her aching neck and sore legs to get the blood flowing before walking back.

All the tías were stationed around Gloria, just as Dena had left them several hours earlier. Today, they would hold the official burial. In DR, bodies were buried as soon as possible to limit the damp heat that seeped into caskets and rotted the limbs of the dead. The room was quieter than before, but felt much more volatile in the same way that the sky became increasingly still before it opened up and a storm tore through public peace.

"Vamos estar allá'lante," Tía Candy pointed towards the front of the church. She had been nervously pacing around the front door, waiting to tell Dena where she would be seated. The room was small enough that Dena could easily find her mother's siblings. But Tía Candy always stood by, her anxiety veiled by kindness.

"Gracias, Tía. Voy ahora." Dena stared down at Candy's navy pants and cream top. As a rule, Tía Candy didn't own black clothing. She said it was too miserable and hot to wear, as if the dye's hue affected her temperature. On the contrary, as a lifelong New Yorker, half of Dena's wardrobe was black. Today, she wore a short-sleeved, wide-leg black jumpsuit that fit snug around her shoulders and hips but otherwise hung loosely. It was meant to be breezy, but she was sweating from the moment she stepped into the crowded church. The poor parish couldn't afford air conditioning, only two dusty fans that spun hot air around in circles.

Jess went to link arms with her as soon as she stepped inside. She always used Dena as a repellent for rude women, guys at bars, and pesky family members. She hoped to use her today for everyone who might want to pull her into their mourning.

All of Gloria's siblings sat side by side in front. They could tell them apart by their hair: Julia's high gray bun, Flaca's jet-black locks, Candy's bright red pixie cut, and Sol's naturally brown curls. Their two tíos sat on either side, holding them up like bookends.

Dena didn't look in the casket this time, figuring nothing had changed from the previous night. The procession felt longer than it was. The priest shared personal stories about his interactions with Gloria. Tío Yunior spoke on behalf of the siblings, since he was the only one who could contain his tears. Afterward, everyone stuffed themselves into various cars and pickup trucks. The parade drove for five minutes to the outskirts of town. Miles of rice fields sprawled out in every direction. Each arrozal was a different height and shade of green. The lower crops, with their large pools of excess water, mirrored the clear blue sky above. It was a gorgeous day for an awful affair.

The air outside was thicker than in the church. Sweat pooled on all the guests. They fanned themselves with leaflets and cheap paper fans. Six men lifted Gloria and walked her through the small cemetery. The rest of the group followed. Dena wrapped an arm around Jess, who had tears streaming down her face. It stung to see her in this state. She decided to be strong for both of them, to hold her tongue and tears back. She walked at a pace that ensured she would not lead nor fall behind the crowd. She did everything right, just as their mother had taught them at their father's funeral years earlier. She would maintain her composure until the end.

Gloria's closest childhood friends started to bawl first, holding each other as they walked. The tías joined shortly afterward. Kids, most of whom Dena didn't recognize, started weeping too, as if they instinctively understood the scene had soured. The men placed Gloria down on ashy dirt: dried up mud from the morning's scorching sun. Dena could hear her mother say, *"Qué cementerio ma feo. ¿Me van a enterrar aquí? ¿Entre todo este polvo?"*

As the priest started speaking, Gloria's closest friends and family—mostly women—draped their arms over the casket. The rest of the group attempted to peel them off. One by one, they sobbed their goodbyes and stomped their feet in the ground all around her. Wet rags collected mixed tears as unsettled dust filled the air.

Dena looked around for somewhere to rest her eyes that wasn't the casket. She saw the guy who had bowed to her the night before standing beside an older woman. His gaze was steady as he nodded towards her. The tender gesture caused her eyes to well up behind her thick sunglasses. She stifled the tears and held her breath. *"Aguanta."* Stay strong.

Then, from the corner of her eye, Dena saw a heavyset, middle-aged woman start to convulse. The cries all around her simmered down as the woman's body continued to jerk. She nearly fell but caught herself with one hand on the side of the casket. Her eyes rolled back for a few seconds, then forward. The woman took a deep breath and spoke.

"¡Ay, Dios! ¿Y ustedes?" It was the undeniable voice of Gloria. Dena trembled. Jess loosened her grip on her sister's arm, startled by the unbelievable scene before her. The woman regained her balance as the crowd stepped back in unison, overwhelmed by her question, which sounded more like an announcement: *"Regresé."*

"¿Quién me eligió e'ta ropa fea? ¡Diablo, que feo! Le' dije que me entierren en algo de color, rojo o rosado." The crowd was silent for the first time all day. Despite the initial shock, it was obviously Gloria speaking. En Campesito, el espíritu de una difunta se pegaba a alguien when they had unfinished business.

"A mis hermanos, dejen de preocuparse. Cuiden la casa. Los veo allá." Her siblings reached for each other, keeping their eyes fixed on the woman. Sol, who had seen this many times, regained composure first. She called over one of the local boys and mumbled something in his ear, pointing to the far left side of the cemetery. He sprinted away as the new Gloria continued speaking.

"Mis hijas, que se lleven bien." She said, her tone more threatening than loving.

The boy ran back and handed Tía Candy a branch of guandules as the crowd began to wake up from their subtle trance.

"¡Juye!" "¡Dale!" "¡Dios mío!" Could be heard all around. Candy approached the woman quickly but hesitated to hit her. She was too gentle for such brutal things. Sol stepped up and swiftly grabbed the branch from her.

Whack! Sol slapped the woman across the back with the branch.

"Me morí soñando con él..." The woman's eyes glazed over wistfully.

Whack! Sol hit her even harder. A couple of leaves floated down upon impact.

"Mi amor..." Her voice cracked, but Sol kept going.

Whack! Whack! WHACK! Green guandule shells burst open. Seeds spilled onto the ground.

"Mi primera hija..." The woman's eyes fluttered as she spoke. "Todas mis hijas..." She held her hand to her chest. Dena couldn't tell if it was her mother getting emotional or the woman regaining consciousness. Sol struck down on her several more times, not relenting until Gloria's voice faded back into the abyss from which it came. The crowd grimaced, but couldn't look away. They knew this primitive practice was the only way to keep un espíritu away. The woman fell silent and began to twitch. Candy knelt beside her and massaged her hands calmly. After a minute, she opened her eyes and looked around, perturbed by all the people glaring at her.

"¿Qué pasó?" She was confused, teetering on mortified.

"Te caíste," Sol spared her the details. Tía Candy and Sol held the woman on either side and walked her over to the fence, her head tucked low in shame, aware alguien se monto. She had heard stories, but she never remained conscious during the episodes. She could tell from the crowd's reaction that her mystical abilities frightened them. Murmurs began to rise all around. The town's ties to Catholicism were too strong to interpret this as anything other than brujería: intentional toying with the spirits from beyond.

"What the...?" Dena caught herself speaking out loud. Her skin was crawling from the echoes of her mother's voice. She had once heard her mother's friend recount a similar story, but she assumed it was a campesino's urban legend. Yet everyone around was calm as if this was normal. The older members of the crowd had seen espíritus enter bodies before. People lived and breathed them in the corners of reality. They were rarely mentioned in daylight to avoid accidentally calling them forth. If they showed up, they were promptly beaten back into the other side.

"Seguimos, ¿no?" The priest attempted to regain control for a final prayer. He signaled the men to lift Gloria again. Fearing the owner's power, they moved cautiously, raising the casket slowly and sliding it into a narrow concrete hole above Antonio. A washed-out portrait was pasted on his mausoleum plaque. Dena recognized it immediately. Her eyes welled again, but she focused her attention on the cemetery worker who sealed the slot brick by brick with an old bucket filled with wet cement.

The tías, who were too exhausted to cook, ordered a couple of roasted chickens and sides from a local pica-pollo for lunch. Jess and Dena poured refresco into little vasitos to offer everyone. Only family members remained. Sol, who usually stayed, returned to her house next door to recover from the day's events. The rest of the tíos and tías sat around the marquesina, enjoying the breeze that squeezed in through the iron bars.

"¿Y quién era esa mujer?" asked Tío Yunior, who always said the first thing that came to mind.

"Pero tú la conoces. Esa era Minerva. Minerva la de Tito,"

said Tía Rosaly, who sat beside Johnny and held his hand. Even as they aged, they remained the most affectionate pair in the family.

"¿Tito cuál? ¿El de por allá?" Yunior swung his arm to the right. He had not lived in Campesito for over twenty years, but he remembered where everyone lived, like the birthmarks on his skin.

"El que vive allá alrededor del río. Esa es la esposa del," Tía Julia clarified, leaning back in her rocking chair and placing her ankles onto a step stool she kept nearby. Like her late mother, Julia's joints were often swollen from basic daily tasks. She spent decades working on her feet in America, and now, retired, she vowed to spend just as much time off of them.

"Ay santísimo, ¿esa fue Minerva? Pero ella tá acaba'a." Tío Yunior spoke his sentiments as facts. "Tiene que ser como veinte año' que no veo a esa mujer."

"Pero Tío, no digas eso." Jess sat in a plastic chair so her aunts and uncles could rock back and forth on the limited mecedoras.

"O sea, 'acabada' no. Rara. Diferente." Flaca defended her brother's words.

"Bueno, perdon, yo soy má viejo que ella y me veo mejor," Yunior insisted.

"Tal vez. Pero no todos tienen la mente para aguantar los muertos," Julia noted, taking off her glasses and resting them in her lap. She was the most well-spoken Vega sibling, always enunciating every word. Dena remembered her constantly correcting her Spanish when she was younger, insisting proper speech propelled women forward, though Tía Julia would never call herself a feminist.

"A mi no me importa como se ve. Solo me importa lo que dijo," Candy interjected. Her sisters nodded along from across the room.

"Es verdad. Y yo les dije a ustedes que no la vistieran así." Flaca similarly took her time pronouncing each word, except she only spoke clearly when she was trying to make a point. "Julia, ¿no te lo dije ayer?" She sought to absolve herself of any wrongdoing.

"Deja eso, Flaca, que ya pasó," Julia dismissed her sister's rant. Unlike her younger sisters, Julia didn't care about clothing beyond utilitarian needs. She was too busy running a household full of kids with their mother. As far as she was concerned, their priorities should align with God's will first and foremost.

"Se los dije a ustedes," Flaca repeated once more as Julia rolled her eyes.

"Pero ven acá, ¿ustede' creen en eso? Esa mujer e una loca." Tío Johnny, the most skeptical sibling, shook his head.

"Pero eso no se dice, mi amor." Tía Rosaly rubbed his arm lovingly. She had heard about Minerva in stories whispered over afternoon café. This was her first time witnessing her transform firsthand. The thought of it sent a shiver down her spine.

"Déjame decirte algo, esa mujer no sabe na. Todo lo que ella dijo lo pudiera decir cualquiera caminando por ahí. No se ilusionen, señore'," Johnny warned. As the only one that never left their small town besides Sol, he was always more cautious than the others.

"No sé. Pero yo la creo," Tía Julia chimed in. She was a devout woman of God, but she had seen too much to disavow la presencia de los muertos. "Además, ella no dijo nada del otro mundo tampoco."

"Pero entonces, ¿qué fue eso al final?" Asked Tío Yunior.

"Hablaba de Antonio. ¿Tú no la oíste? 'El amor de mi vida' y 'mis hijas,' " said Tía Candy, attempting to make sense of the senseless.

"¿Pero cuando en tu vida has oído a Gloria hablar así de Antonio? Dique 'amor de su vida'. Ella…" Tío Yunior stopped when he saw Jess staring back at him. He settled into the back of his rocking chair, uncrossed and recrossed his legs.

"No, te digo yo a ti, esa mujer no sa-be na-da," Tío Johnny cut his brother off, pausing between syllables for dramatic effect. He was unconvinced and unamused.

Dena and Jess looked at each other from across the room. They leaned into the conversation, hoping their mother's siblings would spill as they often did.

"No, pero esa si era la voz de Gloria," Tía Flaca stated.

"Si me das un par de tragos yo puedo hablar como Gloria también." Tío Johnny waved his hand sideways, as if wiping the mere thought away. He disliked funerals in general. They were too rigid; they reeked of forced prayers and old hymns. He preferred retelling stories of the dead while sipping on a bottle of Brugal with the living.

"¿Entonces de quién hablaba?" Tío Yunior asked again, rocking in his chair. His sisters took turns side-eyeing him, mouths clenched tightly. Dena's eyes zigzagged across the room, trying to make out what they weren't saying out loud.

"Oye, dejen eso que se van a volver locos como le pasó a el esposo de Jaquelin hace un par de años," warned Tía Yoselin. She had seen a woman montada at a funeral before. It sent a ripple through the family, and el esposo de la difunta committed suicide two weeks later. It was a cautionary tale for the grieving.

"Ah, sí. Oí eso. Que triste y tan joven que era el muchacho," Candy reflected. Although most of them didn't live there anymore, they were all connected to the stories in town like branches on a tree that stretched towards the sky but drew water from the mud.

"Bueno, yo no sé nada de eso y no quiero saber nada más tampoco." Flaca, visibly uncomfortable, shifted in her seat.

"¡Buenas!" A middle-aged man hopped off a motorcycle out front. He held three plastic bags full of food. Julia placed her glasses back on and went to meet him. Candy followed closely behind. The smell of roasted pollo filled the room as they walked towards the kitchen.

"Dijo algo de mi…" Dena tried to get a word in, but everyone was too busy salivating to speak.

"Claro, porque te quería mucho, mija." Tía Rosaly tried to reassure her before hurrying into the kitchen to help her sisters-in-law with the cups and utensils.

"Bueno, ¿ya?" Tío Yunior remained curious.

"¿Y de qué más quieres hablar? Ella nos mandó todo lo que quería decir ahí," Tía Candy said, stacking plates on the table. Tío Johnny grabbed one right out of her hands.

"No, entonces ta bien. Vamos a comer." Tío Yunior followed his siblings to the table.

Dena looked around the room. It was strange to be around them without her mother nearby, as if the Vegas were a package deal. She watched as everyone loaded up on food. Although they were talking and chewing loudly, she couldn't shake the feeling that something—no, someone—was missing and life was becoming eerily quiet.

In the condensed afternoon heat, Dena sat in her air-conditioned bedroom of Abuela's house, scrolling through her phone. The low-speed internet coming from Sol's house next door slowed as the night dragged on. It wasn't ideal, but it was better than the outside world, full of painfully long stares and sticky embraces.

Tía Candy knocked lightly on her door before stepping in. Tía Candy was Dena's shortest and sweetest aunt. She was Gloria's version of Sombra, and therefore, she always followed Gloria's daughters around, too. Perhaps it was because she didn't have daughters of her own. Or that she had always lived near their apartment in The Heights. Dena wasn't sure, but she tried to be patient with her soft-spoken aunt.

"Mija, vamos a rezar en media hora. Ven a ayudar."

"Ayudar" was Candy's code for placing palms on the

neighbors' backs and making them feel welcome. As a home attendant in New York, caretaking was in her blood. Dena felt that gene had skipped her. Perhaps it was stuck with the one that made her want to carry strangers' babies and regularly cook huge pots of food to share with family and friends.

Manny and Jess were in the marquesina spreading out the plastic chairs from the previous night, since the living room was too small for the gathering. Dena stood by the door, lips pressed together in a tight smile, greeting guests.

It was an intimate assembly. The crowd was a fourth of the funeral's size. By now, the workers had returned to their jobs, the children to their games, and the men to their afternoon gatherings on street corners and driveways. The only people who religiously went to hora santas were older women in worn-out sandals and the daughters and granddaughters they asked to accompany them. People showed their faces at a funeral. At the hora santa, they faced God together.

The guests sat around in a semicircle. The tías sat in the front, facing them. The air smelled like face powder. Motorcycles rumbled past. The setting sun cast a faint glow on the room. Tía Julia, the first sibling to learn all the obligatory prayers, led the proceedings:

*"**Padre nuestro** que estás en el cielo,*
santificado sea tu Nombre;
venga a nosotros tu Reino;
hágase tu voluntad,
en la tierra como en el cielo.
Danos hoy nuestro pan de cada día;
perdona nuestras ofensas,
como también nosotros perdonamos
a los que nos ofenden;
no nos dejes caer en la tentación,

y líbranos del mal. Amén.

Dios te Salve, María,
llena eres de gracia,
el Señor es contigo.
Bendita Tú eres
entre todas las mujeres,
y bendito es el fruto de tu vientre, Jesús.
Santa María, Madre de Dios,
ruega por nosotros, pecadores,
ahora y en la hora de nuestra muerte. Amén.

Gloria al Padre
y al Hijo y al Espíritu Santo.
Como era en el principio
ahora y siempre,
por los siglos de los siglos. Amén."

Julia repeated this five times, eventually tagging in Flaca to read a passage and Tía Candy for closing words. The entire room sang and recited prayers in a rhythm that reminded Dena of her childhood church days. After her father's death, Dena refused to go to church. Gloria, in turn, dragged her out of the house repeatedly and called her out in front of anyone who would listen. *"¿Tu ha visto algo así? ¡Dique 'no quiere ir' a la iglesia! Es por Dios que tú tá aquí. ¡Gracias a Dios!"*

At twenty-one, she moved out and into an apartment with her at-the-time boyfriend, resulting in even more rage and disdain from her mother. Gloria doubled down, blaming her separation from God on her "amiguito" and their sinning. For years, she continued her unprovoked threats to take Dena to church and wash her clean. Needless to say, it left a bad taste in her mouth. Now, religion felt like a childhood friend that she grew apart from but still ran into on special occasions.

The hora santa was a blur. Dena drifted in and out of consciousness, nearly falling asleep a couple of times. Near the end, Tío Yunior entered and asked her "Qué van a servir?" He had only come for the snacks. Tía Julia immediately shot him a dirty look, condemning anything other than solemnity.

Once the food had been eaten and the plastic cups emptied, everyone sat around discussing Gloria. They told stories of her as a child who would run off alone, argue with her parents, and insist on going to la finca, the family farm, because girls could work the land too. She sang at mass, danced at every party, and drank Brugal with the boys on Friday nights, much to her parents' dismay. She was a boisterous little girl que tuvo un carácter fuerte y una risa alta. One of Gloria's childhood best friends claimed Gloria cursed out a local boy in her honor. She told him to keep her friend's name out of his mouth. When they heard the story, the room erupted in laughter. They painted Gloria as a fearless figure. Before the cursing, hitting, curfews, and rigid cleaning schedules that Dena knew, Gloria was fun and free.

"Gloria no era pendeja," said Tía Flaca, a proud sister. "La primera vez que Papá la dejó beber ella le dijo que quería ron con hielo, como él. ¿Tú te imagina'? Una niña a los quince, en eso' año' pidiendo puro romo." The crowd laughed louder than before.

Eventually, one of the ladies pointed to the dark sky outside. It was time to go. The same cushioned soles that came in wobbled out one by one.

"No, Gloria no era pendeja," Flaca repeated when the room emptied out, leaving the Vega family alone again.

"Y Papá no era fácil tampoco." Tía Julia spent the most time with him, not just because she was the eldest, but because she tended to him in his dying days. He requested her specifically. She never knew if it was out of love or punishment. Regardless, she did as she was told. Julia was as obedient as she was tender, as loyal as she was kind. On the other hand, Papá Nito and Gloria were equally stubborn and reactive. Dena didn't have any memories of him, since he passed when she was a toddler. But they said he was the source of Gloria's fire; the volcano from which the lava spewed.

"Gloria le encantaba ir al río cuando era joven," Julia said.

"Sí, ¡yo me recuerdo!" Yelled Johnny, who came in after the prayers looking for food just like his older brother. "Cuando nosotros íbamos a buscar fruta para el dulce, ella iba al agua a descansar. Recuerdo una vez que Papá le preguntó '¿para qué tienes que descansar si eres tan joven? Nunca te has ensuciado tus pies, muchacha'. "

"¡Ay dios! ¡Yo me recuerdo de eso también! Diablo. Ella tenía que tener como quince o dieciséis. Una niña creyéndose mujer."

"Tenía más yo creo. Me recuerdo que fue después que ella comenzó a ponerse pantalones cortos y Mami casi la mató," Candy said, looking at Flaca, Gloria's fellow rule breaker. They both burst out laughing. Gloria was the reason all the Vega sisters were finally allowed to wear short shorts and miniskirts, but not without a couple of beatings.

"¿Y qué le dijo?" Asked Jess, curious about her mother's teenage rebellion, which she coerced out of her.

"Ay, no me recuerdo," said Flaca.

"Yo sí me recuerdo. Nunca me olvidaré. Le dijo 'si tú fuera' a la finca de vez en cuando, también tuvieras que limpiarte los pies'." Johnny was properly nostalgic and laughing out loud.

"¿A Abuelo?" Manny asked in disbelief. He loved his Tía Gloria for her honesty pero esto era otro nivel. No one talked back to Abuelo Nito.

"Sí. ¿Tú te imaginas? Diablo, lo que le pegó ese día. Lo dijo y de inmediato se fue corriendo al jardín atrá'," Yunior said, taking a sip of beer Johnny brought over.

"Y nosotros todos parados ahí en la sala. Nadie quería decir nada. Papá era malo. Si te escuchaba, te pegaba a ti también."

Candy trembled at the thought of her father's interrogations.

"¿Y después qué pasó?" Dena was surprised that her mother never told her this story. She loved to tell dramatic tales repeatedly.

"¿Que tú crees? Él corrió detrá' de ella y la pegó con un palo que encontró atrá'. Diablo, que palo' que picaban." Johnny started to tremble too, thinking about the branches bending and breaking on his own skin.

"¿Y Abuela, qué hizo?" Jess asked.

"Na. ¿Y que iba hacer?" Flaca scoffed at the question.

"¿Se quedó ahí?" Dena thought back to her teenage angst and the chancletas that flew across the room towards her backside. Wood was nothing like foam.

"Claro. Mija, en los tiempos de antes, las mujeres cuidaban la casa, limpiaban y dejaban que los hombres decidieran las vidas de sus hijas," stated Julia matter-of-factly.

"Así era," Candy confirmed.

"Gracia' a dio' que ustedes tienen tanta libertad ahora," Flaca sighed, sounding slightly jealous.

Tía Julia made a thick batida de lechosa and picaderas for dinner. Afterward, all the tías FaceTimed their kids back in the States. Jess watched her favorite anime for comfort. Dena stacked the plastic chairs and looked around the empty marquesina, wondering what her mother would have said if she had heard all the stories.

"Tú sí eres exagera'...No, Papá no era fácil pero no me comparen a ese viejo sangru ...Claro que bailé todo la que tocaron en la 'fiesta'. Si fuimo 'a bailar, ¡íbamo 'a bailar, coño!"

1983

Gloria

Mamá Negra and Papá Nito had six children in twelve years. Having a big family wasn't their goal; it was their earthly duty. By the time the last child was born, the eldest took care of the rest. Each sibling passed down clothes and household chores to the next in line. This is why the boys could often be found in a girl's shirt, and the older kids with no shoes at all.

The firstborn, María Yulissa, or Julia, proudly raised the rest of her siblings, accepting each as a new baby doll instead of toys the family could not afford. Juan José, or "Yunior," didn't resemble his namesake in the slightest. For nearly eight years, he was the only boy in a house full of women. He learned to be soft, to listen, to respect, or be shoved to the side. Fatima la "Flaca," was a twig of a girl but loud and fierce. When Gloria Luz was born, they tried to call her "Luz." She was the only one to fight for her first name, claiming it sounded more powerful. Gloria quickly volunteered for the role of second son. Nito resented a little girl helping out with men's work, but couldn't deny the need for extra hands. The older girls hated getting dirty anyway.

Carina, or "Candy," had a dulce de leche complexion and an even sweeter disposition. She was everyone's favorite baby girl, quick to learn and eager to please. And Emmanuel, the self-proclaimed "best for last," was destined to be a ball-playing playboy from the moment he could walk and talk. Negra listened to El Caballo Negro on the radio for her entire pregnancy, since they couldn't afford a TV. She dubbed Emmanuel her "Johnny." He was Nito's last attempt at another son. Once he was born, Negra "cerró la factoria."

Together, they cooked, cleaned, collected eggs, milked goats, picked fruit, planted vegetables, and lived off the land. It wasn't a bohemian dream; it was survival of the grittiest. The girls were always tasked with household chores. A couple of days after a heavy rain, when the clouds parted, they were sentenced to do laundry. Negra would stack the house's clothes into poncheras and wake the girls up at the first ray of light. Once Johnny was born, she relied on Julia and Flaca to go without her.

"Vayan directamente al río. Limpien todo bien. Mira…" Negra called Flaca over to demonstrate the proper scrubbing technique. She was exhausted from late-night feedings with baby Johnny and had zero tolerance for chores done incorrectly.

"Yo sé, Mamá," the little girl looked back, annoyed. She had been going down to the river to wash clothes with Julia for a few months now, since her mother had been too pregnant and exhausted to go.

"Ah sí, ¿tú 'sabe'? ¿Tú 'sabe'? Entonces, ¿por qué la otra vez regresate con cosa' sucia' todavía?" She smacked the bar of soap into the little girl's palm. "Enséñame." She placed a shirt in Flaca's other hand. Her daughter complied, demonstrating proper washing form.

"Así. Pero más duro. Así. Mira, mira…" This time, Negra held her daughter's hands in hers and rubbed the shirt together. She looked up and eyed her oldest. "Mira, Julia, pónle atención cuando ella lo hace. Que lo haga bien."

"Sí, Mamá," Julia, already standing by the door with a full plastic bin in front of her little toes, nodded respectfully. She had been washing clothes for over half her young life, her small hands had the calluses to prove it. Flaca rolled her eyes at Julia, the perfect daughter.

"Mira, yo casi no he dormido por e'te muchachito aquí," Negra pointed her puckered lips towards giggling baby Johnny.

"Quiero que se lleven a Gloria para que yo pueda descansar un poco."

"¡Mamá, no!" Flaca rolled her eyes again, this time at her rambunctious little sister. Gloria was six years old, itching to go out, play, do anything except work. She wouldn't help them at all.

"Mira, ¡no me hables así! Lleven a su hermana. Vayan directamente al río y limpien todo con mucho cuidado que no se pierda nada o rompe nada. Y después regresen, ¡todas juntas!" Negra watched as they nodded in unison. "Váyanse ya o si no, se va el sol," she said, peeking out the window. Small white clouds were starting to circulate in the morning sky. The weather was temperamental, unpredictable. They took their chances when they could get them.

Julia swung her arms up and raised one of the poncheras above her. She pressed its bottom to the top of her soft head, her hands on either side of it. Flaca did the same with her plastic bin. All three girls walked out in a single file. Their plastic flip flops stuck to the mud beneath their feet then smacked their tender heels with every step. It was the rainy season, and mud was a good sign. It meant the rainwater was still soaking into the earth, not flowing through their home.

"¡Gloria, deje' de caminar tan rápido!" Flaca yelled. Not only did her little sister not have to carry, scrub, or hang clothes, but she was now running ahead of them, mocking their labor.

"Sí, Gloria, ¡espérenos! Casi llegamos y después podemos jugar." Julia hoped the white lie would calm the restless girl. Gloria paused and waited for them to catch up. She scanned the area, but there was nothing to play with, just endless bright green shrubbery in every direction.

Down by the river, the water ran a grayish brown with land runoff from the week's rain. It didn't look clean, but it was the best they had. The older girls placed their bins on boulders and hopped an extra step down to wash. Julia took two bars of half-used jabón de Cuaba from her bin and passed one to Flaca, supervising her closely. She wouldn't let her sister diminish her reputation as a model child and mujer-to-be. They scrubbed, rinsed, and repeated for the next hour until their bony fingers were pruned from the cold Camú waters like an old chinola left in the dark.

"Pero, ¿por donde anda Gloria?" Flaca asked Julia, who was entrenched in her role as instructor. They looked around, horrified to discover that their little sister was gone.

"No sé. Pensé que estaba ahí." Julia pointed left to an empty riverside where she had last seen Gloria just minutes ago. She put on her glasses, which she had previously set down on a rock, and looked around. Julia always felt that poor eyesight was the one thing impeding her perfection. Now it might be the reason for her first beating. "Lo juro, estaba ahí hace no sé...¿cinco minutos?" Julia started to panic. She had miscalculated Gloria's unpredictability.

"¡Gloria! ¡Gloria!" Julia yelled up and down the riverside.
"¡Gloria! ¡Gloriaaaa!" Flaca joined in.

The sisters looked at each other nervously. It was a small town; they knew they would find Gloria. What scared them was that Papá or Mamá might find her first.

As they shouted, Gloria was already seven minutes up the path they had taken down, picking bright red cerezas dangling from a bush. She loved cherries, but they were a rare treat, since her family didn't grow any on their finca. The bush felt like a rare pot of gold she could forage for hours. She stuffed her chubby fists, ate the cherries one by one, and spit the seeds out onto the path. She considered returning to her sisters, but the river was boring: no one wanted to play and Flaca had an attitude. Then again, she usually did. After filling her belly with wild fruit, she decided to go home instead.

Halfway there, she saw her father's motorcycle parked on a side street off the main road. She went towards it, like a safety light guiding her home. The bike was stationed in front of a house she didn't recognize. Curious, she approached the house's front window to peek inside. Standing stiff and shirtless, her father jumped backward when he noticed her wide, brown eyes gazing up at him through the glass. The younger woman he was kissing was just as startled when she turned around and found his daughter watching them from her porch.

In her brief years of life, Gloria had seen her father angry, frustrated, exhausted, even occasionally happy, but this was the first time she had ever seen him scared. It made her uneasy, too; his expression mirrored onto her. Nito pushed the younger woman aside, threw on his shirt, and hurried out the door.

"Mami, ¿qué haces aquí?" He asked, with a tone he usually reserved for pretty young women, never his kids.

"Fui al río a lavar ropa," she said innocently in her squeaky voice.

"¿Tú? ¿Lavar ropa? Pero eres muy joven para eso." He tugged at her dress and patted the top of her head. The loving gesture should have signaled something was off, but she was too confused to notice.

"No, Fati y Juí e'tan lavando," she tried to explain. "Encontre e'to." She held out a small handful of half-smushed cherries. Juice dripped down her fingers and forearm, accidentally brushing against the hem of his clean shirt, staining it pink. He shook his head, declining the offer.

"¿Y las dejaste solas?" He scanned the area to ensure his other daughters weren't coming around the corner too.

"Sí." Her declaration shifted his tone.

"Gloria, eso no se hace." He raised his voice, enough to assert himself but not enough for the neighbors to hear. "Te voy a llevar a la casa para que te quedes con tu Mamá," he said. Gloria pouted. She wasn't sure if she was in trouble, but she hoped she could buy more time away from Negra, who was already in a horrible mood.

"Te dejo allá que yo tengo que terminar algo aquí. ¿Me entiendes?" He asked firmly.

"Sí." She rubbed her arms, which were starting to sting.

"Entonces vamos," he said, looking her directly in the eye and ignoring her wriggly movements. "¿Viste algo ahí?" He asked, hopping on his bike. She was perplexed. What did he mean? Why was he acting so strangely? Why did her skin sting? "Ahora, en esa casa, digo," he clarified.

"Estabas con una amiga," she said, releasing the remaining cherries from her hands, overburdened by the need to scratch her arms. They felt bitten, though she couldn't see any bites.

"No, no mami. Eso fue un *amigo*. Estaba hablando con mi *amigo*," he said before roughly pulling her up on the bike behind him.

"¿Un amigo? Con cabello largo," she said, rubbing her inflamed skin with her sticky fingers.

"No, no. Fue un hombre. Tal vez no lo viste muy bien." He reached back and placed her arms around him for stability.

"Tu 'amigo'." Gloria adjusted her statement and shifted in her seat. Her cheeks and neck began to sting too.

"Sí, así fue. Estaba hablando negocios con mi amigo cuando te vi caminando," he insisted. He turned the key, shifted gears, and jerked them forward, too impatient to drive slowly back home. She bounced in the air as they rode along the dirt road and held onto his thin cotton shirt, unable to reach her arms fully around his large belly. The burning sensation persisted. She wanted to throw herself off the bike, roll around on the ground, find relief.

"Tu amigo," she repeated back to him as they pulled up to the house.

"Exactamente. Mi amigo. Bueno, mami, aquí te dejo. Y no te vayas de nuevo. Te quiero ver entrar a la casa." He looked at her more sternly than before. "Y dile a tu mamá que tus hermanas se quedaron en el río y que yo te traje," he said, hoping she would memorize her mini monologue.

Gloria stepped off of the back seat and towards the house. Her skin burned, but the rash hid beneath her dark complexion. Negra woke up from a nap and found the six-year-old sitting on the porch alone. Once she realized Gloria abandoned her sisters, she told her to get a fallen branch del árbol de naranja agria immediatamente. The fallen were her favorite because they were harder. The previous sleepless night made Negra more intolerant and violent than usual. She lashed the little girl repeatedly to remind her to never run away or disobey orders. The leafless twigs dug into her thin brown skin, leaving soft white drag marks dripping with strawberry blood.

Gloria couldn't distinguish between the branch scars and the cherry bush hives. Her skin burned, begging to be scratched, but the scrapes from the twigs prevented her from moving. She rolled around in her hot bed, before getting summoned to the living room mere minutes later.

"Oye, ¡deja de llorar y ven ayudar a tus hermanas a guindar la ropa!" Negra didn't have time to let Gloria wallow in her pain. As soon as she saw her other daughters arrive, she put them all to work. Soon after, they began making lunch. She needed her soldiers to move swiftly and seamlessly throughout the day. It was her only hope of getting to bed early.

Years later, her sisters would retell the tale of Gloria running off and scaring them to death. But she wouldn't remember most of it: the laundry, the walk, or the beating. It wouldn't be the last time Gloria did as she pleased, upset Mamá Negra, or got beaten with the broken branches of the orange tree out back. Gloria would only remember the look on her father's face when she peeked inside the window and an inexplicable sense of shame for spying on him, as if some secrets were meant to stay hidden.

Day Two

Dena

Slow Wi-Fi and relentless humidity drove Dena to bed early. Once again, she slept deeply and didn't notice when Jess left the bed. She found the house empty in the morning, although breakfast was on the kitchen table. Each plate was covered with another equal in size to ward off any flies. She ate in silence, grateful she didn't have to cook. She wished she could hit the gym or go out for a run like she did back home. The steady, rhythmic pounding of her feet hitting concrete soothed her. It allowed her mind to relax while her legs ached and her lungs fought for air. But she wouldn't get far with the slippery mud and the overbearing heat. Once again, she felt trapped inside la casa Vega.

"Vecina!" Someone yelled towards the home. She didn't respond, assuming it wasn't for her. She stayed in the kitchen, the room furthest from the front door, to try and get some work done. An hour later, when everyone else returned, she had already reviewed and organized most of her outstanding work from the previous two days out of office. She closed the screen as her aunts came into the kitchen.

"Cion, Tía," she repeated three times over.

"Dios te bendiga. ¿Tú tá trabajando, mija?" Flaca's elongated face frowned, distressed by the mere thought of work.

"Solo un poco. Estaba mandando mensajes. Pero ya acabé." She tried to diffuse everyone's worried stares.

"Bueno, cuando termines, deberías visitar a Juana que está mala." Tía Candy suggested, always insistent on doing the right thing.

"Sí, buena idea. O a Juma, el pobrecito siempre pregunta por ustedes aunque ya Jess fue a verlo," Julia suggested.

"Sí, tal vez otro día."

"Debes caminar un poco, no estar sentada adentro el día entero. Estás más llenita que la última vez que te vi," Flaca pointed to Dena's slight muffin top. Everyone had been too emotional the previous two days, but Flaca was finally comfortable enough to be rude.

"Esa muchacha no está gorda. Está fuerte. ¿Tú no ves que ella va al gimnasio?" Candy defended her niece. Despite how much Dena loved working out, her bad eating habits over the last two years were catching up to her. Her once-toned arms had softened and her belly pudged out.

"Muy fuerte. Mirale las piernas," Julia chimed in, pointing to Dena's defined quads. That was the one good thing about running for over ten years: her legs remained toned, her butt full and round.

She nodded awkwardly and attempted to change the subject. "Estaba pensando…quiero saber adónde queda la casa de la mujer de ayer," Dena said calmly, sensing the potential chaos that might commence.

"¿Qué mujer?" Asked Flaca, her right hand already on her hip. Her black hair made her look more serious than usual in the bright morning light.

"La mujer…Creo que se llamaba 'Minerva'." Again, Dena spoke carefully, calculating the amount of energy she would need to combat the defense line already forming in the kitchen.

"¿Y pa qué tú quieres hablar con ella?" Asked Flaca, this

time taking a step toward her. Candy and Julia looked up from either side of her.

"Yeah, what do you want to talk to her about?" Jess came into the kitchen with the last bag of groceries.

"Bueno, tal vez ella..." Dena was not good at speaking slowly. She wondered if this was the right time to reveal her mind's inner dialogue. "Tal vez ella sabe..."

"¿Sabe que?" Tía Julia adjusted her glasses as she spoke as if they might help her better understand her niece's line of questioning. They were Gloria's closest friends. There wasn't anything anyone knew that they didn't already know three decades prior.

"Yeah, what?" Jess put the bag down and stood next to her tías. To Dena's frustration, her sister was joining the wrong side.

"Okay, tal vez ella no sabe nada, pero no sé...tal vez no sería mala idea..."

"Esa mujer trabaja con cosa' rara'." Flaca raised her voice incrementally. "Le meten lo' espíritu' y quien más sabe lo que ella hace. No te meta' en eso," she concluded. Dena thought about how Flaca saged her home monthly and had a small altar in the corner of her dining room. She saw it last time she visited her in Florida. It was after her divorce, when Gloria insisted the three of them fly down there to lift her sister's spirits—not that it worked. Flaca remained inconsolable, reaching new levels of thin and irritable. How was this different from that?

"Mira, esa mujer no sabe nada de tu mamá. Nosotras sabemos más que nadie. Si tienes una pregunta, preguntarnos aquí." As a devout Catholic woman, Julia believed nothing good came of discussing the paranormal out loud.

"Okay..." Dena had already considered another in. "¿Y ella lee cartas?"

"Sí. Yo no sabía que tú estabas interesada en eso," Tía Candy looked up, eager to find alternative solutions.

"Sí, Tía. Tal vez ella me puede decir del futuro. Ayudarme un poco." She lowered her eyes. Her tías looked at her suspiciously, then solemnly. Their nieces were essentially orphans, and they knew firsthand that there was nothing they could do to remove that sweeping pain.

"Bueno, si quieres que te lean las cartas, tengo otra amiga por aquí que sabe mucho de eso. Pero Minerva no," Flaca said in a tone that reminded Dena of her mother. Her aunt had become more snappy post-divorce, more snarky too. She worried about her, but she knew better than to ask. Although she was almost thirty years old, Dena still felt like a child compared to her aunts. She respected their boundaries, mysteries, privacy. It was her mother's life she wanted to pry into.

"Okay. Está bien. Entonces podemos hablar del baño. ¿No hay alguien que podemos llamar para arreglar la llave?" Dena asked.

"Sí. Sí tienes dinero, se puede arreglar cualquier cosa." Julia had been living in DR and looking after Abuela's house for three years, though she could not afford to update the property. She retired early to move back to DR with her husband, but was still too young to collect her social security checks. Her siblings insisted they had too many bills in America. Johnny was barely making ends meet in DR. Sol was the poorest of the bunch, living off small sewing projects and favors. Abuela's house was decaying before their eyes, and no one could afford to save it.

"Sí, está bien. Llama y pregunta a cuánto sale." Dena didn't feel particularly at home there. Years of bittersweet memories filled with water-stained walls and dusty ceiling fans made it feel more like a mandatory summer school program than a home. But she hated feeling like a bystander as the house—a pillar of her childhood—fell apart. It was the least she could do to help preserve this tiny bit of Vega legacy. In some ways, paying to repair it was an offering. It allowed her to give without losing herself.

"El muchacho viene hoy si quieres. Lo llamo ahora mismo," Julia assured her. Dena washed the dishes and waited until her aunts went to sit in the marquesina. Then, she went next door to talk to Sol.

"Sol, ¿dónde vive Minerva?" Dena asked outright when she saw Sol was home alone, rocking in her mecedora. Her adopted aunt took a sip of her limonada and sighed deeply. She was not a woman of many mysteries, but she was a superstitious one. She knew that the more someone ignored a spirit, the more likely it would circle back to finish its unsettled business. She gave Dena the directions and added a warning, "Ojo, mija."

Down the road, Dena made the first left, then a right past the patch of plátano trees. It was the second house on the left, painted pale yellow with light blue trim. She stepped off the powdered dirt road and onto a grassy lawn. The two kids playing outside looked up at her. The little boy, nearly naked, ran around a slightly older girl. They were different shades of brown, but their facial features marked them as undeniable relatives. The girl put down the hose she was spraying and stepped forward. His protector.

"¿A quién tú bu'ca'?" The little girl had a thick country accent. Her tiny hands rested on her even smaller hips.

"¿Está Minerva?" Dena asked hesitantly, unsure if she should be there.

"¡Mamiiiii! ¡Alguien te bu'ca!" The little girl yelled toward the house, her tone mimicking an irritated middle-aged woman.

"¿Quién?" Answered a voice from inside.

"¡No sé! ¡Unaaa señoraaa!" She yelled back, stretching the vowels in her words. Dena looked past the little girl to the open doorway. A straw broom poked out, and a squat, brown woman followed.

"Hola, Minerva. Yo…"

"Sí, yo sé quien eres. Ven, pasa," Minerva waved her in before disappearing into the dark house. Though the outside of the home was surrounded by bright tropical flowers in bloom, the inside was incredibly gray: gray ceilings, gray concrete floors, and gray images glued onto thick wooden boards.

"No te esperaba. Te puedes sentar ahí si quieres." Minerva pointed her lips to a gray wooden chair. The seat was made of cowhide stretched so thin that there were a couple of holes on the wrapped edges. As she sat, her hips spilled over the sides. The chair wobbled, its uneven legs worn down from years of nervous, bouncing guests.

"Sí. No le avisé porque no tengo su número," said Dena, hoping to stay in Minerva's good graces.

"Yo sé. Digo que no pensé que ibas a venir porque…tú sabes…lo de ayer." Minerva spoke more clearly and slowly than her daughter. She appeared strangely uneasy for a woman who just yesterday was so loud and powerful. Dena wondered if her previous demeanor was her mother's energy funneled into her body.

"¿Quieres café?"

"Sí, está bien. Gracias." Dena learned from a young age to always accept what's offered when visiting someone's home. The more you decline, the more they offer, and she needed to get down to business before her presence was required at the next hora santa.

"Lo que pasó ayer…La gente no le gusta hablar de eso." Even she, the blessed vessel, didn't name it out loud.

"Claro. Eh…nunca he visto algo así." Again, Dena tried to lighten the tension but was at a loss for words. She wondered what to say to a body that temporarily held her mother's spirit. From experience, nothing hostile.

"Solo quería saber…si Mami tenía algo más que decir."
She let out a long-held breath as she spoke.

"Por supuesto," Minerva nodded. "Lo que pasa es que yo no controlo eso. Ellos…los espíritus…deciden que quieren decir. Yo no los controlo. Se entran sin avisar y se van así también." Again, Minerva bowed her head mid-sentence. Unlike other practitioners, Minerva didn't work with specific spirits. Nadie se montaba regularly. Instead, the recently dead used her body as a vessel at will. It didn't happen frequently, just enough for rumors to spread and fear to engulf the minds of strangers.

"¿Entonces no recuerdas nada?"

"No. Mi mente se cierra y ellos entran así a su voluntad. Yo nunca los llamo. Y no me recuerdo después lo que pasó." She seemed similarly frustrated. Minerva often wondered if it was more challenging to live with the haunting spirits or the inability to explain them to others. People always looked to her for answers that she did not possess.

"Tengo muchos años con eso encima del pecho. Ellos me mandan, ellos deciden. Yo he intentado ignorarlos pero a veces como ayer, los espíritus son muy fuertes y no puedo."

Suddenly, Dena felt bad for her. She attempted to make eye contact, but Minerva kept her head down, fixated on the brewing coffee.

"Entonces si no me puedes decir más sobre eso, ¿me puedes leer las cartas? Me han dicho que haces eso también." Dena had only done one other reading in her life: her mother's friend read coffee grounds from her mug years ago. All of the woman's predictions struck her as vague, broad statements. After the previous day's display, however, she had faith in Minerva. Perhaps she might inadvertently divulge more about her mother.

"Sí, con eso sí te puedo ayudar." Minerva poured two cups of coffee with two spoonfuls of sugar each and stirred them slowly. "Bebe tu café y después vamos atrás."

Minerva led her to the back of the house, moving slower than Dena expected for a woman her age. In the daylight, she saw a few scars on her arms and legs. But she didn't dare ask how they got there. She thought it best to stay focused on the mysteries pertaining to her own life.

The shack behind Minerva's house was barely six feet wide. The walls were made of overlapping wood panels that often gaped due to their raw, natural edges. Bright sunlight beamed in through the narrow slits, speckling the room like the feathers of a spotted rooster. There was only one small window on the back wall, and it was covered by a black lace curtain.

The only other sources of light were three tall candles Minerva lit as soon as she stepped inside, arranged in a triangle on two parallel shelves. Dena recognized that they were for God, Jesus, and the Holy Spirit, as her mother used to light similar candles on major Catholic holidays. Cluttered around the candles were crochet doilies, wallet-sized photos of saints, glass pebbles, faceless clay dolls, a large Virgin Mary, dried flowers, colorful rosaries, a tablet of alcanfor floating in cup of foggy water, a cobalt blue evil eye, agua de florida, a jar of sand, and a bloodied Jesus hanging from a twelve-inch cross. All the cultures that had been thrown together in the last few centuries on the island were laid out side by side on her shelves. On the right side of Jesus was a Taíno zemi, and an Oshun figurine sat to the left. The totems watched over Minerva, easing her previously tense demeanor.

"Siéntate." Minerva pointed to a plastic chair across from her seat in front of the window. In between them was a small table draped with a burgundy velvet cloth. The table and chairs took up the majority of the space in the room.

"Comenzamos contigo. Me dices tu nombre y tu edad," the matron said, adjusting her position in her chair.

"Me llamo Anadena Luz Rodriguez y tengo veintisiete años." She gave Minerva her legal name, hoping honesty would keep the spirits on her side. It felt strange saying her full name out loud, as if the sounds corresponded to someone else.

While pregnant, Gloria read somewhere that "Anadenathera peregrina" was the Latin name for cohoba, the indigenous mahogany tree of the island. Dena hated that her mother named her after an obscure plant no one knew. Gloria insisted the name represented the tree's tough, durable qualities, only to reprimand her years later for being too strong-willed and hard-headed.

"Bueno, Anadena, ¿qué buscas hoy?" Minerva lifted the baraja espoñola from beside her and placed it between her palms, closing her eyes as she waited for a response.

"Ehh…bueno, quiero saber el futuro. Lo que viene."

Minerva shuffled the deck repeatedly and mumbled an incoherent prayer. She placed it on the table in front of Dena.

"Divídelo en tres."

Dena did as she was told and waited, her right leg shaking uncontrollably.

"Esta a tu izquierda es del pasado. Esta del medio es el presente. Y esta a la derecha es el futuro. ¿Con cuál quieres comenzar?" Despite Minerva's calm gaze, Dena felt pressured. Perhaps it was the dim lighting and figurines taunting her from the shelf.

"¿El pasado?" She sounded unsure.

"Yo recomiendo el presente primero pero es mejor que decidas tú."

"Entonces, el presente," Dena rushed to correct her mis-take.

"No, no. Siempre escuchas a tu intuición con todo lo que digo. Si no suena correcto, está bien. Solo tú sabe' el futuro de tu vida." Minerva was used to people, usually younger women, coming to her for advice, hoping for a clear voice of reason.

But she always reminded them that she was a mere messenger, not the ruler of their lives.

"Okay." Sweat slowly formed on Dena's forehead.

"Entonces, comenzamos." Minerva flipped the first three cards over. "Dos de copas, caballo de espadas y el seis de oro. Estas dos son buenas." She pointed to the first two. "Indican amor, una relación romántica o de amistad. Una pareja que se quiso mucho. Veo alguien con determinación y un carácter fuerte. Y una decisión que cambió todo." Minerva nodded her head slowly as she spoke, as if confirming her own words. Dena was slightly disappointed. Minerva already knew her mother's story. It felt as if she was stating the obvious: her parents loved each other, they moved to America, and it changed everything.

"Y la última...Esta es interesante, sí." Minerva mulled over the card before placing it down in front of Dena, who thought it looked rather unremarkable. "Veo a alguien triste, cansada, tal vez deprimida. Veo que algo le pasó que no pudo pasar."

"¿'Pasó que no pudo pasar'? No entiendo." Dena was perplexed. She was hoping for clearer-cut answers.

"Veo a una mujer fría. Llorando." Dena thought back to her mother, whom she had only ever seen cry four times in her entire life. Perhaps her first New York winters hit her harder than expected. Dena had been a baby when they moved to America, and Jess was already growing inside their mother's belly. Gloria was twenty-one when she flew away from everything and everyone she knew. But she told the story as if she was off on an adventure to a new world, not crying in a blizzard.

"E'ta mujer no sabe na." She imagined her mother objecting to Minerva's analysis.

"Ahora el presente. Una sota de espadas, un cuatro de copas y otro seis. El seis de bastos. ¿El seis significa algo para ti?" Minerva looked up at her.

"Seis...seis...Junio 6 es hoy." Dena noticed dust particles

floating in the thin rays of sunlight around her. The room felt extra stuffy.

"Ah sí," Minerva confirmed. "La primera dos enseñan una mujer fuerte con mucha energía y curiosidad. Busca algo y lo va a encontrar." Dena thought about her mother: loud, aggressive, expressive. Though she supposed those could be synonyms for "energetic" and "curious."

"Sí, Mami tenía mucha fuerza."

"Es que estas cartas son del presente y tu mamá no sigue aquí," Minerva responded softly. The carefully selected words stung Dena. It was the first time someone had said it to her so plainly. "Me imagino que esto está hablando de otra mujer," Minerva clarified. Did she mean Tía Julia? Or Flaca? Or Sol? They were all as vibrant and energetic as her mother.

"En esto veo un momento difícil…complicado." Minerva pointed to the last card. She stared at it for a long time before grabbing the last pile. "Ahora para el futuro. La sota de copas, el ocho de oros. Mira, esa sí es una carta buena y la dos de espalda." Minerva returned to the first. "Esta representa un hombre leal, sensible y fiel." Of course this older Dominican woman would convince Dena to keep her head up, dream big, and, ultimately, find a man.

"Así mismo."

"Ocho de oros. Una carta muy buena. Significa un cambio positivo," she smirked. Dena was starting to get a nagging feeling that Minerva was keeping everything light. "No sé si quieres comenzar algo nuevo, si estás caminando por un camino nuevo, pero sigue ahí. La gloria te encuentra," Minerva said, unironically. "Esta representa noticias importantes que vas a recibir." Minerva rested her index finger on the last card.

"¿Tal vez aquí?" Dena was hoping for something more specific.

"Tal vez. Esta al revez entonces también puede ser un engaño." Minerva casually sprinkled in the bad news, hoping her client wouldn't sulk. "Sigue buscando y vas a saber," she offered another vague response. "¿Tienes una pregunta?"

Dena shook her head no. Minerva seemed sincere, though the reading was trivial at best. What she really ached to know was what it felt like to have her mother's spirit spontaneously spring into her body, if she had heard anything else, and if Gloria had something more to say, since she usually always did.

"¿Algo que está en tu mente?"

"No, no creo." Dena decided. The reading reduced her faith. Perhaps Minerva couldn't conjure up answers; they had to burst out of her uncontrollably.

"Bueno, eso fue todo. Si tienes otra pregunta me avisas. Siempre estoy aquí." Minerva could sense Dena was itching to fall apart. She didn't want her sacred space to be the site of such unraveling. It was best to lead her guest out graciously.

Outside, Dena stumbled around the grass as her eyes readjusted to the aggressively bright sunlight.

Once the second hora santa was over, Dena headed to the backyard for some fresh air. She stood beside the outdoor kitchen, which was slanted from years of flash flooding from the river. Its corrugated tin roof and all the shiny tree leaves surrounding it reflected the purple sky. The air smelled like wet dirt and green mangos.

The concrete path from the outdoor kitchen had been poured out decades ago and no longer lay flat. Weeds reached up towards the sky between the cracks. White petals that fell from the naranja agría tree were speckled on the ground like little stars on a concrete sky. A patch of plátano trees sat to the left. Dozens of plátanos hung low behind 4-foot-long leaves that fanned out from the flaky trunks. The garden looked haunted and holy as the night began to cast shadows all over.

"Sigue," she heard her mother say, but she didn't dare go further. Instead, she looked up to see the moon and a couple of faint stars starting to emerge.

"Hola." A tall moreno stepped out behind her. She squinted, trying to place his face. It took a few seconds but she remembered: the guy who bowed at her at velorio and again at the funeral. He held a rusty wrench in his left hand and extended his right one towards her.

"Hola," she said, shaking his hand in another out-of-place greeting. She looked him up and down. Although he didn't kiss, hug, or dap like every other Dominican man, he definitely dressed like one. He had on flip flops, intentionally ripped jeans, and an obnoxiously bright blue polo shirt. His biceps looked defined beneath his thick cotton sleeves. A thin gold chain glimmered against his protruding collarbone.

"Soy Ariel. Estoy arreglando la llave del baño," he said when he noticed her staring at the wrench.

"Que bueno," she responded, unsure what else to say. Perhaps he thought he needed to greet the woman paying for the job.

"Cuarto creciente."

"¿Qué?" She followed the wrench as he pointed up towards the moon.

"La luna. Casi llega la luna llena. Dicen que e bueno para dar fuerza y para enfocarse." He stared up at the sky beside her.

"¿Tú crees en todo eso?" She tucked a loose strand behind her ear and eyed him up and down again. His skin was cocoa powder brown with eyes to match. His sharp beard and clean shape up framed his face perfectly. At the top of his head rested an inch of tight curls, crispy from excessive gel. He was a few inches taller than her with broad shoulders and a flat stomach. His build suggested a lifetime of endless manual labor, not spiritual practices.

"Claro. Aquí no e como allá que no se ve el cielo ni la' e'trella'. Aquí siempre miramo' pa'rriba. Así navegamo'." He was slightly insulted by her words and side-eye stare.

"Yo soy de aquí." She crossed her arms over her chest. She thought about Minerva's prediction of her finding a man, and she laughed to herself. Minerva probably sent this beautiful campesino herself.

"Me dijeron en el velorio que eres de allá," he said, admitting he already knew about her.

"No, yo nací aquí," she said, suddenly proud of her birth country. No one on the island thought she was Dominican enough, which made her insist upon it even more.

"No te pareces con todos los picados." He pointed to her mosquito bites and laughed. It had only been three days, and they had already covered her. Her mother liked to say the mosquitoes branded her body as having *"sangre dulce."*

"No conocí a tu mamá pero la tía mía la conoció. Me dijo que era una mujer buena. Lo siento mucho." He looked her in the eyes so intensely she took a step back.

"Entonces, ¿cómo se ve el baño?" She changed the subject swiftly.

"¿La llave? Ya la cambié. Eso fue muy fácil. Julia me mandó una foto esta mañana. Yo trabajo así, rápido."

"Perfecto. Muchas gracias." She feigned a smile before heading back inside.

"A la orden."

1993

Gloria

"¡E'pérenme!" Gloria yelled to her brothers. Johnny and Yunior walked 30 feet ahead, eager to start the day's work. The earlier they finished, the earlier Papá would let them go out and play pelota with the local boys en el play. Gloria, however, would spend the rest of the day cooking and cleaning with her sisters back home.

"¡Tu va' muy lenta!" Yelled Yunior, who was moving quicker than usual because one of the local girls was going to go watch him play. A lanky 20-year-old boy with a wisp of facial hair, he was excited anytime a girl looked his way.

"¿Cual es el apuro si van a perder!" Gloria shouted back.

"¡Oye a e'tá!" He scoffed from afar. "Mira, concéntrate en los tamarindos que nosotros vamos a recoger los limones, naranjas y cajuil." He refused to slow down or turn around. Johnny nodded in agreement. They were a decade apart, but as the only brothers in a house full of women, they were almost always on the same page.

Papá always sent Gloria out with the boys while the other girls stayed back to do household chores because, as he often said, "le gusta andar." She preferred it that way. Household chores were aburrido after a while. When she got a chance to be out in the fields, even in the blistering heat, estaba libre. The open land gave her paz entre toda la bulla back home.

The small bit of land owned by la familia Vega sat in the valley of the same name. Their two acres rolled down towards a creek that sprang from el Río Camú. It was huge for a family their size in their little pueblo, where most people only owned a two-bedroom cabin and a handful of chickens. It had been passed down three generations and somehow survived the dark Trujillo days. No one spoke about it, but it probably had something to do with the fact that Nito's grandfather supported El Jefe.

Cashew trees hung low at the entrance. They had been planted years ago by the boys, who loved to snack on the roasted nuts after running around outside. It took a few years for them to reach full harvest. Just beyond them on the right, carambola, naranja, limón, almendra y tamarindo trees were scattered around. The boys marched over to the lime trees in the back as soon as they popped open the wooden fence.

Most of the trees had been planted the year Papá Nito y Mamá Negra took over the land and converted it from a cattle farm to a fruit farm. Piña and chinola plants had been replanted three times since then. On the left side, several mango trees stretched out towards the sky. Their skinny offspring sat in their shadows, waiting for the day they could access more sunlight. The whole family took turns filling sacks of fallen leaves and branches for the goats in the back. The goats had their own fenced area, since they loved tearing the plants apart. Their ruthless munching drove Nito crazy. Coconut trees lined the fence even though no one ever went up to collect them. Negra just loved how they looked swaying in the breeze. That was how la finca grew: part convenience, part business, part para la vista.

The tamarindo trees were 20 feet tall, but the fruits hung low and fell frequently. Gloria had fought the boys to secure this cosecha. Hasta un saco lleno weighed a fraction of a lime or an orange sack. They eventually gave in after realizing it was worse to be left alone in the fields with a nagging Gloria than carrying a heavy bag. She began her work by appraising the ones on the ground, carefully selecting the ripened fruit. Afterward, she used a long pole Papá kept nearby to rock the veiny branches and knock the fruits off their stems. It rained tamarindo all around her.

The tamarindo trees sat close to the water en la orilla de la finca. The creek was too wide and her family was too poor to build a fence around it. There was an understanding with the neighboring landowners que no se crusaba. Whenever Gloria finished her harvest early, she would dip her joints in it. She didn't need to get clean, just soak her flesh en agua dulce. On this day, just to spite her brothers, she decided to spend a few extra minutes lingering around the bank. She took off her shoes and hopped across the flattest rocks she could find. Then, she plopped both feet into a three-inch deep pocket and let out a sigh. The feathery leaves of a cohoba tree swayed above her. She closed her eyes and bathed in the morning light filtering through them.

"Sí, ¡está rica la agua!"

She jumped up, startled by an unfamiliar voice. She squinted her eyes and looked around the riverbank to see who was there. Across from her, with his back against a 30-foot tree, was a guy around her age or possibly older.

"¿Quien tú ere'?" Gloria asked with an instinctively protective attitude.

"¡Marcelo! ¡El jefe de esta tierra!" He spread his arms wide as if they signified his power. She rolled her eyes. At sixteen, she was already tired of boys, their lines, and lies.

"Yo no te conozco," she said with one eyebrow up and her opposite hand on her hip. She was more annoyed by the fact that she didn't recognize his face than his actual presence. She knew everyone around town, including the owners on the other side, and he was not one of them.

"Esta es la finca de mi tío. Vine a visitarlo y me trajo para acá." He smiled so widely she could see all his white teeth against his roasted coffee bean complexion. She walked a few steps along the river to get a better look.

"Ven para acá." He was still grinning.

"¡Ven tú!" She ordered.

"Yo no. Papá me mata si mojo estos zapatos." He shook his head, pointing to his clean shoes. He spoke too properly to be from town.

"¿Y tú viniste a una finca con zapato' nuevo'? ¿Quién ha vi'to eso?" Her sassy remark made him chuckle. That, paired with her country twang.

"Me trajeron de visita. Yo casi nunca ando así," he claimed. She assumed it was another charming lie. She could tell by the amount of product in his thick hair that he was a city boy. He was probably always well-dressed and well-spoken. Her side-eye made him laugh again.

"Qué pasó, ¿no te gusta?" He asked, turning sideways so she could analyze his style from all angles. Now she was the one laughing.

"No. Entonces, ¿el dueño es tu tío? ¿Cómo se llama?"

"Ah...¿Quieres que te lo demuestre? Tío Dario es el hermano de Papá. Se mudó acá hace diez años cuando se casó con Tía." His story checked out. "Mira, ven a ver. Me dicen que me parezco a él." He held out his hand. She grabbed the hem of her skirt and skipped over the rocks until she was on his side. She was a pro at keeping her skirt clean, since, unlike her brothers, she would be the one to scrub down her clothes on wash day. She released her skirt, pressed against a slab of rock, and took his hand.

"¿Y tú, cómo te llamas?" He asked, waiting to release her hand until she answered. She liked his boldness. Most of the guys she knew were too scared to speak to her, aware that Papá Nito waited for her at home.

"Gloria." She took back her hand and stared into his eyes so long she forgot she intended to examine the rest of his features.

"¿Ves?" He turned to show his profile in both directions, then faced her head-on. "Me parezco a él, ¿no?" His features were all sharp: jaw, nose, eyebrows, and cheekbones. Nothing like hers, which were all round and soft. He really did look like his uncle, but she wouldn't give him the satisfaction of knowing she agreed.

"Ni un chín." She shook her head. He was much taller up close than he seemed across the creek. Skinnier too. Like a palm tree swaying gently, her voice the wind.

"¿Por qué nunca te he visto antes?" Her eyebrows furrowed as she interrogated him.

"No hemos venido hace años. Tío y Tía siempre van a la Capital a visitarnos y comprar cosas. Papá dice que está demasiado cansado para venir al campo. Pero Mamá lo convenció porque ahora quieren investir en la finca de Tío." His crisp pronunciations intrigued her. His dress shoes too. She wondered what his life looked like in the city. If he had money, fancy things, girls.

"Tengo como siete años que no vengo acá," he said, nervously placing his hands in his pockets. She scanned her brain, trying to remember if Dario's kids had primos de visita una vez. There were too many distant relatives to keep track.

"¿Y tú? ¿Eres de acá?" Marcelo asked, as curious about her life as she was about his.

"Esa es la finca de mi familia." She pointed to the other side of the creek. "Tenemos mucha' fruta', pero no de esa'." She pointed up to the fruit dangling above them.

"¿Qué son estas?" He stepped onto a rock by the base of the tree, reached up, and grabbed one of the fuzzy brown bulbs.

"Mamey. Tienen que ser media blandita para coger," she

explained. He squeezed it gently before releasing it. He reached for another two before finding a perfectly tender one.

"¡Dale la vuelta y hálalo!" She instructed. Marcelo pulled hard and lost his balance on the rock. As he began to fall backward, Gloria stretched both her arms out and pushed him up, catching him before he hit the ground.

"Tú sí eres fuerte," he said, surprised and slightly embarrassed.

"¿Tú nunca ha' recogido fruta?" She laughed for a minute straight as he attempted to dust himself off and regain composure. He couldn't hide the fact that he was out of his element on a farm. He held the fruit out towards her, waiting for her to accept it. It took her another minute to realize that he didn't know how to cut it open. She started to laugh even more, nearly wiping tears from her eyes. He was such a strange boy: he wore clean shoes to a finca y ni supo cómo partir una fruta. Que raro.

She pulled out a small knife from a pocket she had sewn into her skirt's waistband. He jumped back nervously, though he was secretly impressed.

"¿Quién te dio ese cuchillo?" He teased. Gloria ignored him. Men always had sly remarks about her knife, which was precisely why she carried it. She flipped the blade open and cut straight down the middle of the fruit and around the other side until she ended up back where she started. She twisted the two halves back and forth in opposite directions until they fell open. She held one side out to him, revealing a bright orange flesh and a nearly black core. The narrowing ends made it look like an open eye. He had never seen anything like it before. Marcelo lived a relatively sheltered life in the capital, away from open fields and wild food. Everything he ate was prepackaged or precut by his mother.

She cut a slice, and with the tip of her blade, she slid off the peel in one motion. "Pruébalo," she smirked. He dug his teeth into the edge.

"¿Te gusta?" She cut herself a piece too.

"No sé. Es suave pero un poco desabrido," he claimed before devouring the rest of the piece and holding his hand out for another.

"Ah, pero mejor de ahí se daña." She bit into her own slice.

"La piel se parece al color tuyo." He pointed to her arm as he ate.

"Y la semilla se parece a la piel tuya." She poked his arm back and bit into another piece. Slice by slice, they finished eating the mamey until they were licking their fingertips. She hopped back into the water to rinse her hands and the sticky blade. He went to jump down beside her but misstepped, causing the water to splash up and wet the bottom of her skirt.

"¡Ay! ¡Perdón!"

"¡Me ensuciaste la falda!" She cried, resisting a smile through her scrunched-up face. He laughed louder than before. It was hard for her to remain stone-cold Gloria with a sound like that ringing in her ears.

"¡Riaaaaa!.....¡Gloriaaaaa!" An echo crept in through the trees. She recognized Yunior's voice calling her.

"¿Te llaman?" Marcelo's eyes narrowed as he strained to listen through the wind. They widened again when she held out a hand to say goodbye. He spread his arms out wide in response, his bony shoulders stretching his crisp guayabera. "Pero dame un abrazo." All his white teeth shone across his long, slender face. She placed her knife back into its pocket and hugged him goodbye. He bent over to pick up the seed that fell when she cleaned her hands and held it up against her face.

"Igualito a tus ojos también," he said, placing the seed in her hand, hoping to hold onto her for a moment. But she moved too quickly. He let out a small sigh, barely audible over the birds and the breeze. As she crossed the shallow creek, she heard his stiff shoes shuffle around dried leaves.

"¡Vengo todos los sábados si te encuentras por aquí de nuevo!" She yelled without looking back.

Day Three

Dena

When Candy found Dena sitting alone in the kitchen at 8 a.m., she asked, "¿Cómo amaneciste, mija? ¿Qué quieres comer?" Candy always woke up early to paint her face and look for something to do. Today, she wore papaya colored eyeshadow and a matching lip.

"No, Tía, ya comí un pan."

"Oye eso. Pero eso no es comida. Ven, vamos a cocinar algo bueno." Tía Candy straightened her back and rubbed her eyes. She had been running around the kitchen since she was two and was considered the best cook in the family. Cooking removed the grogginess from her limbs, awakened her senses, focused her nervous energy. She opened the cabinet under the sink and pulled out a machete.

"Ven tú, que eres más joven que yo." Tía Candy stepped outside and pointed to the patch of plátano trees. "Mira, corta uno que vamos a hacer un mangú." She used the blade to point before handing it to Dena, who refused to take it.

"Pero llama a un muchacho, Tía. Yo no sé usar eso."

"No dique eres 'una mujer moderna'," her mother's voice mocked. Candy laughed out loud. It was a prank to see

103

if she would really try. Dena was happy to see Tía Candy was maintaining a sliver of silliness, all things considered. Her vibrant aunt was slowly returning to herself. At least someone was.

Candy went to the front of the house and asked a random teenage boy who was passing by to help. With three strikes, he cut a bundle of two dozen plátanos and carried them into the kitchen.

"Tía, déjame ayudarte," Dena insisted, crouching down beside Candy and grabbing an olla from under the sink.

"Ay, gracias. Tú sabe' que mi cadera no sirve pa na," Candy frowned, both hands on her hips. Twenty years of lifting elderly patients in and out of bed had weakened her.

A few minutes later, Sol came over and the three of them cracked, peeled, scraped, and cut until their hands were stained and the plátanos were floating in a pool of murky, salted water. When they were done boiling, they took turns smashing the olla full of plátanos into a pulp. They released their grief by pounding into metal over time—every meal like therapy.

"Ven y corta el salami." Candy handed Dena a smaller knife this time. For a split second, her round, speckled arm looked like Gloria's. It startled Dena. She was reminded of the last time she had been forced to cook there, under her mother's gaze, trapped by her duties. Except now, the kitchen felt quiet without her singing merengue in between shouting orders. Emptier too. Dena was swept up by a sudden sadness that was hard to describe and made it hard to breathe.

"Pero ese salami tá tan fino que se puede ver el sol por esa rueda." Sol came up behind her, grabbed one of the rounds, and held it up to the light. She promptly took the knife back from her niece.

"¿Cómo te sientes, mija?" Sol asked over the sound of the frying pan spitting hot oil into the air.

"Bien, Tía," Dena lied. She hated the idea of her aunts, deep in grief, worrying about her. Whatever she felt was her own to deal with. She would not burden them. Before Sol could ask again, Julia and Flaca came in glowing with a thin layer of morning perspiration.

"¡Buenos días! ¿Y ustedes por donde andaban?" Candy asked her sisters.

"Caminando por ahí," Julia said coyly.

"¿Por dónde? ¿Por ese puente?" Candy frowned at the idea. The makeshift pipe bridge was just down the road from the house, and even though the entire town crossed it regularly, her older sisters were too old for that nonsense.

"¡Ni loca cruzo yo por ahí!" Flaca was appalled at the mere idea. "Fuimos a visitar a Mary y Lurelis. Pero me duelen las rodillas. No dormí bien." Flaca was starting her list of complaints early, her voice gravelly from days of nonstop talking.

"Yo le dije a ella que si no estira las piernas se va a pudrir más rápido," Julia chimed in.

"Buenos días. ¿Hay café?" Jess stepped into the kitchen in her PJs. The coffee's aroma had traveled through the house and woken her up.

"Yeah, grab some before it's gone." Dena directed Jess to the stovetop. She poured a cup, sat across from Dena, broke a galleta in half, and handed her sister a piece. They dunked them into their mugs and watched as they soaked up the sweetened, black coffee.

"Tal vez hoy podamos limpiar la casa y arreglar algunas cosas," Dena suggested.

"What? Why?" Jess looked back confused and accidentally dropped her cracker into the coffee where it drowned helplessly. "Damn it." The liquid was too hot for her to grab it. It was annoying enough to make her want to crawl back into bed for the rest of the day.

"Ustedes siempre dicen que hay un reguero y demasiado coroto en el medio. Entonces podemos organizar un poco." Dena hoped to spin this as an act of kindness.

"¡Buena idea!" Mumbled Tía Julia through a banana-filled mouth.

"¡Oye a e'ta! Tú lo que quieres es poner a esta' pobre' niña' a trabajar," said Flaca, pouring the last bit of the coffee for herself.

"Bueno, e verdad. Siempre hay cosa' que hacer aquí," Candy agreed. Finally, Julia might dejar de amenazar everyone into cleaning every time they came back to visit.

"Uh, Dena, are you sure you want to do that? There's a lot of stuff around here." Jess frowned at her sister's suggested plan and her crumb-filled coffee.

"The Wi-Fi's down. We don't have a car. What else are we going to do?" Dena didn't mention that it was the weekend and without any work or gym or friends nearby, she had nothing else to do. Inactivity gave her more time to think and feel. She craved a distraction. "We can start with Mami's room."

"Is that a good idea?" Tía Candy asked in her thick accent. She looked to her sisters for backup.

"¿La habitación de Gloria dicen? ¿Y no es un poco temprano para eso?" Flaca's face returned to its default state of worry. She put her hair in a high ponytail, tightening her features and pulling her eyebrows higher, exaggerating her look of concern.

"Bueno, no sabemos cuando vamos a regresar. Mejor lo hacemos ahora," Dena explained. Her aunts looked at each other just as they had yesterday when she mentioned the psychic reading. They weren't buying her story, but they preferred her con un trapo en la mano over sitting around staring at a screen.

"Si las muchachas quieren ayudar, déjenla. Por fin alguien me quiere ayudar por aquí," Julia praised as she chewed her food. If there was one thing Julia loved more than praying, it was cleaning.

"Podemos comenzar allá por ahora." Dena grabbed a large garbage bag from the pantry.

"Right now? You want to start right this second?" Jess couldn't tell what Dena was up to, but she knew she would inevitably be involved. This was always the way with them: Dena had a plan, Sombra followed. For most of their lives, Jess did whatever her sister told her to. But she was weary now. It was unnerving the way she held back tears at the funeral and needed to purge first thing in the morning.

"Mira, vamos a comer antes que se enfríe la comida." Candy smoothed out the top of the mangú like icing on a cake before pouring grilled onions on top.

Three hours of cleaning felt more like a turf war with a sulking Jess and a fuming Flaca, who refused to lift a finger but had endless things to say. Every time Dena felt like tossing or donating an item, they claimed it had been beloved by Gloria.

"¡Ese no! ¿Pero cómo vas a botar eso?" Flaca maintained a bewildered expression for the better part of the cleanup.

"Tía, yo no he visto a Mami en esto desde la última vez que estuve aquí. ¡Hace diez años!"

"But Dena, Mami used to wear that shirt all the time when we were kids. That's her favorite color."

"Then, she only wore it to clean the house. That's why she sent it here."

And so it went, back and forth until Sol called them into the marquesina for lunch. She and Candy had been cooking all morning.

"¿Cómo va la limpieza?" Candy was as peppy as ever, her bright red hair dancing in the light breeze flowing through the marquesina. She was the only sister who wore her hair out since it was too short to gather. The rest used hair ties, clips, and pins to combat the climate.

"¡Horrible! Tía y Jess no quieren dar nada. ¿Cómo podemos limpiar así?" Dena looked across the table at them, annoyed. She was swiftly distracted by the moro and rabo in between them. They all dug into the food, arguing in between bites.

"Lo que yo digo es ¿como ella va a botar la ropa favorita de Gloria? Si ella estuviera aquí te gindara." Flaca grit her teeth as she poured rabo sauce on top of her rice.

"Pero Tía, ¡todo no era su 'favorito'!" Dena sucked the tender meat off of a bone.

"Flaca, es verdad, no podemos dejar todo aquí. Mejor donarlo o regalarlo. Lo único que va a hacer todo eso aquí es acumular polvo." Tía Julia tried to reason with her sister as she loaded her plate with salad and then proceeded to eat around it.

"Ven a ayudar entonces si quieres limpiar todo," Flaca shot back.

"¿Y yo no limpio todo aquí? No. Hoy tengo que arreglar algunas flores allá atrás. Mejor deja que esas niñas hagan su trabajo y ven *tú* a ayudarme a *mi*." Julia and Flaca had been butting heads their entire lives. While others believed them to be endlessly arguing, it was just how they spoke: fiercely, bluntly. On the contrary, they shared a mutual respect for each other's honest, stubborn nature.

"No. Mejor voy a ver a Rosaly que el ambiente aquí es demasiado pesado," Flaca said, digging into another piece of rabo.

Flaca left promptly after lunch. Candy and Sol returned to the kitchen to clean up. Julia went out to tend to the family garden. Jess lay down to watch downloaded episodes of her favorite anime. Finally freed from all the opinionated women, Dena went back to the room to start the real digging.

Most of Gloria's belongings were back in The Heights. The spare items her sister and aunt fought to keep were a mix of old clothes too *"feo para andar en Nueva York"* and items from her mother's childhood. The further back she went into the closet, the deeper she sank into Gloria's life. She filled three donation bags with used clothes, faded sheets, raggedy towels, and dusty curtains. Beyond the house linens, she found a box of childhood toys and trinkets Gloria considered too precious to donate to other kids. She didn't dare touch her mother's homemade cloth dolls that sagged from years of living in a wooden box, nor the matching ribbons and bows she used to put in her hair as a kid, since Jess would want to keep them as mementos.

One of the boxes contained a photo album covered in yellow fabric and a thick plastic sleeve. Abuela Negra made an album for each of her kids in a distinct color. She didn't realize until years later that Gloria hated yellow because, according to her, it was too *"chillón."* Dena opened the album to find a frowning Gloria at age two with her older siblings, a couple of photos of her at age six. She could just hear her mother complaining *"Diablo, eso' vestido' que Mami me puso siempre me picaban. Mira ustede' ahora poniéndose lo que les den la' gana',"* as if the mark of freedom was high-waisted denim shorts.

At her quinceñera, Gloria wore a strappy, light blue satin dress cut just above her knees. Her mother always mentioned it, claiming she was the talk of the town in the provocative slip. Dena had seen these photos ten years prior, but this was the first time she was struck by how beautiful her mother was. Her face was perfectly symmetrical with big brown eyes, full lips, and a broad nose. Her skin was smooth and clear. It didn't have any of the scars or creases etched in over the last two years. Unlike the previous photos where she was frowning in her lace collars and white tights, she was beaming in front of her three-tier birthday cake. Her bright white teeth, which she used to say were a personal gift from God, were perfectly straight without any dental intervention.

Even at Candy's quinceñera two years later, she was radiant. There was a photo of her and Tía Candy alone; one of her and all her siblings again, including Tío Johnny just before the growth spurt that made him taller than all his sisters; a couple with primos and primas Dena vaguely recognized from visits over the years. There was even one of Gloria smiling widely and dancing with a guy in the middle of the dance floor. The center of attention, even at someone else's party.

The next couple of pages included photos of her with Antonio. She wrapped her arms around him, but her smile was always with a closed mouth. Her father, on the other hand, looked happier than Dena had ever seen him. In one photo, he was mid-laugh as a thin Gloria clung to him on a motorcycle. In another, his thick hand sat on her belly, proudly declaring himself a father-to-be.

Dena thought about her parents' marriage, filled with constant disagreements, cursing, and getaways, often taken separately. They always seemed to want to get away from each other. The last photo in the album was taken in DR just before they all set off for America. Dena sat on her father's lap, while Jess was concealed inside Gloria's nearly flat belly. They looked like a happy little family.

She organized the boxes and stacked them on the top shelf. Finally, she could see the white tiled floor of the closet. With a broom, she swept the spider webs and dead moths so as not to touch them directly. Nothing was worse than accidentally getting caught in a web and not knowing where it began or ended.

"Gracias a todos por venir." Tía Julia closed out the third day of rezos a few minutes early. La luz se fue again, and it was too hot to keep going.

"Nos vemos mañana." Flaca was a bit less gracious.

"Sí, muchas gracias a todos. Que se vayan con Dios." Candy attempted to recover the crowd that was already buzzing about.

"Tía…" Dena approached all her aunts in the marquesina as the last neighbor shut the iron gate out front. They looked up in unison. "Encontré esto cuando estaba limpiando." She passed her aunts the photo album.

Flaca grabbed it first. "¡Ay, Dios mío! ¡Mira esto! ¡Pensé que Gloria se llevó esto hace año'!" She said, shocked and ecstatic.

"¡Déjame ver!" Tía Julia wiped her glasses to get a better look. Flaca brushed her sister's hand away and opened it up. Her eyes welled up from the very first image. "¡Mira que cosa más linda!" Julia pointed to Gloria's little white stockings. She gushed over her younger siblings as if they were her own children.

"¡Jesu'! Cuanto tiempo tengo que no veo este álbum," said Candy, also fawning over the weathered images. The few that existed of them as children were dispersed across three states and their hometown. Dena patiently waited until they reached the page with her father.

"Quería saber la historia de Mami y Papi. No recuerdo muy bien cómo se conocieron. Ustedes saben que Mami nunca hablaba de eso."

"Tu mamá y papá se enamoraron joven. Después se casaron y se fueron allá a vivir conmigo," Julia said. "Flaca se quedó a ayudar a Mamá y Papá aquí con el negocio. Pero Gloria no era fácil. No quiso trabajar aquí."

"Sí, ¿pero cómo conoció a Papi?" Dena asked again.

"Ellos se conocían de antes. Es un pueblo pequeño," Tía Flaca said as if it was obvious.

"¡Buenas!" Tío Yunior came in through the front door. He spent the last day en la Capital visiting un primo. He would leave after the weekend, since his job didn't allow him much time off.

"Cion, Tío," Dena and Jess said one after another.

"Dios me la' bendiga. Diablo, estoy cansado de ese viaje." He sat down and crossed his legs.

"¿Quieres algo de tomar?" Candy asked.

"Jugo, si hay," he leaned back into his rocking chair as his younger sister went to fetch him a drink, a habit they never shook off. "Y ustedes, ¿en que 'tan?"

"Aquí mirando el álbum de Gloria." Julia passed it to him.

"Mira a Gloria y Antonio. Que feliz ese tipo con su visa," he chuckled. Tía Julia smacked his arm and sucked her teeth.

"¿Cómo así, Tío?" Dena asked. Her aunts' eyes moved like daggers in Yunior's direction.

"Sí, bueno, se querían mucho pero tú sabe'. Tu papá quería ir a los Estados Unidos. Los dos. Todos nosotros en verdad." Julia began explaining what her brother had just blurted out.

"Antonio estudió con Gloria. Él la llevaba un año en la escuela." Candy answered the previous question that everyone else had ignored.

"¿Y así comenzaron a conocerse? ¿De un día pa'l otro?" Dena asked.

"Bueno, estaban junto' por un año. Es que en eso' tiempo' la gente se casaban rápido. No como ahora que se conocen por diez años, tienen hijo' y a vece' nunca se casan," Flaca frowned.

"Sí, además Gloria supo de una vez. Tú sabes cómo era. Cuando le cogía con una cosa, no lo dejaba." Julia raised her eyebrows and let go of the album. She was done flipping through the pages of the past.

"So, ¿se casaron para una visa?" Jess, who had been listening from a corner, was also curious about the finer details of her existence.

"No, no, no. Claro, para ir a vivir allá tu papá necesitaba una visa, pero ellos se querían mucho," Candy insistió. "Ella fue la que quería casarse temprano y arreglar los papeles para irse."

"También los padres de Antonio conocían a Mamá y Papá hace año'."

"¿Cómo?" Dena was looking for a thread to pull. For a moment, she missed her mother. Gloria would have known how to guide the conversation to get information out of them. She would have filled the room with light and laughter until they spilled their secrets uncontrollably.

"Tenían negocios juntos," Yunior said.

"¿'Negocios'?" Dena kept her eyes on him, assuming he would be the one to crack. Tío Yunior was infamously, helplessly honest.

"Sí. En eso' tiempo' Mamá y Papá estaban perdiendo mucho dinero con el negocio. Y ellos les ofrecieron comprar parte de la finca. Y después, tú sabes, Gloria se fue." He disclosed as little and as much as he needed to.

"Tus padres se querían mucho." Candy placed a hand on Dena's shoulder. "Tuvieron tiempos difíciles pero nunca se separaron," she said, as if the glue of marriage could only ever be sincere and not oppressive.

"Me voy a dormir." Dena looked at Jess, who was watching quietly from a corner.

"¿Tan temprano?" A worried Candy looked at Dena's face for clues. Her niece was as hard to read as Gloria.

"Sí, Tía. Estoy cansada de toda la limpieza. Me voy a bañar y descansar." Frustrated, Dena retreated to her bedroom. She could hear the worried mumbles of her aunts—who were incapable of whispering—outside the door.

"How are you?" Jess came in a few minutes later.

"I'm okay," Dena said though her sister didn't believe her.

"It's sad getting rid of Mami's stuff. Made me realize I

have to go home and do it again." She sat down beside Dena on the bed.

"Well, you're not going to do it alone. I'm going to help you. We can call Tía Candy to help too. And you don't have to do it right away. We just did it here because we won't be back for a long time."

"You think so?"

."Of course. Of course, I'm going to help you," Dena repeated, slightly insulted by the implication. She spent her life devoted to helping Jess.

"No, I mean you really don't want to come back here for a long time?" Jess always held more affection for their native land. She craved familiarity. It was one of the reasons she joined her mother and began working at the salon, even after earning an associate's degree at a community college. Dena and Gloria constantly nagged her about continuing her college career, but she refused.

"Yeah. Don't you think it's time we traveled to new places? All we do here is get eaten by mosquitoes and wait for the Wi-Fi to turn back on."

"I guess." Jess didn't have the energy to argue. Though Dena found their childhood oppressive, it comforted her. The apartment, the salon, Abuela's house, and Campesito always felt safe.

1994

Gloria

Eighty-six chinolas pressed onto each other in two large buckets on the kitchen floor. The boys picked them at the farm earlier that morning. The girls had to crack them open, scoop out all the seeds, and place them into a paila before lunchtime. Candy was cooking with Mamá. Young Sol, who had moved in a year earlier, was helping Julia clean. Flaca and Gloria were on fruit duty.

"Ay, ¡pica!" Flaca squealed after the third or fourth one. She cut her hand earlier in the week and was now complaining about the sour juice dripping into her wound.

"Ay Flaca, e'tamo' comenzando. ¿Vas a e'tar así el tiempo entero?" Gloria swatted several pesky flies away. The more she swatted, the more they swarmed, accepting her resistance as an invitation.

"Sí, porque me arde. Si prefieres, te puedo dejar sola," she snapped back. Gloria rolled her eyes. Flaca loved any excuse to work less. Responding would only trigger her.

One by one, they cut the passion fruits in half and scooped them clean, chewing on a couple seeds to pass the time.

"¿Como van?" Mami walked outside to check on the status of their respective buckets.

"Bien. Casi terminamos," said Flaca, who had slowed her pace down dramatically.

"Me avisan cuando terminan." Negra went back inside to check on Candy, who didn't need much supervision at all. At fourteen, she could already outcook everyone else in the family. Within an hour, all the girls finished their chores, and the boys came inside from playing with their friends. Sol set the plates down, her sisters brought out the food and juices, and everyone except Negra sat around the dining room table. Mamá always stood by in anticipation of any missing items.

"¿Mami, tenemos aguacate?" She went back to check.

"¡Pásame el jugo!" She went over to grab it.

"¿Dónde están las servilletas?" She made sure to bring enough for anyone else who might ask. For Negra, motherhood mainly consisted of whirling in circles and completing tasks. Though she had enough kids to help out each day of the week, she never took a break. Her joints were constantly aching from keeping everything together, but her mind remained sharp.

"Negra, siéntate." Nito looked up at his wife. The kids barely heard him through all their chewing and talking. "Niños," Nito spoke, breaking their chaos with his deep voice. They tensed up at his sudden attempt to regain order mid-meal. "Ustedes saben que Tía Estefany le consiguió una visa a Julia," he said, pausing for their response. When he didn't hear one, he continued. "Y por eso la agradecimos mucho." Another forced pause contained their awkward silence.

"Sí," Flaca said, hoping his speech would move along.

"Pero sin Julia aquí, tu mamá va a necesitar más ayuda en casa," he said, causing everyone to freeze.

"¿'Ayuda'?" Gloria realized he was looking directly at her.

"Sí. Sin Julia, no podemos seguir con todos los pedidos de los dulces." Selling produce had become a limited income for the family. The market was oversaturated with industrialized farms expanding across the valley. They didn't have enough hands to work or enough money to pay for more hands. One of Nito's brothers gave him the brilliant idea to sell dulce made from the fruit. The Vega family now turned out more dulce than anyone else in a ten-mile radius. They were the "Dulceros del Valle," with no patent pending, no logo, no labels, not even a single sign out front. Their marketing was all word of mouth— mouths that had been left watering after just one bite. Negra had a gift, Nito had the land, and their kids had enough time to work before and after school. Except now that Julia was leaving, there was a sudden gap in the workforce that someone had to close.

"Es la única forma que tenemos para ganar dinero. Tu mamá y Flaca solas no pueden."

"Pero Yunior ya terminó el bachillerato," Gloria pointed to her older brother, who was attempting to ignore the conversation.

"¿Y tú ha visto un hombre trabajando con dulces?" Her father said, coughing up a piece of chicken.

"Yunior no es un hombre," she scoffed back.

"Claro que sí. Mira, ese muchacho solo le falta terminar la universidad. No va a dejar de estudiar pa cocinar," he said adamantly. "Él va a estudiar pa no tener que trabajar en una finca el resto de su vida." Apparently, only the Vega men had the privilege of higher pursuits.

"¿Y yo? ¿No puedo estudiar?" She looked at Yunior enviously. She always imagined going to college just as he had. Julia had begun studying education, although she would stop now that the U.S. held a better future for her. Flaca had chosen not to go of her own accord. No one ever told Gloria it was off the table for her. Not until now.

"Ya te dije lo que vas a hacer," her father's voice steadied. Her siblings attempted to stare at their food to avoid provoking him. Gloria did not have the same restraint.

"Entonce, ¿Julia puede ir a los Estados Unidos y Yunior puede estudiar y yo me tengo que quedar aquí pelando fruta?" She raised her voice even higher. Her father's betrayal rattled her bones. Didn't he want a better future for her too?

"¿Y Flaca?" She said, moving on to the next sibling.

"Flaca sola no puede. Ella no trabaja tan rápido como tú," he said, growing more irritated by her back talk. "Tú sabes recoger las frutas, cortarlas, pelarlas y cocinarlas." They always knew when Papá was upset because he would speak slowly, dragging out his words for emphasis.

"Gloria, nosotros hemos trabajado la vida entera para que ustedes tengan una casa, comida, ropa y tiempo libre. Ya eres una señorita y necesitamos que trabajes," her mother chimed in semi-compassionately and semi-annoyed that she had to say anything at all. Gloria was always the most rambunctious child of the bunch.

"¿Entonces ya decidieron?" Gloria hated that they were using her skills and work ethic against her. She looked back and forth between her parents, appalled by their calm demeanors.

"¡Sí!" Her father pounded the table with one closed fist. He couldn't believe that after he had broken his back for this child every day of her life, she wanted to opt out of his orders. "Nosotros te hemos dado todo. Ahora es tiempo que trabajes también," he said, daring her to utter another word. "¿Tú crees que esto es gratis?" He pointed to the food on the table with his dirty fork.

"Lo único seguro que uno tiene en la vida es la muerte. Por el resto tenemos que trabajar, ganar y luchar para seguir adelante," he said pointing around the table, reminding her of the hungry mouths that needed feeding. "Julia se va en dos meses, si Dios quiere. Antes que se vaya, te va a enseñar todo lo que sabe." He spoke clearly, making sure she heard every last word. "Vas a trabajar con tu mamá y no quiero oír nada más sobre esto. Y otra cosa, mas te vale que no estés andando por la calle con fulanito por ahí," he said, swinging his dinner knife towards the window. "No quiero que nadie me hable de ti. ¿Entendido?"

One by one, her siblings tried to make eye contact with her to offer reassurance. Even Sol, who was fairly new to the family dynamics, stared wide-eyed from across the table.

"Nunca sabes lo que Dios tiene guardado para ti," her mother said, but Gloria was beyond comforting. She got up quickly, fuming from her father's final words, and nearly knocked her seat over. She went to her room, making sure not to slam the door. The last time she did, Nito kicked it open and slapped the calm back into her. She changed out of her slimy clothes and went out the back door.

The high afternoon sun beamed on her forehead as she walked through the garden. She resisted tears, stomping her way to the back concrete wall. She had never thought about what she wanted to study, but not having the choice to find out was almost worse. Who was she? What did she want? Who could she be? It didn't matter to them. It didn't matter to anyone.

She thought about Marcelo, whom she had seen at the farm a dozen Saturdays over the past few months. He cared. He asked about her. He listened carefully. She barely knew him, but she had never wanted to be beside someone as much as him at that very moment.

Day Four

Dena

At seven in the morning, Tío Yunior brought two chickens over from la finca. Tía Julia was in charge of killing, cutting, and seasoning them. By nine, white feathers were floating around the backyard. Tío Johnny came over to ignite the fire in the fogón around ten. He collected a few wide branches from the back to slide in slowly as the fire crackled. Candy and Jess cut the vegetables and boiled the viveres. Sol sprinkled in the cilantro and oregano she grew behind her house. Rosaly made white rice in another caldero. Flaca, not to be left out, gave herself the task of stirring. She claimed her self-diagnosed arthritis was too bad to do anything else. Around noon, the tías placed the sancocho, rice, fresh avocados, toasted casabe, picante, limón picado, water, and two kinds of juice made fresh that morning along the center of the table in the marquesina.

Hernando, Julia's husband, came in from Santiago for the first time since the funeral. Julia had been going back and forth from Abuela's house to her own, but he had stayed home, overwhelmed by all the prayer circles. Sol's sister came over, along with her husband and two kids. A couple more neighbors dropped in as the family was eating. Everyone went around the table discussing the weather, their upcoming plans, and the food's spectacular seasoning. Tío Yunior nearly clapped as he sucked the marrow out of his chicken bones.

"¡Ay, que jartura!" Tía Flaca exclaimed.

After the last of the stew was scraped from the bottom of the pot, the tías began cleaning, Dena and Jess served the afternoon café, and the men sat around the table sipping and chatting.

"Prima, ¿qué lo que?" Manny went to sit next to Dena when he noticed she was staring out into the backyard, her mind deep in thought.

"Tranquila aquí."

"¿No has visto a un muchacho por aquí que te guste?" Manny smirked. "Yo conozco a todo el mundo. Solo tienes que preguntar."

"Pshhh," Dena scoffed, but remembered the handsome handyman from two nights earlier. She was curious if he was really as good as he claimed. "¿Conoces al tipo que arregló el baño? Se me olvidó su nombre."

"¿A Ariel? Sí, yo lo conozco hace muchos años. Juego beisbol con él de vez en cuando. Buena gente. Y sabe bailar." Manny nudged her arm with his elbow.

"Oh my god." English uncontrollably spilled out. "No para salir con él, para arreglar cosas de la casa."

"Ahhh. Sí, claro. Es buen trabajador. ¿Y tú no viste la llave que él arregló?"

"Sí." It was true: Ariel's fix had been quick and seamless. She considered contracting him out to do more work, perhaps after she returned home, so Tía Julia could oversee it instead.

Almost as if he could read her mind, Tío Johnny pointed to her from across the table. "Cuida'o contigo," he said, curious if his accusations led him anywhere.

"Cuida'o si te enamoras por aquí," Yunior joined in.

"No, yo no me caso todavía," she assured them.

"¿Y cuanto' año' tú tiene'?" Johnny probed with a sudden look of concern.

"Veintisiete."

"Ah, po ya tú ta pa casarte," said Yunior. Both brothers nodded in agreement.

"Deja tu relajo y encuéntrate un hombre serio." Tía Flaca, despite her hoarse voice, spoke loudly enough for everyone around to hear.

"Pero no te cases aquí. Estos muchachos no tienen nada para ofrecerte," Tía Julia said as she collected the empty coffee mugs.

"Tía, pero yo soy de aquí," said Manny, betrayed by her declaration.

"No. Tú no, Manny. Yo digo los otros. Solo te quieren para una visa. Encuéntrate un hombre con dinero. A man with money," Flaca translated in her thick accent in case the message was unclear. She had refused to learn English in all her years in America except for a few important phrases.

"Dejan esa muchacha," Tía Candy interjected. "Una muchacha así—fina, elegante, trabajadora—puede tener a cualquiera. ¿No es verdad?" She winked at Dena as she sipped her tacita de café.

"¡Claro que sí! Los hombres solo dan dolor de cabeza," Sol, the only sibling who never married, responded. Though Sol never had kids, she raised two of her nephews after one of her biological sisters died tragically. But the boys were teenagers by then and barely needed any parenting. The block was her inherited family. All her time was spent helping others, cooking, and cleaning. Truth be told, she never wanted any man, but Campesito was not progressive enough for her to live freely. Instead, she grew her curly hair into a long lion's mane, stuck to the same handful of clothes, and dreamt of lives she would never live.

"Bueno, cuando tú viene' a ver, el tiempo pasa rápido," Johnny commented.

"Sí, mira a Papi. Sembró una mata de cohoba antes que nací para regalarme un mueble cuando me iba casar. Y quién supo que me iba a casar tan joven. Las cosas no se planean," Rosaly said.

"Oye eso. ¿Y qué pasó con ese árbol?" Yunior asked.

"Na. ¿Qué iba pasar? El pobre viejo la tiene ahí todavía. Dique se lo va regalar a Manny un día. Imagínate tú." Johnny laughed at his father-in-law's long forgotten dream.

"¿Y cómo sigue el viejo?" Yunior asked .

As the group went on a separate tangent, Dena turned to Manny again, this time more discreetly. "¿Manny, podemos salir esta noche?" She asked under her breath.

"Prima, no sé si eso es buena idea." He shook his head, knowing full well he would do whatever she asked.

Later that night, after la hora santa was over and the tías retreated to bed, Dena cornered Jess in their room.

"I think we should go out."

"What are you talking about? We can't go out. Tía Flaca will kill us," she whispered so as not to inadvertently wake her up.

"Listen, I need a drink. A strong one. And the only thing with alcohol here is a mango pudrido under the kitchen sink. You know how Tía Julia is about drinking in the house. Please," Dena pleaded. Since retiring early, Julia dedicated most of her days to worship. Abuela's house was now a dry zone except when Tío Johnny was around, and even then, he always took his leftover alcohol to go.

"Listen, I want a drink too, but we can't go out. The whole town is watching us. Can't someone bring alcohol here?" Jess's worry lines deepened as she spoke.

Gossip en Campesito spread faster than cancer. Rumors were born from a good baile. Kids from them, too. Jess knew it would only be a matter of hours before someone somewhere would start a sentence with "Vieron a las hijas de Gloria…" They would whisper about the girls who went to a party after their mother died. "Una mujer que trabajó tanto para darles una vida buena." She could see them scowling now.

"Okay, but what did Mami say over and over again the whole time she was sick? 'No caigen luto. No dejen de bailar. No dejen de comer por cuenta mia'. Right? She would want us to go out." She looked over at Jess, whose eyes were starting to swell with tears at the mere mention of their mother's deathbed requests. Although the memories moved Dena too, she remained steady in her request. "Being rebellious was her thing." Dena doubled down in desperation.

"But we don't even know where to go. We don't even have a car. Mami would not want us to go out alone. It's dangerous here. She literally banned us from doing that our whole lives." Watching the nightly news with Gloria had turned Jess into an anxious, middle-aged vieja.

"Manny said he could pick us up and take us to someone's house. Very chill. Not a bar or a party. Nothing crazy. Tía Julia returned home to Santiago, and Tía Candy and Tía Flaca are snoring as we speak." She pointed to the other side of the door, where Jess could hear them. "We will get one, maybe two drinks, and then he will bring us back. You decide when," Dena assured her.

"So, when I say 'It's time to go,' we go?" Jess asked, her mouth already watering for some rum and Coke.

"Yes, exactly. You're the boss."

"And we're going to someone's house? Not a bar?"

Dena nodded.

"Okay, but tomorrow you're going to explain to Tía what happened," she said. Dena did not know which "tía" she meant and didn't care. All that mattered was that she could escape the repressive air at Abuela's for any amount of time.

They put on a touch of makeup and long jeans, and waited for Manny outside. He quietly rolled up to the house in his jeepeta, which looked newly washed and shiny in the moonlight.

"¿Lo lavaste?" Dena asked, knowing it would get on his good side. He seemed hesitant to take them out when she asked earlier.

"Claro. Yo cuido lo mío." They could see his teeth gleaming from inside the darkened car.

"Dena y Jess, está es mi novia Rubi. Como la piedra. Mira que brillante." Rubi wore a short, fitted dress that matched her name. She was young and gorgeous, exactly as Dena expected.

"Lo siento por lo de su madre. No pude ir al velorio porque estaba estudiando en la Capital," Rubi frowned apologetically.

"Ella va ser doctora. Vino a pasar el fin de semana pero regresa mañana," Manny grinned widely again. At least he was just as proud of his girl as his car. "Entoce', na de teteo hoy. Vamo' pa la casa de mi amigo. Todo tranqui," Manny promised.

They drove across the main bridge to his friend's house downtown. A small group had formed on his poorly lit lawn, if a patch of dirt with scattered fallen leaves could be considered a "lawn." White plastic chairs were placed in a semicircle with two guys sitting on boulders on either end. The back of someone's old beat-up SUV was opened up and facing the group. It had a state-of-the-art stereo system with massive speakers. They listened to dembow, ate fritura, and sipped rum from white styrofoam cups. Music pounded all around them, but Manny insisted that because they were not inside a bar, they weren't actually partying. When the bottle they were drinking from emptied, he pulled another out of his bag.

"¿Cuanto fue?" Dena asked, pulling her wallet out to pay him back.

"No se preocupen. Yo me encargo," he said proudly. Even though Manny had significantly less money than they did, for the first time in his life, he could afford to treat them. He swore to them every future bottle would be on him to make up for all the sneakers, sports gear, and electronics they sent him in cajas over the years.

"Mira primas, ustedes me dicen a quién quieren aquí y yo te lo traigo. Conozco a todo el mundo. Y lo que no conozco, puedo preguntar. Así es. Soy el jefe aquí. ¿No es verdad, mi amor?" He looked over at Rubi, who giggled and pushed his shoulder playfully.

It didn't take long for Dena to realize she was amongst a group of the neighborhood kids she used to play with, all grown up. She barely recognized the guys behind their facial hair and the girls beneath their curves. Small-talking with them felt like running on mud: sticky. They asked questions about her life in New York, assuming she was well off and happy. It didn't matter that she had student loan debt, worked nonstop, and barely had time for herself. She was "una americana" and thus her blessings were endless. Then, they wanted to recount the past. But she was too far removed from that version of herself, from this town, from her childhood.

"Voy al baño," she announced abruptly after a fourth person tried to chat. The bathroom was nothing more than a glorified outhouse with no toilet paper, lock, or tiles. The guy who invited them over said they couldn't go inside the house because his mom was sleeping, although that seemed impossible given the noise. She lingered in the backyard afterwards, hoping to avoid the awkwardness out front. She wished she had a vape to pass the time, like she did back in college before Gloria found one in her drawer and threw it out the window. *"¿Te quieres morir antes de tiempo?"* She laughed to herself at the irony.

As she stood there, she heard crunching leaves. Ariel, the handyman, was walking towards her. His broad shoulders in a plain white tee reflected the moonlight.

"Damn, again?" She mumbled to herself. Either Manny invited him, or the town really was as small as her mother claimed.

"Hola, ¿cómo tú tá?" He asked in his crisp, deep voice.

"Bien, ¿y tú?" She smiled politely, searching for his eyes behind the shadow of his cap's brim.

"Mejor ahora," he replied smoothly. "Te vi en el frente."

"Mhmmm." She didn't know what to say. Had he followed her looking for something? If so, what? "¿Manny te dijo que estabamos aqui?"

"No. ¿Por qué? ¿Estaban hablando de mí?" He flashed a bright smile. Her stomach fluttered at the sight of it.

"No," she responded quickly. Ariel was the type of handsome that was aware he was. This usually turned her off, but he wasn't presumptuous about it. Even now, when no one else was around, he kept his distance from her and spoke calmly.

"Conozco a todo el mundo aquí." He explained.

"Yeah…Me tengo que ir. No puedo dejar a mi hermana sola," she pointed to the front of the house. Jess always provided a perfect excuse to leave.

"Parece que está en buena compañía." He pointed his chin in the same direction. Dena turned around and looked past a row of bushes. Her sister was surrounded by multiple men. One of them was Jess's old childhood crush. She would fret over every word he said to her or around her. That was before the street was paved and they paid for their own flights. Now, they wouldn't dare date anyone from Campesito.

"Sí, tienen muchos años que no la ven a ella. A mi también."

"¿Y por qué?"

"Estaba estudiando. Ahora trabajando. No sé…" The statements sounded more like questions. She wasn't sure what kept them away for so long. Sure, they were busy, but there was something else too, something she couldn't quite explain.

"Te puede' quedar aquí a hablar conmigo un ratito," Ariel

suggested. He wanted her to linger. "Nadie no' va a ver si tá preocupada por eso."

She turned her back to the floodlight next to the house so that when he looked at her, she could see his whole face. Bugs danced above them, smacking the lightbulb periodically, causing it to softly flicker. An old feeling fluttered across her belly. Was it the rum or his body inching closer to her? When was the last time someone looked at her like that? Her family, her boss, even her friends back home all looked at her like she was a victim of something. Ariel wasn't giving her one of those long, pained stares. He didn't pity her. He looked happy to be in her company. Eager.

"Ta bien," she said, leaning against the back of the house, hiding from the crowd out front.

"¿Te gusta esta canción?" He asked, swaying his hips side to side, doing a little three-step and tap to the Aventura song playing on the speaker. She watched but remained still.

"Y ahora por un segundo me ahogo en los mares de la realidad..."

"Sí." Dena remembered the summer *The Last* came out. Her father was still alive. "Quería ir a verlos cuando salió este álbum. Pero no pude."

"¿Por qué?"

"Mami dijo que no había dinero. Papi estaba de vacaciones aquí. Y bueno, nunca fui," she sighed.

"Qué pena."

"Al final me quedé en casa con mi hermana. Nos maquillamos y pusimos el álbum en un CD player...no sé como se dice en español," she smiled thinking about their dinky pink radio covered with fifty cent stickers from the bodega vending machines. "Tuvimos una foto de Romeo pegada a la pared." She remembered how she would practice kissing it at twelve when no one else was around. She pressed one hand to her cheek, blushing from the memory.

"Entonces tuvieron su propio concierto." Ariel smiled as if he was blushing too, though she couldn't tell from his dark complexion.

"Sí, más o menos. Anyway, fuimos hace cuatro años atrás. Siempre dicen que es el último tour pero siempre siguen."

Someone hit a drunk man's transition and dropped a dembow beat in the middle of the melodic vocals. It snapped Dena back to reality. Suddenly, she was keenly aware she was oversharing. She peeked over the bushes to check on Jess.

"No te preocupes. Nada ha pasado en los últimos tres minutos," Ariel teased. Dena knew he was right, but she couldn't help but worry. Ever since they were little, Jess always needed an extra pair of eyes on her.

"Tá bien. Te veo por ahí entonces." He paused for half a second before adding, "O si quieres, me puedes dar tu numero y no' vemo' a propósito."

The rum must have fully made its way through her body because she took out her phone and said, "Dame el tuyo mejor."

At the front of the house, the boys had returned to a corner of the lot, and Jess was scrolling on her phone. She barely looked up when Dena returned.

"You want to go?" Dena asked, hoping for a "yes."

"Sure, I guess. Let's tell Manny. He's over there talking to some guy. Why are you smiling like that?"

"Like what?" Dena feigned confusion.

"You're being weird."

"I'm kind of drunk."

"How? It's only been...wait, how many have we had?" Jess tried to count but couldn't remember. "I might be too." They started giggling, their lungs filling with fresh, orchid-scented air.

"Where were you?"

"I told you. I went to the bathroom." Dena pointed towards the back of the house.

"That was a while ago." Jess was tipsy, not stupid.

"I ran into our handyman. I didn't realize there would be so many people we knew here," Dena shrugged and avoided eye contact with Ariel, who was now sitting on one of the boulders.

"It's a small town. What did you think would happen? Also, we saw a lot of them the other day. You didn't notice?"

"Not really. There was a lot going on."

"Yeah..."

"So, what's up with...Doug?" Dena pointed her nose discreetly at Jess's old crush.

" 'Doug'? You think his name is 'Doug'?" Jess burst out laughing as Dena had hoped. "It's Miguel. He's good, and he looks it. Did you see him? Oh my God." Jess sighed loudly. "And a father of two. He showed me photos. I think that was his version of flirting." Jess quickly looked away as Miguel caught her eye from across the yard. Dena's jaw dropped open in disbelief. She couldn't imagine the same little boy who used to pull pranks around the neighborhood now raising human beings.

"From the same mother?"

"I don't know..." Jess laughed again. Dena missed that sound—her giggle, which sounded exactly the same even though it should have deepened years ago. She still hid behind her hair and covered her mouth when she laughed, as if joy was a secret she had to keep.

"I bet one of his baby's moms is somewhere around here," Dena joked. They looked around and giggled like little girls whispering at church. Dena gazed at her little sister, who was glowing even at night. Jess always said Dena was the prettier one. It was true that guys liked her, but it was because she was bold and confident. She commanded rooms just like their mother. But Dena knew she looked like any other mixed girl with wide hips and bouncy curls.

Jess, however, with her almond-shaped eyes, kinky hair, and slender body, was rare and striking. She inherited most of her features from Abuela Negra, who loved carrying her around as a child and telling everyone who would listen that she was *really* hers. For as tough as Negra was as a mother, she was an equally tender Abuela. And she didn't pass down any of the internalized colorism often found in Dominican homes. She loved her brown skin and mini-me granddaughter.

Most impressive of all, Jess's hazel eyes that could be seen from a mile away. Dena couldn't wait for the day her sister's face would return to normal without the added redness or puffiness of prolonged grief. To hear her laugh loudly, wildly.

"Look, Manny's coming back." Jess waved him over. They chugged what was left in their cups and pouted at Manny. He understood immediately. The same sets of eyes that had convinced him to climb up and cut down bundles of limoncillos when they were young were now the ones requesting a safe ride home. He had a soft spot for them. Unlike his other cousins in America, the girls used to visit every summer without fail. They grew up together. He liked to joke that his mother didn't need any more kids because he was the best. The truth was, he always wanted sisters to help, tease, prank, and save.

"Vámono' mujere'," he declared as if it was his decision.

In the car, still proud of having paid, Manny made an announcement. "No le' digan a Mami, pero 'toy feliz que u'tedes salieron hoy." They looked at each other confused. "Tía e'tuviera feliz que salieron de la casa. Ella hubiera dicho que estaba demasiado deprimido allá y que faltaba música." He laughed, imagining his Tía Gloria hating her own mourning.

"La trauma se quita con el baile," Dena remembered her mother yelling before dancing with a mop soaked in detergent and dirt.

Back at the house, Jess knocked out as soon as her face touched the pillow. Dena, however, buzzing from the alcohol, couldn't get her mother's voice out of her head. She went to the closet and pulled out her mother's photo album again.

Dena flipped back and forth through the pages and noticed that one of the plastic edges was slightly undone. She carefully peeled back the crinkly plastic and slid the faded photo out. It was the one of Gloria dancing with a guy at Tía Candy's birthday party. She couldn't make out the guy's face because he was turned away from the camera. But when she flipped it around, the other side of the image had "Marcelo" written in blue ink with a heart next to the name.

1994

Gloria

The Vegas were hitting their stride in the dulce business. Soon, Julia would go to America and Yunior would move to Santiago to study. The rest of the kids could practically run the business themselves. Nito was living his dream. To celebrate, he offered to throw Candy, his beloved baby girl, a blowout quinceñera. With each daughter, the parties got bigger and flashier. It wasn't just that Nito had more money, he wanted to show it off.

On the day of the party, the Vega sisters crowded into Gloria and Candy's bedroom to get ready. They all sat around the room, sensing that it might be their last time partying together for a long time.

"Gloria, déjame pintarte las uñas"," begged Flaca. "Te vas a ver más bonita."

"No, ya yo me la' pinté."

"Pero azul, eso no va. Déjame pintártela' rosada'," Flaca frowned. "O por lo menos, déjame arreglarte el pelo." She only loved to work when it involved beauty products.

"O a mi…me lo puedes dejar a mi," said young Candy, excited they were getting dressed up for once.

"No, tú no. Eres la cumpleañera, no puedes estar trabajando," Julia said. "¿Y tú maquillaje, Gloria? ¿No me vas a dejar pintarte?" Julia, the one who taught her how to use makeup in the first place, felt personally insulted.

"¿Y yo no tengo mano'? Preocúpate por Candy," Gloria snapped back. Julia lived to assist her siblings, but this one resisted every bit of help she offered.

"Gloria, no seas así," Candy tried swaying her softly.

"Ven, permítame," Sol walked over and started brushing Gloria's stubborn hair. She initially swatted her away, but eventually gave in because Sol, with her luscious locks, knew how to do the prettiest updos.

"¿Y tú con todo esa sombra?" Flaca laughed at Candy who had just smeared pink eyeshadow all over her eyes. "Ven acá," she waved her over with one hand.

"¿Cómo te sientes?" Julia asked Candy as she applied some powder onto the girl's face.

"Bien. ¡Mi vida entera se va a cambiar!" She exclaimed. The rest of the girls burst out laughing.

"No seas exagerada tampoco, Candy," Flaca said. "Eso piensas y cuando tú vienes a ver, todo sigue igual."

"Pero no le hables así a la niña," Julia said.

"No soy una 'niña'. Soy una mujer," Candy said, tripling her sisters' laughter.

"Y ustedes, ¿en que están?" Negra waddled in without knocking.

"Nada, Mamá. En una hora ya estamos," Julia assured their nervous mother.

"Muy bien. Yo sigo allá afuera. Todavía estoy organizando con el señor de las flores y la comida." Negra wasn't a very affectionate mother. Her love revolved around daily tasks, not hand-holding. Her kids found ways to comfort each other while she cooked food and mopped their footprints off the floor, this day included. "Entonces, quédense aquí y ayuden a su hermana." Negra shut the door behind her and returned to making calls on the only phone in the house. She prayed all week that the electricity stayed on for the big day.

"Yo nunca he visto a Mamá tan nerviosa."Candy said what they were all thinking.

"Sí, parece que Papá invitó a mucha gente."

"Sí, ¡qué divertido!" Candy squealed.

"Tranquila, que no he terminado," Flaca pushed her shoulders down to keep her still. Candy kept wriggling around as Flaca tried to place mascara on her lashes.

"Bueno, lo que yo quiero saber es ¿con quién van a bailar?" As the adopted daughter, Sol wouldn't get her own quinceñera. This party was as exciting for her as it was to Candy.

"¡Con todos!" Ever since Flaca finished el bachillerato and started making dulce full-time, she barely saw any boys. Papá forbade them from going out past dark. Even though she and Gloria managed to sneak out a couple of times, the local bar owners stopped letting them in after a hostile word from their father.

"¿Y tú, Gloria?"

"Yo, ¿qué?"

"¿Con quién quieres bailar?" Candy asked innocently.

"¡Contigo!" Gloria said, although images of Marcelo flashed through her mind.

"Pero mírale la cara," Flaca teased. "¿Qué pasó ahi?" Her sisters all looked at Gloria's flushed cheeks.

"Na," she responded coyly. It was impossible to hide anything from them.

"Cuida'o si tienes un amiguito por ahí," Flaca said, excited about anything remotely romantic. She spent most nights watching novelas on their new TV with Mamá and Candy.

"¿Es Antonio?" Sol guessed. "Ese muchacho siempre habla de ti." The only thing Sol loved more than hearing firsthand gossip was sharing it.

"¿Quién es ese?" Julia asked for more details.

"El bajito medio gordito."

They spoke too fast for Gloria to correct them.

"¿Quién?"

She didn't want to anyway.

"El hermano de Nelson…"

She was lost in her own mind.

"Sí, yo lo conozco," another sister offered, describing the intricate social dynamics that linked him to their family porque todo el mundo era un hermano de un amigo de un primo de por ahí. Meanwhile, Gloria was daydreaming Marcelo would waltz in and ask her to dance.

"Si es él Antonio en el que estoy pensando, no es tan guapo," Flaca said, frowning. Perhaps it was a good thing that her sisters guessed incorrectly. Gloria knew they judged everyone too quickly and harshly.

"No digas eso. Tal vez ella piensa que sí," suggested Candy, looking for clues in Gloria's withdrawn face. She was thinking about Marcelo and his hands in the rushing river water. He liked to scoop it up and offer her some as if she didn't have hands of her own. He was always giving without expecting anything in return, always finding small ways to get closer to her.

Since they met over a year ago, Marcelo's father began officially investing in his brother's land. This meant he came around more frequently. Gloria, who hated surprises, started praying to run into him every Saturday she stepped onto the farm. It was rare, but each time he did, they sat behind the old mamey tree and talked until her brothers called her back. The boys were too lazy to go down to the creek and get her. Their friendship remained a secret. Her secret.

"Ese muchacho vive preguntando por ti," Sol spoke about Antonio again.

Marcelo was the only boy Gloria knew that didn't ask for anything directly—not her time, secrets, or even a smile. "Sonríete," the guys in her class would say when she had a stank face on, making her roll her eyes in disdain. Everyone wanted something. She just wanted to stretch out those tranquil Saturdays.

"¡No seas exagerada!" Flaca yelled across the room.

Marcelo never asked her to smile or laugh or speak. And yet, when she was around him, she couldn't stop herself from doing just that. Even now, a smirk spread across her face. Only Candy noticed, but she kept it to herself. Candy learned from a very young age that she could not talk above her older, louder, more exuberant sisters. However, if she got quiet enough, she could pick up on the things they didn't say, the things they couldn't shake off when they were too emotional to keep their bodies in check. Things like tight fists and crossed arms. She could see warmth and affection oozing from Gloria's soft gaze. And she was happy for her.

"Ten cuidado o Papá te mata como casi me pasó a mi," warned a less than pleased Julia. She had always been too cautious to bring a guy around the house. The one time she did, Papá forced her to send him home. He never said why, but it was with enough rage that she never dared to do it again. Even at twenty-three, she had not yet had a formal boyfriend.

"Pero Julia, tú eres una adulta. Tú puedes bailar con quién sea. ¿O estás esperando a ver si te enamoras pa'llá?" Flaca teased.

"Ojalá," she responded while brushing through Candy's hair.

"¡Ooooo!" Her sisters cooed in unison.

"Si te encuentras uno, el pobre va a tener que viajar para acá a ver la locura de e'ta familia," Flaca smiled deviously.

"Habla por ti misma, ¡yo soy normal!" Julia shot her a sideways look and accidentally poked Candy's head with a bobby pin.

"¡Ay!"

"Mira, dejen su relajo y terminen que casi nos tenemos que ir," Julia looked around the room.

"Sí, Señora," her sisters chorused before hearing a knock at the door. Unlike Mama, Papá always knocked when the girls were in a room together, ensuring they felt safe in their bedrooms, secretly hoping they stayed longer.

"¡Sí! Puede entrar," Julia spoke on their behalf.

"¿Cómo están, mis hijas?" Papá stepped in and took a head count, making sure all his girls were there. "¡Mira cuánta belleza!" He declared. Candy stood up and twirled around in her dress. "Salieron a su mamá, no como yo que soy un viejo feo."

"No, Papá. No digas eso." Candy hugged him. She was the only one who was still affectionate with him. Gloria and Flaca rolled their eyes before looking at each other.

"Solo me quedan mujeres. Acuérdense de mí cuando se casen y se vayan de acá." He was uncharacteristically emotional. Nito had spent so much time planning the party that he nearly forgot it was a celebration of his baby growing up. He had a house full of women, and he knew it was only a matter of time before they all left him.

"Tú sí estás emocional," Julia teased.

"¿Y cómo no?" He said, patting her shoulder. "Bueno, las dejo aquí a terminar."

The girls continued to gossip until they spilled out of the car downtown. The party was located at the only hall in Campesito. It was a round, open air cement block beside the rice paddies. Their dresses were all rentals except for the birthday girl's, which was made for her specifically. The food was buffet style. A four-tier cake sat in front of a freshly painted white wall. A perico ripiao band played on a small stage. The photographer was un tipo de Santiago que "sólo vino a trabajar" and later kept flirting with Flaca. Three separate times, Antonio had to tell him to focus on his job and not his daughter.

Gloria wasn't sure Marcelo could make it. She told him about the party the last time she saw him, but she had no way of confirming his attendance. She watched the door patiently as guest after guest arrived. Her heartbeat would quicken then instantly drop as another primo showed his sweaty face. It was two hours into the party when she finally saw his tall, lanky silhouette trailing behind his uncle. It took all of the energy in her body to look away and play it cool. She ignored him as best as she could, dancing with other guys, chatting profusely, and making her rounds. She wanted to make sure no one caught on. But with every step she took, she could feel his eyes on her from across the room. After an hour, just as the tension was becoming unbearable, he strolled over to her.

"¿Quieres bailar?" He held his hand out.

"¿Y quién tú eres?" She gazed down at the palm that had fed her water several times and forced a furrowed brow. Her sisters were scattered around the room, but she could sense them watching from afar.

"Marcelo, el sobrino de Dario." He played along and turned his long index finger towards his uncle. She looked across the room then back at him, avoiding eye contact, paranoid that one of her sisters might see. She didn't want anyone catching her with an unclenched jaw unless it was because she was laughing loudly.

"Está bien." She followed him. On the dance floor, he placed her hand in his, and her body lit up. She put her other hand on his shoulder, her eyes looked towards the empty field outside.

"Te vez increíble," he whispered into her ear.

"Yo sé." It took everything in her body not to lean into him. Her feet felt weightless as he guided her front, back, left, and right across the dance floor. Each time he pulled her closer, she stepped back, refusing to close the gap.

At seventeen, she didn't have the words or insight to explain her worst fears: that her father's misadventures had robbed her of hope, that she burned with such a rage that she might never put out, that she didn't trust her body's desires or the fingertips that set her on fire. Instead, her thoughts raced around in her mind. *No me quiere. Claro que sí. Todo el mundo nos ve. Ellos saben. Tal vez a nadie le importa. Sólo estamos bailando.*

"En diez minutos…" He said loud enough for only her to hear. "Voy estar…" *One, two, three, and they stepped back.* "atrás…" *One, spin, step, back.* "Te encuentro afuera." He looked into her eyes to make sure she heard him. What was right? Or wrong? She wasn't sure. But as soon as he invited her outside, her tension gave way to joy. She nodded silently. *Sí. Claro que sí.*

There were two separate bathrooms behind the party hall. Beyond them, a patch of unkempt plátano trees. Gloria stepped into the patch hesitantly, unable to see beyond the dark shadows they cast. Instantly, she felt an arm grab her and pull her into the trees. In one motion, Marcelo pulled her towards him in the dark and kissed her on the lips. The feeling was electric and calming. Her heart raced as he breathed into her.

He pulled himself back to speak, "No sabes cuánto tiempo…"

She pressed her lips back onto him before he could finish his sentence. For the first time in her life, Gloria's mind went completely quiet.

Day Five

Dena

After discovering the image with "Marcelo" written across the back, Dena immediately returned it to its sleeve in her mother's album.

"No toques cosas ajenas," her mother had said to her too many times.

She stepped onto the closet ledge to place it on the top shelf, but her foot slipped in the dark. As she lost her balance, the tile inside the closet floor clamored, revealing a small concrete hole beneath it. She crouched down to pick up the tile and found a pocket journal the size of her hand inside. Every page was filled with a much neater version of her mother's handwriting.

The diary started at age fifteen. Dena found a handwritten note from her great-aunt offering it to Gloria as a quinceñera gift. The first few entries were short and brief until she met a boy: Marcelo. She wrote about his laugh, his strange shoes, and the softness of his lips. Most of all, she wrote about their long conversations by the water. For over a year, they would meet up at la finca. She even admitted, *"Lo quiero, pero no le voy a decir hasta que él me lo diga primero."* It was exactly how she imagined her mother at seventeen: openly prideful and secretly romantic.

The entries were filled with naive fantasies, teenage frustrations, and an undercurrent of angst that her mother carried to her dying day. After her parents made her drop out of school, she became even more restless and reckless. She would skip work, stay out late at la finca, party on the weekends, and wait for the day until she could see Marcelo again. In the last entry, she wrote that he told her he loved her. That he saw her "completamente."

The remaining pages had been ripped out, leaving frayed edges behind. She closed it, feeling icky about invading her mother's privacy. That feeling was quickly replaced by betrayal. Her mother could not sit quietly for more than two minutes straight. She shared every emotion, idea, and vexation that simmered in her mind. Having a secret boyfriend at sixteen made sense. Never mentioning him was insane.

Although her mind spun with more questions than answers, she needed to rest. She placed the old diary at the bottom of her backpack and went to bed.

Later that morning, Dena answered emails in bed. In the kitchen, everyone kindly reminded her that the bags under her eyes were darker than usual. It was a tragic mix of mascara residue and lack of sleep. The coffee had run out. The electricity was gone too.

"Eso pasa," Candy said to her in her usual chipper mood. "Pero no te preocupes, regresa ahorita. Por lo menos hay luz afuera, gracias a Dios." Tía Candy loved praising God in the midst of bad circumstances.

"¿Ustedes salieron ayer?" Tía Flaca's voice was becoming

raspier by the day. Dena could see her aunt straining to keep her composure. It wasn't even 10 a.m. and she already knew.

"Sí, por un rato," she hoped to come across nonchalant.

"¿Qué?" Tía Candy did a dramatic double take. "¿Pa dónde?"

"Eso quiero saber yo." Flaca stood with her arms crossed. Dena was happy Julia went home to Santiago the day before. She couldn't deal with all three of them without a full night's sleep.

"A beber un chín. Fue solo una hora...o dos..." Jess sat with her shoulders slumped and her elbows on the kitchen table.

"¿Salir a beber o salir a bailar?" Flaca asked, although she disapproved of both equally.

"A bailar no puede ser." Candy, still confused, looked back and forth between the girls.

"No bailar. Solo beber un poco." After her late-night discovery, Dena couldn't focus enough to argue. She wished her mother had been there to joke around, lighten the mood. She was brazen enough to get away with it. While it led to many arguments in their household, Dena always admired that about Gloria: she could talk up anyone in any room, lift the air pressure, soften people's edges. Without her around, rooms felt denser, harder to move through.

Flaca looked at her with clear disgust. "¿Y tú crees que eso es justo? Después de..." She couldn't bring herself to say it. "...todo lo que ha pasado. Julia no va a poder creer esto." She went to find her phone to send her older sister a long voicemail detailing everything she knew thus far.

"Miren, mis hijas, está bien que quieran relajarse. Pero mejor váyanse al río o la playa," Tía Candy tried to reason with them. "Si ustedes quieren, podemos ir todos juntos un día." It was against Candy's nature to reprimand anyone. But they could tell by her drawled words that she was disappointed.

"Sí, Tía. Perdón." Jess mumbled, looking hungover and guilty, regretting having gone out. She was becoming a cartoon version of herself with her dark circles, oversized T-shirts, mismatched socks, and nails chewed down to the quick. She tucked her messy hair into a claw clip, grabbed a banana, and staggered out of the room.

Jess and Dena spent the rest of the day avoiding the aunts and each other. The few moments of laughter they had the night before dissolved in the heaviness of the day. While Jess remained glued to her phone, Dena attempted to catch up on work. Mondays were always hectic for her, but the electricity going out in the morning set her back even more.

In the afternoon, after the hora santa, Dena went into the backyard, hoping the dense garden would distract her. She finally stepped off the crooked concrete and down onto the narrow dirt path, created entirely from stomping feet. Both sides of it had an array of vaguely familiar plants. The mango tree, the oldest living member of the Vega family, had at least two hundred bright green mangos, announcing the start of the season. Just past it, there were a couple of lime trees and one skinny carambola tree twisting up towards the sky. She picked a starfruit and bit into it. It was more tart than she remembered. She tossed the half-eaten fruit onto the ground like her Abuela Negra, who taught her that feeding the garden was as crucial as taking from it.

A cinderblock wall wrapped around the entire backyard. Untamed vines slithered onto it, leaving imprints when they died and dried off. The rest of the plants sprouted awkwardly, constantly fighting each other for sunlight, hoping to fill the garden with their swirling stems. A chinola vine wrapped itself around another tree. In the back right corner, chickens clucked about. She remembered the breadfruit tree she and Jess used to play next to as kids. Several orchid plants grew adjacent to its trunk, all bending towards the light. She couldn't believe she used to find comfort there. In her memories, the backyard was a lush jungle oasis. All she saw now were wilted plants, dried flowers, and patches of dirt. It looked more dead than alive.

She thought about her mother's journal: proof that Gloria was good at keeping secrets. After her father died, Dena heard whispers around town. Unlike Jess, she was old enough to know what they meant, along with the awkward stares from wrinkled church ladies in pressed button-ups. She loved her father. She didn't want to believe he was capable of such deceit, but she thought she deserved to know the truth. Years later, when Dena finally mustered up enough courage to confront her, Gloria slapped her across the face and went to bed in silence. It was a classic Gloria move: avoidance concealed by violence. That memory always made Dena uneasy because she never technically denied nor confirmed it.

Similarly, her aunts were too upset to have an open conversation. Even sweet and honest Candy wanted to sugarcoat everything. Jess was being passive-aggressive. She couldn't get any work done. And she was stuck there for another five days. That's when it hit her: just because she had to be there, didn't mean she had to be *there*. She wasn't a trapped teenager anymore.

"¿Qué haces?" She sent Ariel a voice note, knowing full well she could have typed it out instead. She liked the idea of him ignoring all of his surroundings just to listen to her voice.

Dena met Ariel down the street from Abuela's. She directed him to meet her there, lest the nosy neighbors see her and notify the Vega sisters. It reminded her of her teen years, when a guy from around her block would stand below her fire escape and try to convince her to come down. Except back then, she never went; Gloria would have slapped her with a chancleta at the first sound of a sliding window.

Ariel was leaning against a streetlight when she saw him. His brown skin glowed like copper under the warm amber light. He smiled and kissed her cheek as soon as she was close enough to touch. It was the first time he greeted her formally.

"Hola. ¿Cómo estás?"

"Bien," she said unconvincingly. He could tell by the hour of the night and the curve of her lips that she wasn't fine at all, but he didn't follow up.

"¿A dónde quieres ir?"

"No sé. Lejos de aquí," she replied, looking over her shoulder to ensure no one was watching. He bowed his head like he did the first time she saw him at the velorio, only this time he kept it there deep in thought.

"Conozco un lugar." He pointed down a small dirt path up the road. She nodded, grateful to get away from the center of town.

As they walked, mud pushed up into the crevices of her shoes. By the end of her childhood trips to DR, her shoes would be covered in thick brown mud. She would want to throw them away, convinced everyone in NY would clown her for wearing beat-up sneakers. Gloria refused, insisting they were salvageable. She would make her hover over a large bucket and scrape out the mud bit by bit until they were clean enough to pack in a suitcase full of clothes.

After a few minutes, Ariel stopped in front of an empty concrete edifice. "Llegamos." He pointed up towards the abandoned dwelling.

"¿Aquí?" She looked around the side as if there was more to see. "Pero aquí no hay na."

"Exactamente. No sé porque querías salir a e'ta ahora, pero me imagino que no quieres que nadie que te conozca te vea. Bueno, aquí no hay nadie ni nada."

"Nada de nada." She was nervous. Perhaps she should have listened to Flaca and avoided the campesinos.

"Mi mamá y yo vivíamos aquí ante' que falleció. La casa tiene mucho' año' abandonada pero nunca pude vender la tierra o tumbarlo," he explained, sensing her hesitation. "Hay un techo arriba. Podemos subir y hablar allá."

She followed his pointer finger up to the rooftop. It had metal poles sticking up from the corners as if they had intended to build another floor but never got around to it. The cracked, stained walls looked strangely beautiful in the moonlight, like ripples in a tide.

She considered his offer. Jess always had her location, her phone was fully charged, and the house down the road had lights on. From the brief moments she had with him, Ariel seemed sincere. She wasn't hesitant because she felt she was in danger. She was struck by how nice he was and how good he looked. His thin cotton shirt revealed his defined chest and draped over his waist perfectly. His previously stiff curls looked softer than before, worn from a couple of days post-wash. His eyes glistened as he bit his bottom lip, waiting for her to decide.

"Vamos." She bit down on her lip too, unintentionally.

Inside, there was a thick blue blanket used for protecting furniture from paint jobs, though not a single wall showed remnants of paint. Ariel grabbed it before heading up dusty, crumbling stairs. On the roof, he opened it up and sat down on top. Sweat moistened his collar and forehead. Layers of dirt covered the ground. The view behind him consisted of banana trees and run-down homes. It was the least romantic scene Dena had ever seen. She thought about the meetings her mother wrote about with Marcelo, featuring riverside rendezvous on sunny afternoons. Meanwhile, she was on an abandoned slab of concrete with a guy whose last name she didn't even think to ask.

"¿Crees en alienígenas?" Ariel asked. He had lain down, crossed one leg on the other, and stared at the sky with the same look of wonder from the first night they met in Abuela's backyard.

"¿En qué?" She sat down beside him, her back upright, her legs crossed like a pretzel.

"Como otro ser que existe afuera de e'te planeta." He pointed his chin up at the stars, which were slowly revealing themselves one by one as their eyes adjusted to the darkness.

"No lo he pensado mucho." She placed her hands down on the cloth behind her, leaned back, and tilted her head up too.

"Yo sí. A mí me parece que existen pero tal vez no como en la' película'. Tal vez no con tres ojos y manos de cuatro dedos, pero en formas que ni siquiera podemo' imaginar."

She laughed at the thought of this grown man pondering alien lifeforms. Ariel was not what she expected. Then again, she didn't expect to be there at all: on a random rooftop with the local handyman.

"Primera vez que te oigo reír así. Tienes una sonrisa hermosa." He gazed up at her. Flirting felt foreign to her after spending so many years single, stressed, and overworked. She clumsily repositioned her hands and stretched her legs out in front of her.

"Gracias." Her cheeks grew warm. The bun holding back her hair felt tight. She had gelled down her hair when her blowout became too poofy to sustain after days exposed to constant humidity.

"Es como la gente. Pensamo' algo de ello' pero ni podemo' imaginar por lo que han pasado."

"¿Y qué te ha pasado a ti?" She asked.

"¿Qué quieres saber?" He sat up beside her, ready to offer whatever she wanted.

"No sé. Empieza desde el principio." She was genuinely intrigued. She couldn't quite pinpoint his personality, which made sense considering she had known him for less than twenty minutes total. But she didn't like elusive mysteries. She preferred concrete answers, collecting data, analyzing the facts. It made her great at her job—not great at following her heart.

"Bueno, estaremos aquí la noche entera," he smiled like he wouldn't mind that at all.

"Entonces comienza con eso." She joked, pointing to the slash in his eyebrow. Dominican guys loved making a razor cut there to look tough, though it always struck her as more feminine than masculine. "O ese." She pointed to another scar on his cheek that extended to his right ear. That one seemed less intentional. Now that she had more time to study his face, he seemed to have more ridges and marks than she first realized, like a leaf held up to the light.

"¿O este?" He said, pointing to the center of his nose.

"¿Qué pasó ahí?" She could barely see that one in the dark.

"Una pelea cuando tenía dieciséis." He turned to the side so she could get a profile view. He explained that his nose was slightly crooked, knocked sideways by an aggravated blow from a fellow angry teen. "Este fue una pelea cuando tenía trece. Pero se abrió de nuevo a los quince." He pointed towards his eyebrow. She leaned in to inspect it. It wasn't an intentional razor cut as she initially thought. The twisted skin showed signs of tearing. It was long enough for two, maybe three stitches.

"Este fue una pelea a los veintiuno con un cuchillo." He pointed to his cheek. "Él tenía el cuchillo, yo no," he shrugged causing his shirt to scrunch up on his shoulders. The skin on his cheek was raised slightly, but his low-cut beard covered most of it. She squinted trying to follow the scar beneath it.

"¿Me permites?" She asked, reaching to touch it. He nodded, looking her in the eyes as she traced her index finger over it slowly, gently parting his thick facial hair. "Entonces, eres peligroso," she said, returning her hand to her side.

"Era." By the looks of his arms, he could easily knock someone sideways or pin someone down.

"¿Ya no?"

"Yo peleaba mucho cuando era joven. Tenía solo doce años cuando Mami murió. Mi papá decía que yo no era del. Tenía otra familia. Tú sabe' como es." He spoke of his life matter-of-factly, as if it was someone else's.

"No sabía, perdon," she nearly whispered, knowing words were not enough. "Mi papá se murió cuando yo tenía quince." It was a strange offering of condolences—an acknowledgement that he was not alone. They locked eyes. For a moment it felt like it was just them on an endless open valley in the middle of the island.

"Entonce' entiendes que no es fácil," he continued. "Fui a vivir con mi tía y lo' muchacho' de allá se juntaban a pegarme." He looked away and grimaced. "Después de un tiempo, aprendí a defenderme. Comencé a pelear para ganar dinero." From their brief encounters, Ariel always seemed effortlessly calm. Everything she would have guessed about him would have been wrong. She felt slightly ashamed for assuming so much so soon. She wondered what he assumed about her.

"Quería ser profesional, pero me estaba haciendo más daño que bien y lo tuve que dejar."

"¿Así tan fácil?" She asked, unsure she believed someone's life could change so drastically or quickly even though hers already had.

"Sí. Ahora trabajo reparando casa'. Todo tranqui. Todo relax," he said, flattening the air around him with his hands. "Antes, no me importaba morir. Ahora sé que quiero vivir y no voy a malgastar mi tiempo viviendo en guerra."

She understood exactly what he meant. Every day since Gloria's passing, she grew more frustrated. The worst part was that it wasn't about the death itself, rather everything her mother lied about before it. The things they could have resolved in person. Nothing was ever easy with Gloria, but at least she had someone to fight with. Now, it felt like she was fighting herself.

"Algo pasa cuando peleas todo el tiempo. Te cambia tu forma de ser, de pensar." He reflected. "Ahora cuéntame de ti."

"No hay mucho que decir."

"Imposible. ¿Después que te dije tanto?"

"No sé qué decir. También perdí a mis padres." Her voice cracked as she spoke. She paused to think about how strange it was to say it out loud. She lost her parents. Both. Plural. "Perdón, no me he acostumbrado a decirlo todavía. Pero tengo la suerte de que me queda mucha familia: tías, tíos, primos y mi hermana sobre todo."

"Sí, tu hermana. La del otro día, ¿no? Dique la llaman 'Sombra'. ¿Por qué?"

"Cuando éramos niñas ella siempre andaba detrás de mí: escuchando la misma música, viendo los mismos programas en la televisión, poniéndose mi ropa. Además, ella era más bajita y más tímida que yo. Entonces los muchachos acá la pusieron el nombre 'Sombra'. Como si fuera mi sombra."

"¿Y todavía sigue atrás de ti?"

"No, ahora ella anda en su propio mundo. No sé…a veces no sé nada de lo que ella está pensando. Nunca quiere hablar de lo malo. Igualita a Mami," she said, sadly.

"¿Y tú? Me parece que te gusta hablar mucho," he teased. "¿Dónde están las cicatrices tuyas?" His directness and intensity caught her off guard. She couldn't gather her thoughts fast enough to come up with a quippy, flirty response. She held her breath, nervously.

Sensing the tension in her body, Ariel leaned in, hovering just above her lips. They locked eyes just as he pulled her towards him. His kiss was softer than she expected. She placed her hands on his face, the tips of her fingers digging into his low cut fade, her thumbs on his beard. Her body felt lighter than it had in days. She leaned into his arm, which he had wrapped around her lower back. He gently laid her down, pressing his chest against her, squeezing her waist with his one hand and holding her face with the other.

"Cuando quieras, no vamo," he said.

"Sigue." She tugged at his gold chain, which dangled between them.

They kissed until her bottom lip was tender. Then, holding her chin down with his thumb, he started kissing her temple, cheek, and neck. When he reached her collarbone, she held his face in between her hands, signaling him to stop.

"Perdona, a vece' me paso." He sat back up, and placed his elbows around his knees.

"No, me gustó."

Ariel nodded quietly, staring at his interlocked hands, restraining himself. He didn't want to lose control or make her uncomfortable. He didn't yet understand that his stories of violence—the fact that he understood pain and loss, yet maintained a sense of grace—comforted her.

"En todos los años que he venido aquí, nunca he hecho algo así." She giggled. She had always wondered what it was like to sneak out at night in DR to make out with a boy. Gloria's grip was too tight on them on the island.

"¿Entonce' e'to fue un experimento?"

"Mas o meno'," she teased, feeling like herself again, like the teenage Dena that had boys chanting her name during volleyball games and track meets, fighting for her attention.

"¿Y?"

"Y…fue divertido. Pero creo que debo regresar."

On the walk home, she kept her hands at her sides. She did not want to get wrapped up in a mere fantasy, not physically and definitely not emotionally. She needed a stranger to distract her until she was temporarily out of breath. She needed a good night's sleep, though she probably wouldn't get one for a while. She needed to desahogarse de todo.

Ariel stood still when they arrived back at the streetlight down the street from Abuela's house. "Yo sé que no puedes andar mucho pero si quieres, podemos ir al río un día," he offered.

"¿Tienes un motor?" She pictured her hair, untied, whipping in the wind.

"Claro."

"Vamos a la playa mejor." She imagined rinsing her scalp in the saltwater, releasing all her tension into the sea.

"Cuando quieras."

"¿Manaña?" She thought about all the times she was stuck in the campo when the beach was just a short ride away.

"A la orden." He looked down at her lips like he wanted to tug on them again. Instead, he kissed her goodbye on the cheek and waited for her to slip back into Abuela's house before going home.

1994

Gloria

It had been two months since her family broke the news that she would have to drop out of school. Though the finca was brutally hot and the house felt increasingly claustrophobic, Gloria got used to her new routine. She spent her days picking and grinding ripened fruit while daydreaming about Nueva York. Soon enough, Julia would formally request her and turn her into una americana.

Mientras tanto, she had Marcelo. His sporadic visiting schedule was as exciting as it was frustrating. One August morning, just before his first university semester began, she found him tossing pebbles towards her side of the creek.

"Cuanto tiempo," she said, visibly annoyed. She hadn't seen him in the four weeks since Candy's party and even then, they didn't get to talk much. He simply pulled her into a kiss and ignored her the rest of the night. What now?

"¿Cómo estás?"

"Mal. Gracias por preguntar," she responded sarcastically.

"¿Qué pasó, mi amor?" He calculated his steps towards her, trying not to trip.

"¿'Mi amor'? ¡Ja! Pero casi nunca te veo," she projected across the water. He stood holding his hand out to her, waiting for her to cross. She huffed and puffed and inevitably went towards him.

"¿No te gustó la última vez que nos vimos?"

"Sí, pero nunca sé cuando te voy a ver de nuevo."

"Tú sabes que Papá nunca me avisa cuando viene." He always claimed he was just a kid under his father's rule. "Pero dime de ti. Casi no pudimos hablar en el cumpleaños de tu hermana."

"¡Na'! ¡Que tengo que estar aquí por el resto de mi vida!"

"¿Qué?"

"No puedo ir a la escuela o estudiar o vivir mi vida o ser nada menos que estar aquí," she said pacing back and forth on the small bank.

"¿Y qué querías estudiar?" He followed her footsteps with his eyes, trying to keep up with every abrupt switch and turn.

"No sé. ¡No importa! ¡Algo! ¡Algo grande e impactante e importante!"

"¿Pero 'impactante e importante' no son la misma cosa?" He scratched his head.

"¡No! ¡No sé! No sé na porque no estudié. Voy a ser una de esa' mujere' que no sabe na, solo cual jabón funciona mejor para sacarle una mancha de la camisa de un hombre."

"Bueno…"

"¡Estoy jarta! Jarta de limpiar y pelar y pelear!"

"Gran poder de Dios, Gloria…" He was getting dizzy trying to follow her.

"Me voy con Julia." She stood still, announcing it to the entire creek and every living creature within earshot. "Me tengo que ir con Julia para no quedarme aquí. Aquí lo que hay es lodo y polvo y pajaritos…"

"Y yo…"

"Y trabajo y me duele…"

"Pero tú no te vas a vivir en los Estados Unidos. ¿De qué hablas?"

"Y solo estoy comenzando y…"

"Te vas a quedar aquí conmigo." He tried cutting her off again, but he spoke too softly to command her attention with just his voice. He held out his open palm, pleading with her to stop pacing.

"¡Ahhh!" She rubbed her face and yelled.

"Gloria, está bien si quieres llorar."

"¿Y quién dijo eso?" She shouted angrily before picking up a fruit and throwing it in his direction. He ducked his head and heard a hard thud behind him.

"¿Pero estás loca?" He yelled, slightly amused by her powerful throw. "Ven acá," he held his hand out again, this time turned up towards the sky, hoping she would take it. Instead, she picked up another fruit and threw it closer to his head. This time, he caught it. He was a city boy, but he played ball too. Most guys would have thrown it back, called her crazy, run away. Not Marcelo, he smirked and pulled out a pocket knife from his pants. "¿Quieres probar?"

"¿Y eso? ¿Quién te lo dio?" She went to inspect his shiny blade.

"Mi novia en la Capital," he teased. She went to push his shoulder, but he grabbed her hand instead. He placed her open palm on his lips and kissed it.

" 'Toy sucia," she said, "Estaba recogiendo fruta por una hora antes de que te vi." She wiped the sweat off her forehead with her free hand. He grabbed that one too and kissed her fingertips. She couldn't pull herself back. She wanted to feel his lips all over.

"Perdón que me estabas esperando tanto tiempo," he said, bending down to kiss the sweat dripping down her hairline on her cheek. "No decido cuando puedo venir." He kissed the tender spot under her ear. "Pero debes saber que siempre te quiero ver." He left a trail of kisses down her neck to her collarbone. He pressed his forehead to hers. "Te quiero," he whispered. He sat down on a boulder beside them and pulled her onto his lap. She looked around nervously. She knew no one else was on her side of the farm, since she had come alone, but she wasn't sure who was on his.

"No hay nadie. Vine solo. Papá está con Tío comprando algo en Macorís."

"¿Seguro?"

"Seguro," he said, holding her steady with one hand on her waist and the other on the back of her neck.

"¿Estás bien? ¿Quieres seguir?" His thumb traced her jawline until she released the tension. She nodded, got up, and went around the back of their tree where a couple of bushes made it impossible to see anything from her side of the creek. She took off her skirt and placed it on a rock before lying down and digging her fingertips into the black dirt. Small twigs dug into her flesh, but she didn't care. He matched her every move.

"¿Segura?" He asked.

"Segura." They finished undressing under the shade of the mamey tree and pressed into each other's skin.

"No te detengas."

"Ni tú tampoco." Her body softened under his weight. Her pleasure multiplied exponentially like moths after a heavy rain. Afterward, she washed herself in the river, catching glimpses of her reflection in the still water. The girl staring back looked different. His touch had permanently changed her. She couldn't decide if it was a good thing or not. Her mother's voice rang in her ear *"Ten cuidado. No te dejes llevar."*

When he stepped into the river behind her, she turned around to splash him.

"¡Ah! ¡Que frío!" He said, still adjusting to the countryside and its fluctuating temperatures: fiery air, icy waters. She stared at his quivering lips and pressed hers to them to calm him.

"Mi Gloria," he whispered when she pulled away.

"¿Tuya?" She laughed out loud, secretly loving the sound of it.

"Mia," he confirmed. "Ven, vamos a ponernos la ropa." He said, anxious to get out of the cold water. As she dressed, he reached for the fruit she threw at him earlier. He pulled out his knife but struggled to get it all the way around. When he ripped the two sides apart, the interior was pale and dry.

"Está seca." He handed her half the fruit, frowning.

"Claro, pero estaba durísima," she said as if it should have been obvious to him. "Lo cortaste antes de tiempo." She tossed her half onto the ground.

Day Six

Dena

In the morning, Dena messaged her boss that there were some unplanned things she needed to tend to. It wasn't untrue. She just didn't mention it involved a beautiful man, not her mother's recent passing.

"Voy pa la playa," she announced to no one in particular in the kitchen.

"¿Qué?" Flaca was the first to pry. She was still upset about her outing two nights earlier. "¿Y qué afán es el tuyo? Antes no querías salir y ahora quieres salir todo' lo' día'." She demanded answers.

"¿Sola?" Candy asked.

"No, con un amigo." Dena hoped they wouldn't read into it too much, though she knew they already had.

"¿Cuál amigo? ¿Tú tienes amigos aquí?" Sol asked.

"Es el muchacho que arregló la llave," Dena answered with as little detail as possible.

"¿Quién?" Candy was as confused as ever.

"El sobrino de Doralis," Sol filled in the blanks.

"Hmmm. Ten cuidado. Dicen que son amigos hoy y

cuando vienes a ver…" Flaca crossed her arms and raised both eyebrows dramatically.

"Sí, Tía. Ustedes me dijeron que salga a descansar. Entonces voy a hacer eso."

"Bueno, que gozen mucho y gasten poco," Candy encouraged.

"You're just going to leave me here?" Jess walked into the room already frowning.

"Sorry, we can go out another day," Dena promised, although she didn't really mean it. Jess was still hovering around like a cloud, ready to burst at the mention of anything remotely nostalgic, which was practically everything. When went into the bedroom to change, Sombra followed her in.

"I feel like we shouldn't have gone out." Jess hung her head in shame. "I'm not saying you shouldn't go out again, but…I don't know. Are you okay?"

"I'm fine. Everything's fine. I just want to go out for a day. I don't think that's crazy."

"Well, you seem really tense."

"I mean, this isn't a very calming place." Dena slapped a mosquito on her arm.

"So, you're going out for the whole day? Where were you last night?" Jess hated that she sounded like their mother, but she didn't know what else to do. Dena took a deep breath, triggered by the slew of questions. "I know the tías seem calm, but they were talking about you yesterday. They think it's weird that you're asking so many questions, trying to clean up." Jess hated confrontation, but she hated being alone with all the tías even more. They asked her questions that she never had the answers to, as if she knew the inner workings of Dena's mind.

"Okay…" Dena changed her T-shirt, revealing a swimsuit underneath. She had already made up her mind.

"Now you're going to the beach with a random guy. Can I at least go?" Jess asked again, nervously. Her heaviness was weighing on Dena. She did not want to be a babysitter. She wanted to tan and swim, preferably with an ice-cold, sweaty cerveza in her palm.

"No. You don't fit. He only has a motorcycle, and it's an hour-long drive. You can handle being alone for one day."

"So, you like this guy?"

"Girl, I don't know…" She really didn't. "No. It's not like that." She decided. "I just want to relax. How much time did we spend stuck in this house as kids, locked up when there were white sand beaches less than an hour away? We don't have to do that anymore." Dena grabbed her bag and started stuffing sunscreen, bug repellent, and sunglasses inside.

"Going out on an adventure with a random campesino… That's not like you at all." Usually, Sombra didn't press, she hovered. But since their worlds had turned upside down, she was starting to pry more than Dena liked.

"And what am I like?" She went into the closet to grab an old towel.

"I don't know…organized. You plan everything you do months before you do it." Sombra immediately regretted her words.

"Solo quiero nadar. ¿Ni eso puedo hacer?" Dena spat in Spanish, all her rage tied to her mother tongue.

"But you barely know this guy."

"Manny knows him. You met him too when he was here. He seems nice. And you can always check my location," Dena reminded her, although none of those things comforted Jess.

"Yeah, I just thought we could spend more time together here."

"But you hate new places, and I don't want to be here. Everyone wants to pretend like everything's fine, and it's not." Dena tried to slow down but she was already too worked up. "You're on a vacation. But my job's not like yours. They expect me to keep working even when I'm away, and the light keeps going out, and I'm tired. This trip has not been relaxing at all.

So yes, I want to go to the beach alone. We still have three more days to hang out here."

"You think this has been a vacation for me? I know you guys had your problems, but I spent every day with Mami, and now she's…gone." Jess stared at the dirty lines between the floor tiles. "It's been almost a week and…You want to get rid of stuff and go out and…" Jess's voice trailed off as if it had somewhere else to go.

Dena took a deep breath in to control her tone. "We have to get rid of stuff because we don't know when we'll be back. And I'm not ignoring you. I just don't want to be stuck in here anymore," she insisted. "You know, you can go out too. No one's stopping you."

"Alone?" Jess was appalled by the idea.

"Yes, you don't have to be scared of everything all the time. Mami's not going to yell at you. Go outside. It has to be better than sitting in here all day depressed."

Jess wiped her imminent tears. It wasn't helpful bringing up Gloria, but they knew it was true. The heavy burden of having to sit still and keep quiet was gone. They could do anything, go anywhere—sans the constant nagging.

Dena slipped on her flip-flops and walked over to her sister. She squeezed her in her arms, but Jess did not squeeze back. She seemed deflated and lost. Dena decided it was all she could do for the day. For once, she wanted to prioritize herself.

Dena climbed on Ariel's bike hesitantly, her fingertips gripping the back seat below her hips. She couldn't remember the last time she sat on the back of a motorcycle. *Estos motoristas son locos y peligrosos.* Her mother always said.

"¿Ya?" Ariel waited for her arms to wrap around him.

"Ya," she confirmed. As handsome as he was, she would not give him the satisfaction of having her body wrapped around him so easily. He rode gently onto the asphalt and sped up as they got closer to the main road. He pressed down on the gas hard and fast, causing her body to jerk forward and press up against him. She rolled her eyes at this obvious, well-played move.

They passed the party house from two nights earlier, a couple miles of rice fields, and, finally, the cemetery where her parents were buried, before they were officially out of Campesito. She couldn't help but smile on the drive as she watched the mountains shrink behind them. She felt relieved, like she was entering a new dimension where the problems from her past didn't exist.

The ride was flat and breezy. The fauna grew denser as they rode from the lime green rice fields to the deep emerald seaside forests. When they reached the water, they turned left and rode up the coast. The land smelled like perpetual rainfall and peppered saltwater. Palm trees lined both sides of the road. On the right, the sea crawled up and crashed along the shore. It sparkled like glass beneath the bright morning sun. The current looked rough, but the breeze was crisp and cool.

"¿Adónde vamos?" She asked after they had passed a couple of postcard-worthy white sand beaches.

"Casi llegamos," he assured her with no clear answer.

After a few minutes, they pulled up to a gated community. He spoke to someone at security, who let them into a narrow road with a few houses along the right side. They stopped at the end of it, at the edge of a rocky cliff, definitely too high up for them to go swimming. She got off the bike and looked at him sideways. He laughed when he saw her face.

"Abajo es más bonito," Ariel said proudly, as if it were all his land to show off.

"¿'Abajo'?"

"Sí, ven." He went towards a janky wooden stairway pressed up alongside the cliff. The narrow path cut straight to the water. At the bottom, the rocks were completely empty. She thought about the beaches of her childhood: hot, crowded, full of fried fish, and slimy seaweed that stuck to her arms. This was a private watering hole exclusive to extranjeros with private estates.

"Arreglé una casa por aquí hace dos años. Me hice amigo con el guachimán y él me deja entrar de vez en cuando," he explained as he headed down the stairway. She followed as fast as she could, careful not to stumble over the rocks. By the time she reached the bottom, he was sitting on a boulder in nothing but his swim trunks, ready to throw himself in.

"¿No te vas a poner protector solar?"

"No, olvídate de eso. Ya mi piel se acostumbró al sol. Además, todo eso le hace daño al medioambiente," he said before gracefully diving in headfirst. "¿Sabes nadar?" He yelled over the loud crashing waves once his head popped back up.

"Sí, ¡claro!" Dena left the sunscreen in her bag, deciding to put it on afterward. She untied her hair from the tight bun, freeing it to the wind. It was the first time since arriving that she didn't put a drop of makeup on her face, not even her standard under-eye concealer and lip gloss. She felt naked, in a good way, like none of the extra layers mattered.

As she walked towards Ariel, she thought about the last guy she hooked up with. He held her together throughout a string of bad nights when all she had for dinner was old takeout and anti-anxiety medication. She told herself dating was boring. Her friends called her a workaholic with high expectations. The truth was, Gloria's disease bombarded her life. Between the paperwork, doctor's visits, family interventions, and death scares, there was no room left for play. Ariel was all play. He looked like a giddy child splashing around in the water.

"E'ta agua e fuerte y tienes que tener cuida'o." He looked at her with wide eyes and a huge smile.

She jumped in but swam away from him. She did not want to sway hand in hand. She wanted this familiar sea to cradle her in its arms, like it did when she was a child. She soon realized, however, that this was not the same cove from her memories. She could not touch the sandy bottom, let alone see it. That would be fine if she knew how to float, but she never quite learned. She was used to running on hard concrete sidewalks. She liked pounding the earth, bouncing up, stretching her physical capactiy. Floating was different. It required her to surrender in a way she was not accustomed to. She never mastered the waves, the insurmountable water pressure, the quickly changing current.

She tried to lay still on her back, but the waves were too choppy. They slapped her across the face as she attempted to breathe, making her swallow water involuntarily. As she turned her body, trying to get closer to the boulder that held her clothes, she realized it was getting smaller and smaller. The current was pushing her north. Saltwater invaded her throat. Every kick was draining, dragging her farther away from Ariel, who seemed completely unfazed.

She thought of her mother screaming every time she went towards something dangerous: open water, boys, motorcycles. Gloria may have spoken loudly, but she lived cautiously. She spent two years nearing death and cursing everyone who suggested it was true. Two whole years, and Dena couldn't even make it two minutes without completely panicking. She was dizzy from spinning around, trying to find her way. She cried out towards Ariel.

"¡Nada!" Was he saying "nothing"? She swallowed more saltwater.

"¡Nadar!" No. He was telling her to swim. She felt nauseous.

"¡Allá!" He yelled. Though she could barely hear over the waves, she saw his arm point to the right. The shore was hidden behind another jagged cliff wall. She had no choice but to trust him. Dena turned her body around to swim up the coast in sync with the current. The ocean pushed her towards land at a wide angle. By the time she saw the sandy cove between two cliffs, the one she had just come from and the next one over, she was practically getting thrown onto it by the waves.

She dug her toes and nails in when she finally touched down on sand and immediately started coughing up saltwater. When she was done heaving, her cough turned into an uncontrollable laugh. She dropped her back onto the ground and stared up at the daunting cliffs. It was a comically horrible situation. There weren't any houses, boats, or people around. The cove was probably unreachable by road. Someone would have to rescue her, possibly helicopter her out. The tías would emphasize this was why she shouldn't go out with desconocidos.

"Te dije," rang in her ears. As she scanned the area for her next move, Ariel's dark figure emerged from the water a few feet to her right.

"¡Me dejaste!" She smacked his calf when he reached her.

"No, ¡nunca! La corriente siempre te iba llevar a la costa," he said with a level of certainty that made her doubt her previous fears. He offered a hand to help her stand up, but she shook her head.

"Necesito un minuto." She sat up with her legs bent in front of her, placed her elbows around her knees, and intertwined her fingers to hold herself up.

"Tá bien. Coge tu tiempo. Yo sé como regresar de aquí." He sat down next to her, mirroring her position. He noticed a tear he initially thought was saltwater sliding down the side of her face, and gently wiped it away. The tender gesture moved her, but she swallowed the other tears trying to come up. This wasn't the time or place.

"Perdón," she said, slightly embarrassed. In less than the time it took to get there, she had already ruined their day.

Ariel inched closer to her and rubbed the side of his arm with hers. "No tienes que decir nada. Sé cómo se siente perder el control." He remained quiet until her breathing returned to normal. She wondered what he meant by "lose control." In life? In nature? In a fight? With oneself? Which one of those was this?

"Querias relajarte pero no pudi'te." He laughed, attempting to lighten the mood.

"Por lo menos hay sol y brisa aquí." She closed her eyes to enjoy the sunlight on her skin, the breeze on her back.

"Sí, Campesito no tiene mucha brisa, no," he agreed.

"¿Tú nunca has querido venir a vivir por el mar?"

"Ay, ¿y tú cree' que e fácil?"

"Pensé que sí." She felt ignorant of the inner workings of the island.

"No. Como no trabajo para una compañía, no gano tanto. O sea, gano suficiente para vivir pero no para mudarme así de un día pa'l otro. Además, ¿no ves que la mayoría de las casas frente al mar son mansiones y los dueños son extranjeros?" He pointed to a mansion up the coast. "No vale lo mismo que vivir en el campo. Y tú, americana, ¿nunca has querido venir acá a vivir cerca al mar?"

"No soy rica tampoco." She looked at him sideways for the intentional "americana" comment.

"No, pero puedes coger tiempo libre, tomar un vuelo y quedarte dos o tres días de vacaciones."

There was a silent understanding that they had different lives and means. Sure, he actually lived in DR, but there were certain parts that were easier for her to access even though she lived two thousand miles away. In the same vain, she could buy as much land as she wanted, but she would never be as connected to it as he was, not after he depended on it for decades to survive. It stung both of them to think about.

"Mi trabajo es complicado. Tengo una semana aquí pero sigo trabajando." She sighed, rubbing sand off her legs.

"Pensé que estabas libre," he said, surprised. "¿Con todo esto sigues trabajando?"

"Sí. Bueno, lo que puedo con ese internet que casi no sirve. Pero así es la vida allá. Siempre hay trabajo, problemas, deudas."

"Debes de estar descansando." He joined her in rubbing sand off her limbs.

"Sí, se supone que vine aquí a hacer eso y mira cómo acabé," she joked now too.

"¿Sabes lo que necesitas? Una buena comida de playa. Pescado frito, tostones y una fría." He opened his eyes widely, exciting himself with his own idea. "Con el mar al frente. Así puedes descansar bien."

"Buena idea." She hoped to salvage something of this trip. Ten minutes later, he was guiding her up the rocky wall with his smooth voice. He knew not to let her run off on her own. Though she had Dominican blood, she was clearly a New Yorker at heart.

"Espérame aquí que yo bajo y busco la ropa," he said once they reached the top. Then, he headed back down to the jagged cliff they had initially descended.

At the restaurant, they ordered a whole fish each with all the sides, and sipped Presidentes while they waited for their food. He looked over at her, curious if she would talk without being asked anything directly. She accepted his silent stare as a challenge, examining him instead.

The more she stared at him, the more details she saw: a small nick in his ear, a couple of gray hairs in his beard, and brown eyes that looked lighter now that she saw them up close in the daylight. His hands were calloused, though his fingernails were clean. They read like a man who had learned to take care of himself after years of neglect and violence.

"¿Qué fue?" He was the first to break the prolonged silence.

"Nada."

"Bueno, algo será por esa mirada." He sipped his beer, looking at her inquisitively.

"Eres lindo." She sipped her beer too.

"¿Ah, sí? ¿Tú crees?" He cocked his head back, proudly.

"Fuerte. Y buena gente. Esa combinación es rara."

"Tú tambien."

"Bueno, tal vez fuerte no. Parece que no puedo aguantar las olas," she joked.

"No, tú sí puedes. Mira, todavía sigues aquí." He pinched her forearm. She jumped back from the playful move. "Lo que pasa e que la' tienes que sentir. Querías controlar tu dirección pero el mar no funciona así."

"¿Entonces cómo funciona?"

"Por ejemplo, si ves un bosque qué tú cree', ¿que todo' los árboles están ahí solitos bajo del sol? No. Ellos están conectados. Comunican. Así sobreviven una tormenta, una sequía, un animal que viene a atacarlos."

"¿Qué?" She was even more confused than before. What was he talking about? Trees? The ocean? She hoped he wouldn't start talking about the moon phases again like the first night they met.

"Todos los árboles que ves tienen raíces que están interconectados abajo de la tierra. Hablan. Así funciona el mar. Así funciona la gente. Hablamos en muchas formas que ni se ven."

She didn't know what to say. Yet again, Ariel was proving to be wiser than he looked. But maybe that was the problem: she kept judging him by his rusted wrench and ripped jeans, and he was none of those things.

"Sabes mucho de la naturaleza."

"No, yo no sé na. Yo sé un poquito de mucho."

"¿Como qué más?" She leaned her face into her palm, resting her elbows on the table between them.

"Plátano maduro no se vuelve verde."

"Eso me lo sabía."

"También sé un poco de santería." He nearly whispered the last word in his statement. She laughed at his fake tense demeanor. "No, en serio. No me recuerdo mucho pero vi a Mami trabajando con los santos cuando era niño."

"¿Qué viste?" She asked bluntly, forgetting how taboo the topic was.

He looked around, leaned in, and placed his index finger over his mouth. "Shhh. De eso no se habla." He appeared serious for about two seconds before cracking a smile. "No vi gran cosa. Mami tenía un altar y rezaba mucho. Eso sí me recuerdo."

"Creo que vi uno parecido el otro día."

"¿Dónde?"

"En la casa de Minerva. La fui a ver el día después del funeral," Dena admitted to him. It was the first time she told anyone about her visit. It was easier confiding in Ariel than her family. He absorbed information calmly, quickly.

"¿Y qué te dijo?"

"Muchas cosas. Me dijo que iba a encontrar un hombre."

"¡Pero mírame aquí!" He smiled before taking another swig of his beer.

"Que mi mamá estaba triste en el pasado. Que pasó por un momento difícil. Que 'pasó que no pudo pasar'. ¿Sabes lo que significa eso?"

"Ni la menor idea. Pero si no entendiste algo, debes regresar."

"¿Crees que debería?"

"Claro. Ella trabaja en eso. ¿Quién má va a saber?" He refilled their plastic cups with beer. "Nadie elige esa vida. Esa vida elige a uno. Ella ayuda a la gente porque no hay nada más. Es su deber."

Dena thought she had been imposing during Minerva's visit, mostly because she spent a lifetime feeling like she was imposing on her mother. Perhaps Minerva wanted her to gain clarity too.

When they were done eating, they sat on the patch of sand between the restaurant and the sea. He put his arm around her as he had been waiting to do all day. She leaned into his embrace.

"Es raro estar aquí sin ella," Dena reflected. The orange color in the sky, which preempted sunset, made her unexpectedly nostalgic. "Aunque nací aquí, no conozco este país sin ella. Es como si fuera de ella y necesito su permiso para verlo. Pero no está…"

"¿O sea te hace falta?" Ariel said what she could not. She didn't respond. Instead, she held back the tears forming in her eyes for the second time that day and kissed him. She ignored the sea of extranjeros and the staff effortlessly weaving through them carrying platters of food. She didn't care who saw. As they kissed, she imagined she was on a tropical vacation, far away from home, resting in the arms of a man she loved. She imagined her life unfolding in new and spectacular ways. Maybe there was more to DR than what she knew, more worth exploring. Perhaps she could live out there on the shore of her previous reality, dancing with a new tide.

On the drive back, Ariel smiled when he saw her spread her arms out in the rearview mirror. She could hear his muffled laugh through the loud wind. She didn't mind being a tourist cliché like the photos posted in the airport that allowed for-eigners to envision the freedom that awaited them en el aire libre del Caribe. A large pothole made her arms retreat to his waist. She effortlessly tucked her chin between his shoulder blades, the only pocket where the wind wasn't infiltrating her space. The rigid creases of his body held her in place. She felt more relaxed on this bumpy, winding, chaotic road than she had in the last two years.

The tías sat in mismatched chairs in the garden after the hora santa ended. Dena was heading back to her bedroom, as she did every afternoon, when she heard one of them yell.

"Dena, ¡tráeme un té!" Flaca croaked from her rocking chair.

As Dena went to hand her a cup, the tías exchanged looks like giggling school girls who had been gossiping beneath the mango tree. Spiders dangled from the leaves trying to listen in on el chisme del día.

"Entonces, ¿estás disfrutando de tu país?" Candy tried to play coy.

"Sí, ¿con tu amiguito?" Julia was more direct.

"Sí," Dena was prepared to walk away.

"Siéntate. Cuéntanos," Candy encouraged.

"Sí, comparte con nosotras." Flaca's eyebrows perked up as she rocked back and forth in her chair. "¿Y a qué playa fueron?"

"No sé muy bien. Cerca de Cabrera, creo." Dena felt slightly ashamed that she didn't know the geography of her native land.

"Que divertido. Me hace falta una aventura, andar así sin responsabilidad," Flaca said, a tinge sarcastically.

"Tú tá muy vieja pa eso. Esa muchacha debe andar y conocer su país," Candy defended her niece.

"Viejo es el viento y sigue soplando," Flaca declared, sipping her tea slowly.

"Deben ir a un río," Julia suggested unexpectedly. Dena assumed they would all be upset she had left the house, mainly because Gloria always forbade it. But her aunts seemed happy for her. And yet, she wished she could hear her mother chime in, even if only to argue against them.

"¿Y cómo se ve?" Candy asked.

"Bonito. Pero las olas estaban fuertes."

"No, tu amigo, digo," Candy laughed at the misunder-standing. Dena blushed.

"¿Y no lo viste el otro día cuando vino a arreglar la llave?" Julia asked her sister. "Tú sí eres lenta."

"¿No lo viste, Candy? El muchacho la recogió por allá," Flaca pointed down the street. Dena wasn't sure how she knew that, and she didn't want to find out her sources.

"¿Y es buenmozo?" Candy looked at Dena for an answer. She was the only sister who hadn't done prior research.

"Sí. Joven, guapo y dicen que tiene dinero invertido en la Capital," Julia updated everyone on her findings.

"Puede ser." Dena wondered if she should have asked him more questions. How did her aunts know more than she did?

"¿No te habló de lo que hace? Entonce' tan amigos no son," Flaca criticized. "Bueno, te digo, mija, no importa cuánto dinero tiene ni lo que guapo es, no te cases con alguien que necesita papeles," she warned her for a third time. Flaca loved repeating herself. It was why her voice was often raspy. It was also why her husband claimed to want a divorce: her nagging, though she knew it was really his lying and wandering ways that had strained their marriage. After everything fell apart, she decided she wouldn't let anyone hold her voice back. If she had something to say, then she would say it—ten times over, if need be.

"No le diga eso, Flaca. Deja que la niña se enamore con quien quiera." Candy's affectionate and tender marriage shaped her differently than the rest of her sisters, made her softer, more hopeful.

"¿Y ustedes? ¿Están hablando de visas?" Sol came out from cleaning up in the kitchen. "Déjala que gane dinero. Tal vez ese muchacho quiere pagarle por una." Sol had her own theories on marriage.

"Ay Sol, esa muchacha tiene su carrera, su apartamento y su propio dinero. Ella no necesita eso," Julia rolled her eyes beneath her glasses.

"Olvídate de eso. Esa muchacha e demasiado vieja para pensar en eso. Para hacer eso, ella va a perder cinco años de su vida. ¡Mínimo! Y después se le hace tarde para conseguir un esposo y tener su' propio' hijos." Flaca was only good at math when it came to fertility. She once told Dena she needed to marry by 32 in order to have three kids before 40, lest they be endangered by her deteriorating womb.

"Tía, yo ni sé si quiero hijos," Dena said, causing her tías to gasp simultaneously. She looked around at them. There seemed to be an empty space in the circle where her mother should have been, her legs kicked up onto the metal coffee table, her laugh echoing in the backyard. She would have agreed with them, as motherhood was the only subject that united them all. Even single, childless Sol, who helped raise her two nephews, thought motherhood was the defining characteristic of womanhood.

"Los hijos son la mejor cosa en la vida."

"Claro que sí."

"¿Quién te va cuidar cuando seas vieja?"

"Mira la pobre Madely."

"Que no tiene a alguien para cuidarla."

"Después que se murió el esposo no tiene a nadie."

"Los hijos son lo más importante en la vida."

"No sabes nada antes de tener hijos."

"Un regalo de Dios."

"Amen."

1994

Gloria

Eleven days after the day they made love beneath their tree, Gloria could still taste Marcelo. She could feel his arms wrapped around her, his coarse hair pressed into her neck, his thumb tracing her hairline. She felt him more clearly than ever before, as if her limbs held onto memories stronger than her eyes. They parted ways under the pretense that he would visit when his father permitted. She counted every passing day.

Twenty-eight days was about the time they usually spent apart. She went to the creek early in the morning and waited to hear his feet squishing mud. He never came. Then again, he didn't always come. He couldn't warn her either. Calling her house was impossible. And the mere thought of Nito finding a love letter, however vague, sent a shiver down her spine.

Thirty-seven days passed when she started to feel woozy in the morning. She counted backwards to the last time she saw blood leaving her body. She looked up at the moon at night, her loyal clock that never failed. She prayed it was true.

Forty-three days was when she decided it must be true. She rubbed her soft belly and imagined him humming tunes and kissing her neck when he paused to catch his breath. Nostalgia consumed her thoughts. She longed for his soft hands. She prayed he could sense from one hundred miles away that she needed to be rescued, that she needed to be held. She dreamt he barged through the door, declaring in front of her family that she was his and he was hers. He would take her to the capital. They would build a new life together from their scraps.

Fifty-six days, two full moons, and no response. He still hadn't shown up by the creek. She continued to count the days, wondering if he was doing the same. She assumed he was busy, but wasn't she important too?

She gritted her teeth and worked harder, hoping her calloused hands and feet made her worthy. She scribbled in her journal at night, attempting to release her pain through the ink. Her cravings forced her to pick and binge eat cherries. She liked the stinging sensation from the bushes. She slurped chinola at night. The cracked, black seeds scraped against the inside of her mouth. She picked at her cuticles until they bled. Her skin was itching with impatience. The pain refocused her attention.

Sixty-four days, and she imagined him coming into her room, lying down next to her, rubbing her belly with Vivaporú, and reminding her she was loved. But he didn't. She forced herself to make dulce for nine hours straight. The hot cauldron's smoke spread black ash in her hair. She had to wait behind four siblings to get a turn at the cold shower. She felt like a guest in her own home. She felt like a guest in her own body.

In bed, she cursed herself for having silly fantasies that gave her nothing to eat. With every growing millimeter of her waistline, she became more irritable. Her chichos hid her minuscule bump. Her fierceness hid her sadness. No one knew, and no one thought to ask.

Seventy-two days, and it was the size of an aguacate pit sinking in her stomach. He should have been there. She didn't have a plan. She needed him so they could come up with one together. He would have been happy hearing the news. He would have loved her harder.

Or, maybe not. Maybe he was the kind of twisted guy who would ask her whose it was. Maybe he didn't trust her. She had heard stories of lovers glued together until an umbilical cord split them apart. The men shrank in fear, the women repelled them with their round bodies. She would become a single mother, then no one would want her. The neighbors would whisper that they had known all along who she truly was.

Eighty days, and the light coming in through the window was too bright, especially during sunset when the sun glared directly into the cracks. The walls seemed thinner than before. Everyone's laugh was irritably loud. She was both exhausted and restless. She wondered if she should have it at all. Perhaps God's little plan was better planted in another body, by another man who wasn't a child himself, in another family with more food on the table, on another island that didn't make everything endlessly pegajoso.

Eighty-nine days, and he wasn't coming. He probably got what he had always wanted: he had used and discarded her. She should have known. She sweated her body weight, dredging through everyday tasks. Her shoulders felt heavy. Her hair wouldn't sit right. Her cravings tortured her out of bed at night to scour the half empty fridge and suck on ice that melted far too quickly.

Nito made comments about her constant consumption. Flaca said her face looked hinchada. Her mother told her she could stand to rebajar un par de libra'. She felt fat and ugly. She could hear the spirits laughing at her in the dark when she lay down at night. They knew she deserved this misery for her carelessness.

Ninety-five days, when she saw blood. It wasn't much. She sent herself to bed to rest.

Ninety-six days, and she woke up sweating in the middle of the night. The entire street was sound asleep. As she went to brush the sweat away from her neck, a current of pain spread across her belly. She turned over in bed and saw Candy spread out beside her. She lifted herself gingerly off the bed before tiptoeing to the bathroom.

Her lower back was hot and heavy. She threw cold water on her face to cool down. Her eyes, still blurry, readjusted in the bathroom mirror. Her face looked foreign, twisted, and stretched from the roaring pain in her lower abdomen. Beads of sweat pooled around her face. Her body trembled as liquid trickled down. She stuck her index and middle fingers in between her legs and pulled them out to reveal a dark film. She rinsed her fingers quickly. The face in the mirror looked shocked, though her mind was numb.

Adrenaline kicked in as she pulled herself away from the sink and out of the room. She grabbed the keys and a flashlight from the kitchen, opened the back door, and gently closed it behind her. She felt like a headless chicken looking for somewhere to go. She opted for the far back wall so no one inside could hear her rummaging around. As she reached it, the weight of her legs doubled. Her belly quivered like overflowing trucks that roared down mountain roads. Her load was too heavy. Her body betrayed her, spasming in place. She dropped to her knees and started clawing at the dirt. Moving her arms kept her from screaming and crying. The dripping turned to leaking. She pulled off her underwear and hiked up her thin nightgown.

She crouched down into the hole she had just made and readjusted her footing as the pain increased. After a few minutes, she went back on her knees, clenching her abdomen, arms, face, the ground. Nothing soothed her. Every position was awful. There was nothing she could do to stop it.

Minutes turned into an hour, although she was not keeping track of the passing time. All she could think about was the small hole she had clawed out that was absorbing her blood, the color of a dark cereza that had stayed on the stem too long. She stood up and looked inside. A thumb-sized knot lay at the center. She couldn't get herself to touch it.

As the shedding slowed, tears began pouring down her face. She cried soundlessly, covering her mouth with her bloody hand. The vecinos loved an episode of midnight madness. She did not want to make a spectacle of her misery. Eventually, she took a deep breath and grabbed two fistfuls of dirt. She bent her tired, deflated, and heartbroken body over the hole and threw dirt in over and over again until the soil around it had been repositioned into a flat mound, converting her backyard into a cemetery.

She said a silent prayer, mourning the life that never was. The faded Milky Way mocked her from above. If only it had been raining, like in the movies when something horrible happened. Then she could scream into the thunder, and no one would hear. Her sorrows would drown in the puddles by her feet. But no, this night was crisp and clear, blowing cold air on her open wounds.

"Nunca sabes lo que Dios tiene guardado para ti." Her mother's words lingered heavy and ominous in her mind. Her body sank into the dirt around her. Ten minutes was all she gave herself to grieve before she dragged her legs, covered in dust and dead dreams, to the garden hose. She turned the knob slowly and washed her dress and body clean.

Who was to blame for her broken body? Her? God? The jungle that wore her out day and night until her fingertips were scraped raw from its sour fruit? Was her love podrido from the inside out? Was she unworthy? Was God punishing her? Or was He merely granting the awful wish she asked for one night in quiet desperation? Was this a gift granted or a curse? One thing she knew for sure: God did not make mistakes, only people did. Whatever mistakes she had made before, she would correct them moving forward.

For the first time ever, Gloria was too tired to fight anyone, including herself. She went to bed heavy and exhausted, shivering as the once hot air suddenly felt unbearably cold. She held her breath so as not to cry out loud. Tears streamed down her face and drenched her baby pink sheets.

In the morning, she forced a laugh as she told her sisters she must have sweat all through the night. "Que calor. No lo pude aguantar."

Ninety-seven days, and she ripped out the last pages from her journal. They burned en el fogón's fire as she cooked the day's dulce.

Day Seven

Dena

Before she heard it, Dena smelled the rain flooding the earth. There was a sweetness in it, like honey dripping from the clouds. She stayed in bed on her back with her laptop at a 45-degree angle, facing down. She got up around noon when the rain finally let up and the clouds began to part. She headed out unannounced and sloshed down the muddy street towards Minerva's house.

The grass out front was still slippery from the rain. A puddle pooled around Minerva's doorstep. Dena hopped over it and onto the concrete step leading up to the open door.

"¡Hola!" Her voice echoed inside the seemingly empty home.

"Sí, ¿quién es?" Minerva's raspy voice could be heard from the kitchen.

"Dena, ¡la hija de Gloria!"

"¡Entra!" Minerva waddled over and waved her in. This time, she led Dena to her living room, which felt much more comfortable than the outdoor shack. Dena could hear her kids watching TV in one of the bedrooms. She was much more at ease than the first time she visited a week ago.

"Te estaba esperando," Minerva said unexpectedly.

"¿Sí?"

"Sí. Primero, ¿quieres beber café, jugo o agua?" She offered.

"Jugo está bien."

"¿De qué? Tengo chinola, cereza, tamarindo…"

"Tamarindo."

Within a couple of minutes, Minerva was back with two full glasses.

"Entonces, ¿me esperaba?" Dena reminded her before taking a sip.

"Sí. El otro día te fui'te de aquí medio rápido. Y yo sé que a tu familia no les gusta estas cosa'. No me deja'te un número. Entonces, te esperaba aquí."

"¿Pero por qué?"

"Tengo muchos años trabajando en e'to. Y me he dado cuenta que cuando alguien comienza a preguntar, nunca encuentra la respuesta de una vez. Nada es fácil," she exhaled deeply and pointed to her arms and legs. "¿Tú ves todo esto? Son marcas de ellos. Cuando ellos quieren hablar, les tengo que poner casó o se enojan." She spoke more clearly now, her eyes fixed on Dena.

Decades of Minerva's life were spent retreating to the darkened outer edges of society. Raised by a single mother and abandoned by her Haitian father, she was a lonely only child constantly teased for being poorer and darker than the rest. She spent hours wandering riverbeds and shaded forests alone. She never intended to work with los espíritus. But once they started tapping into her, she could not shut them off. Each time she attempted to ignore them, they grew louder, more violent. She would get into accidents, trip, fall. Her right arm held the patchwork scars of burning oil from a pan she mistakenly tipped over. On her leg was a long slash from coiled barbed wire. She explained all this to Dena as they drank their juice.

"¿Esa también?" Dena pointed to the tip of a scar that was peeking out from the top of Minerva's blouse. She lowered her neckline slightly so that Dena could see it more clearly.

"Sí, esa dolió más que los otros." The five-inch-long bubbled scar—directly in the center of her chest—was from open heart surgery for an irregular heartbeat. But she had been living con los espíritus so long she believed it was them at work. It was not a coincidence that it came after she neglected to tell someone of a vision she had involving a truck accident. They were reminding her that they were in control; she needed to take heed. Since that surgery twelve years ago, she never neglected them again.

"Los misterios vienen sin avisar y he aprendido a escucharlos en vez de correr." She stated this in a strangely calm tone that reminded Dena of Ariel. Life had washed over and numbed them. Minerva had accepted her fate and the mystic lore that followed. She seemed at peace, no longer afraid of her own destiny.

"¿Y son todos malos?" Dena asked, careful not to overstep.

"No, ¿quién dijo? No son malos. Es que los ángeles se enojan también. Así juegan y así te enseñan. Y si no le' pones atención son capaces de quitarte todo para que entiendas."

Dena shuddered. Minerva was battling another world while she could barely manage this one.

"El día que te fuiste de aquí, Gloria me vino a visitar." Minerva abruptly changed the subject. "Vino tres noches seguida'. No creo que regresará de nuevo."

"¿Y qué dijo?"

"El primer día me habló de ti. Dijo que te vio cansada, que estabas preguntando muchas cosas. El segundo día me habló de un amor que la esperaba, un árbol, un río. Me habló en imágenes, no con palabras. A veces son así." Minerva pressed her lips together as if she was sucking an imaginary lime. She was struggling to deliver the information across realms. "El tercer día me habló de un bebé o dos o tres. Creo que fueron de ella. ¿Sabes si estaba embarazada antes de ti?"

"No entiendo nada. ¿Qué árbol? ¿Qué bebé?" Once again, everything sounded cryptic and vague to Dena.

"La verdad es que ella no dijo mucho. Parece que tenía secretos que ni ella quiso revelar."

"¿Y no preguntaste que significaron?" Dena could not hide her growing frustration.

"No me gusta preguntar mucho. Prefiero que hablen y vayan a su voluntad," Minerva said. "Todos tenemos el poder de ver y saber como yo. Lo que te dije ese día: tu intuición es más importante que todo lo que te puedo decir."

"Gracias por todo, Minerva," Dena said as politely as she could manage before putting the cup down and getting up.

"Donde hubo fuego, ceniza queda," Minerva offered final words, but Dena was already halfway out the door.

The tension around the Vega house was a thick fog that rolled out and back after the day's hora santa. Dena and Jess faked smiles in front of the guests, then retreated to their own corners. They had not spoken since their fight. Manny, convinced he could lift their spirits con un par de cervezas, picked them up and brought them to his house or, rather, his parents' house.

Tío Johnny's home was set on the outskirts of town, one block away from his ferretería. It was the only house he had lived in after moving out of Abuela's. He was the youngest, wildest Vega and the one to settle down the fastest. He and Rosaly were childhood sweethearts who met at the age of five, fell in love at ten, and had Manny at sixteen. Due to complications in labor, they only ever had Manny, though rumor had it Johnny had two more kids with a woman in Macorís. His sisters tried confronting him over the years, but they didn't press too hard, aware of the ways of men.

Dena, Sol, Jess, Manny, and Rosaly's father sat in a small circle of matching rocking chairs in Johnny's small marquesina. The wicker chairs scraped the rough floor tiles as everyone rocked back and forth. Lime green geckos ran across the butter yellow walls. Neighbors could be heard in their homes nearby along with Merengue playing down the street.

"Sol, ¿hiciste los cojines?" Asked Jess, pointing to the identical cushions they sat on.

"Sí. Hace varios años ya," Sol said, proudly.

"Sí, debemos hacer uno' nuevo'," yelled Rosaly from the kitchen, aware that sewing projects were Sol's only source of income, excluding all the money the Vega siblings sent to her from America over the years.

"Aquí estamos." Rosaly walked in with a tray of plastic cups filled with icy Presidente.

"Gracias, Tía," Jess picked up a cup. She glanced over at Dena, who had been strangely quiet all day. After her sister spent the last few days asking questions about their mother's life, her sudden silence was even more unsettling.

"Gracias," Dena smiled and chugged, avoiding Jess's eyes from across the room and focusing on the group discussion of new cushions and predicted rain for the upcoming days.

"Dena, are you okay?" Jess tried to slip in casually mid conversation.

"Yeah, I'm just hot," Dena lied, fanning herself with her empty hand. Minerva's words kept replaying in her mind. *Embarazada. Árbol. Bebé.*

"¿Caliente, dices? Prendemos el abanico entonces." Rosaly pointed to Manny. He got up and turned the dial.

Dena looked over at Rosaly's dad to try and distract herself. She pointed to his leg and shrugged as if to say *"What happened?"* He shrugged back. He had worked every day in the fields until he was 76, hacking away and working like a horse, just not like his horse, Grillo, who he claimed was the laziest animal "en el mundo entero."

"Es cáncer," Rosaly said.

"Pero no lo sabe. No te preocupes, él no oye na," said Sol, sipping her cerveza. They explained that his leg gave way one day when he was coming off of his horse. Since then, he sat and waited for the moment he could go back out to his land. No one told him the truth. The Dominican healthcare system valued secrecy above full disclosure. Doctors and families kept medical records from the elderly, hoping blind faith would keep them alive longer than the treatment they couldn't afford. He was practically deaf as well, so they spoke about it around him, but he never realized. He sat and waited, feeling the vibrations in the room: a car driving by, a speaker booming, a thunderstorm striking land. Not much else caught his attention, as he drifted in and out of consciousness.

Dena wondered what it was like to live in such silence. She always wanted to know and understand everything around her. Lately, everything was becoming unbearably loud. But he seemed unaware of his own demise, staring off into the distance, gently rocking in his chair. Maybe it was best he didn't know the turmoil within his own flesh. Or perhaps he felt it in his bones and had come to terms with it already.

The more she stared at his sagging limbs, the more she was reminded of Gloria withering away in their living room, quieter than she had ever been, disappearing slowly. But this old man had a peace about him that her mother never had, even in the last days when it was obvious what was coming. Gloria always fought even—almost especially—in the end.

When Rosaly went to the kitchen to grab a third Presidente, Dena followed her.

"Tía."

"¡Ay, mi hija! Me asustaste," Rosaly jumped back from the open fridge.

"Tía, ¿Mami tenía otro novio antes de Papi?"

"¿Qué? ¿Cómo?" Rosaly looked around, but no one was there to redirect her attention.

"¿Marcelo? ¿Ella nunca habló de él?" Dena continued as Rosaly's wrinkle-free face tightened and her jaw clenched.

"Puede ser."

"¿Sí?" Dena kept her tone light, her words minimal.

"Mejor ven a mi habitación y hablamos ahí." Rosaly walked her over to her bedroom and closed the door behind them.

"Ella tuvo a alguien, pero nunca me habló mucho de eso. Tú sabes cómo era tu mamá. Casi no hablaba de lo de ella." As a sister who married in, Rosaly desperately wanted to be accepted into the family. She was always a bit gentler with the girls, always more forthcoming.

"¿Y nunca preguntaste?" Dena spoke softly, hoping it would make her aunt divulge more information.

Gloria was probably rolling in her grave, angry that anyone would have the audacity to demand answers from her past. But Rosaly couldn't help but feel moved by her niece's persistence. She held Dena at nearly every age, excluding the last ten years. The little girl she once knew had become a bold woman, just like her mother.

"Tu mamá era una mujer complicada. No le decía sus cosas a nadie. Quería hacer todo ella sola. Me recuerdo una vez cuando éramo' niña', se cortó el brazo con una piedra en el río y no le quiso decir a Negra o a Nito. Dique se iban a enojar si supieran que ella andaba sola. Tanta sangre y ella misma se limpió. ¿Puedes creer eso?" Tía Rosaly rambled when she was nervous.

"Sí… ¿Entonces no sabes más sobre Marcelo?" Dena tried again.

"Dios, perdóname," she shook her head as she spoke. "Eran amigos. Lo vi solo una vez en la fiesta de cumpleaños de ella. Pero nunca más después de eso."

"Creo que fue la quinceañera de Tía Candy," Dena said, realizing she knew more than Rosaly.

"Sí, puede ser. Pero ellos dejaron de hablar hace mucho' año'," Rosaly restated. For the first time all week, Dena considered that her aunts weren't being evasive—they simply did not know.

"¿Cómo estás, Dena? Sé que e'ta semana fue difícil para ti," she rubbed her back lovingly. Dena relaxed her shoulders under her aunt's gentle touch.

"Estoy bien, Tía. He podido descansar un poco en los últimos dos días," she reassured her with a half smile. "¿Entonces, Mami se quiso ir a vivir en Nueva York?"

"Claro que sí. Todos queríamos en esos años. Pero ella especialmente. Tenía un afán de ir a vivir allá, ser americana y tener dólares. Y lo hizo. Se fue y trabajó mucho para no tener que regresar pa'cá. La vida de ella fue muy difícil. Todo lo que tuvo le costó mucho."

"¿Y nunca más habló de Marcelo?" Dena's eyes reminded Rosaly of Gloria's. Goosebumps spread all over her arms. She remembered how much her sister-in-law struggled raising this little girl—now woman. It was the same reason Rosaly was struggling to respond to her now. Dena was confident, assertive, and brilliant. She didn't hold back, just like her mother.

"A mi no. En eso' tiempo' no había internet o celulares como ahora. Había poca forma de comunicarse. No era algo que me iba decir por teléfono en una casa llena de gente," Rosaly reasoned, before quickly adding, "Además, ella estaba feliz con Antonio, contigo y con Jess. Me recuerdo que le pregunté una vez, después de que se casó porque alguien me dijo que la vio en camino a la Vega un día….Pero ella me dijo que no había pasado nada y que Antonio era su media naranja."

"Su, ¿qué?"

"Su 'otra mitad'. Me dijo que estaba feliz y se iba a vivir allá. Tú sabes que cuando se puso algo en la mente, ella no lo dejaba hasta que lo hacía."

"¿Y sabes dónde está él?" Dena avoided repeating his name as it obviously made her aunt uncomfortable.

"La última vez que supe de él, me dijeron que estaba viviendo en Jarabacoa. ¿Por qué no regresamos a la marquesina? Los demás deben estar preocupados." She stood up abruptly and Dena understood that everyone was only comfortable sharing up to a point. The rest was whispers, rumors, and vintage diary pages scribbled in faded ink.

"Te pareces igualita a tu mamá cuando era joven. Sé que crees que era dura pero ella las quiso mucho e hizo todo por ustedes," Tía Rosaly concluded with tears in her eyes.

At night, as the sky finally cleared, Dena stomped through the backyard, looking to escape everyone inside. An orchestra of insects buzzed all around her as leaves fell sporadically. She wondered if the trees were sending signals to each other of all the craziness going on, just as Ariel said. Perhaps, they were absorbing her family's secrets and lies too.

Dena made it to the back for the first time all week, where a couple of trees hovered over the cinderblock wall. A bougainville plant was pressed against it, dangling papery fuschia leaves. Everything had grown a lot taller in the ten years she had been away. One tree in particular had a thick, short trunk. Its branches spread wide and hung low from its heavy fruit. She stepped forward to inspect a large, brown orb hanging from one of its lower branches. She remembered seeing Gloria standing before this tree twenty years before. Dena was a twiggy six-year-old, and the tree was a fraction of its current size. She only recognized it because of the fruit that dangled before her now.

"Mami, ¿qué haces?" She asked Gloria curiously. She had

never seen her mother stand so still. Gloria, startled, jumped back and dropped the fruit in her hand.

"¡Coño, Dena! ¡Mira lo que hiciste!" Her mother pointed to the busted fruit, cracked open on the ground. "¡Muchacha del diablo que no sirve pa na! ¡Te dije que te quede' adentro jugando con los otro' niños!"

Dena stepped back, confused. The tree before her was full of fruit. Why couldn't she just pick another?

"¡Vete de aquí!" Gloria was acting as if Dena had interrupted a private moment. As if she did not belong there or anywhere but in the confines of the house. Gloria picked up the fruit and threw it at her. It fell a few inches away from Dena's skinny legs and splattered all over the ground. Orange bits splayed at her feet. Fear coursed through her body. Dena took off just as her mother picked up another one. Gloria never missed twice. On the way back inside, Dena tripped on a rock hidden beneath a fallen banana leaf. She felt a sting but kept running. Only when she got inside and Tía Candy pointed to her leg did she realize blood was dripping from her knee.

Dena thought back to all the times Gloria smacked her or Jess's hands if they tried to touch her things. Everything was sacred except for their skin. They trained themselves to stop touching and cautiously tiptoe around their own home. That was why she had moved out at twenty-one, not because of her boyfriend. And that was why she never returned, even after the disease took over her mother's body and their lives, even after her entire family told her she should.

The low-hanging fruit taunted her now. She grabbed it viciously, digging her nails into its flesh. She thought about the mess her mother had caused, leaving it scattered all around her. She swung her arm back and hurled the fruit towards the trunk. She missed. She picked up another and tried again. It splattered, but no liquid fell. Mamey was infamously unjuicy. She tried again and again until her arm was sore and the lower branches were emptied. All she had was pent-up rage and no-where to place it.

Damn, Mami. ¿Por qué no me dijiste nada? You always had to know more than everyone else. Siempre la que lo sabía todo. Now you're gone y mira el reguero que dejaste.

She thought about her mother yelling every Saturday morning when the girls wanted to go out or watch TV. *"Los oficios no se dejan para ahorita. Se hacen temprano."*

Everything had been left undone.

1994-1997

Gloria

A month after the darkest night in Gloria's life, Antonio José Rodriguez Cruz bumped into her at the colmado. She looked nothing like how he remembered her from school: uncharacteristically quiet and fidgety, hair unbrushed, skin ashy.

On his walk home afterward, he couldn't stop thinking about her laugh, the one that constantly interrupted the class and made la profesora yell, "Señorita Vega, tranquilícese por favor." He only had one class with her, since they were a year apart. But it was enough for her to haunt his daydreams. He craved hearing that laugh again. When he asked around about her, he learned she was working for her family and, more importantly, still single. He began hanging around the colmado, hoping to see her again. Whenever he did, he walked beside her until she banished him. But as independent as she was, he could tell she was lonely.

The fourth time, he bought her chocolate, which was gooey before she even opened it. She sucked on the wrapper, squeezing it slowly. The candy stuck to the roof of her mouth and kept her from talking. Meanwhile, Antonio went on and on about her beauty, wit, and energy, which he claimed were missed by everyone since she stopped going out. She wiped her sticky lips as she laughed. The sound was music to his ears.

It was the first time seventeen-year-old Gloria had laughed deeply in months. The night in the backyard replayed in her mind every single day. She wanted to scrub her mind clean, to sink to the bottom of the river and have it wash away her pain. Or, at the very least, wash away the black residue she could never quite get out from under her fingernails. She felt perpetually icky from picking and peeling ripened fruit. Faith and habit kept her going, but on long days, she would collapse onto her bed and pray to her hollow belly. More than anything, she wanted her baby back, to be blessed once more, and to not take it for granted this time. She breathed for her future children. It was the only thing that kept her from digging a bigger hole and surrendering her entire body to it.

She avoided going to la finca on Saturdays, claiming to have headaches or cramps, then picking fights with her brothers so they wouldn't want to take her. It was all she could do to avoid Marcelo. But they made her go back eventually.

When she saw him, he only had excuses: he had been studying, working, and waiting for the right time. She didn't care. She had already convinced herself it was just an insidious infatuation. His love was too risky, his power too potent. She vowed never to give anyone else that power except God.

Antonio, on the other hand, was eager to dote on her every move. Him, she trusted. He made her feel strong, sexy, smart. He made plans to see her and showed up early. He was a good kisser, and when she told him she refused to do anything more, he respected her wishes. He was the kind, devoted man she deserved. Week after week turned into month after month, until one day, he went to see her parents. She had been wary of his intentions, since the entire town knew she had a visa coming her way. But when he sat down in front of her parents and professed his love, she felt more precious than the gold the colonizers scoured the entire island for. Here was a man unashamed and unaware of his desperation—or possibly unfazed by it.

It wasn't a fairytale romance. It was a concrete foundation mixed and poured over time. Not only did he support her dreams of moving to America, he wanted to help make them come true. He promised she could give up working for her parents. In turn, his parents offered to buy part of the Vega's land, since la finca and the dulces were falling short on profits each passing year. Nito didn't have a backup plan. And he was in even worse shape than the business. He couldn't do as much as he used to and, truthfully, he didn't even try. No one could tell if his pains were exaggerated, but they all felt the wrath of their effects. Mamá was stressed, Flaca didn't want to do more manual labor, and Yunior, the strongest member of the family, was busy with college.

Nito had spent most of the business money on parties, a car, a large TV, and other things that made him feel rich but left his pockets empty. His desire to flaunt was suddenly replaced by the need to have enough food on the table. As his dreams dimmed, Gloria's blossomed. She would finally be untethered to her father's land, leave her tiny home, and become an American woman who stomped through Nueva York con un marido que la adoraba.

"¿Te casas conmigo?" Antonio asked her after having received her father's blessing, not that she cared about his opinion on the matter.

"Claro que sí." She had waited months to hear the words leave his lips.

The ceremony was held in March, a few weeks after her nineteenth birthday. At least thirty family members from each party's side along with friends and vecinos crowded into a small hall. They spent the night at a hotel. It was their first time in a room alone, as she had been working to right her wrongs with God. She paced around, unsure how to position herself. But Antonio was patient. He let her call the shots and go at her own pace. It was clumsy and awkward, but she hoped, through time, they would learn each other.

They moved into his parents' home while Antonio worked to save money. He insisted she should stay home; he wanted to provide for her. But Gloria had never known a life outside of work. Alone all day in the small and stuffy house, she grew inquieta y ansiosa. In turn, Antonio and his family became careful around her, using the pitch in her voice to guide their footsteps.

When she became pregnant, everyone was relieved. She moved more softly in response to this greater calling. But when God took that child too, she was unpredictable and predisposed to tantrums—a vicious cycle of victory and defeat. She couldn't escape the feeling of fear; it hunted her down, keeping her prisoner in her own mind. Antonio remained calm, insisting they keep trying, as if it were easy, as if every loss didn't take something from her, too.

It wasn't until her third miscarriage that she sought outside help. Her friend, known for reading tazas, mixed a special baño de limpieza with fresh water, chunky salt, leaves, cinnamon sticks, cloves, and herbal oils. For three consecutive days, she poured the thick liquid from the top of her head to the soles of her feet, releasing all the malignant energy that had been stuck in her cells, praying with her entire mind and body to be free. Three months later, she was with child. This time, for good.

Antonio kissed her belly and hummed songs every night, as she always envisioned. His family catered to her like a goddess. She gave birth on a cool November night. When they placed Dena in her arms, she refused to let her go. When they tried to take her to a separate room to sleep, she started crying louder than the baby, raging until they brought her back. She wouldn't let her out of her sight. Gloria had hoped Dena would cure her heartache. Instead, she cried for all her losses more than ever before, consumed by an overbearing grief that wouldn't let her rest.

"Antonio," she tried opening up one afternoon.

"¿Qué fue, mami?" He smiled, though the pet name made her skin itch.

"No, na." Instead, she retreated and stared down at the floor. Dena began to cry in the corner, sensing the tension in the room.

"Búscala, por favor." She waved her hand at the baby, and he complied.

"Shh, mi niña. Todo está bien," he whispered to Dena.

"Tráemela." She motioned to him to bring her the baby, but he kept her in his arms.

"No sé, Gloria. Lo encuentro raro que nunca quieres dejar a nadie con la bebé" he said, holding Dena close to his chest.

"¿Me tá diciendo cómo ser mamá?"

"No, solo digo que es raro. Mis hermanas y Mamá dicen lo mismo. Puedes confiar en ellas si necesitas ayuda. No tienes que hacerlo todo sola."

"Antonio, tú va' a trabajar todo' lo' día' y yo me quedo aquí cuidando a la niña. Tú ni sabes el trabajo que he pasado. Yo no trabajo, no hago nada, solo me quedo aquí día y noche haciendo la misma' cosa'." She stood up from the bed and approached him as she spoke.

"Sí, pero se supone que si no trabajas, tú vida es un poco más fácil." He regretted his words immediately.

"Claro, ¡porque las mujeres solo sirven para limpiar y cuidar niños!" She bellowed louder than either of them expected. They were home alone, a rare occasion in the crowded home.

"No, yo lo que digo es que ahora que no tienes que trabajar en la finca haciendo dulces, puedes descansar de vez en cuando. Si quieres ir a la tienda a comprar algo, puedes dejar a la niña con la familia. No tienes que estar asustada todo el tiempo."

She wasn't sure what she hated more: that he called out her fears or that she had any at all. "No tengo problema con eso," she lied. "Estoy aquí cuidando mi hija porque quiero. Eso es normal. ¿Qué crees? ¿Que me salvaste? ¿Que porque tus padres compraron tierra y no tengo que trabajar ya no puedo estar cansada?" She glared at him, daring him to speak.

"Bueno, 'salvaste' no. Pero…" He refused to finish his sentence.

"No necesito que nadie me salve o me cuide. He trabajado mi vida entera."

"Sí…" He couldn't get another word in.

As sad and miserable as she might be, she was always more prideful. "Yo no tengo problema con nada. Me voy a la casa de mis padres," she said, putting on her shoes. "Y para que veas que no tengo problema, quédate aquí con la niña mientra' tanto."

"¿Qué? Pero, ¿cuándo vas a regresar?" Occasionally, Antonio bit off more than he could chew with her, and it never failed to surprise him. She liked that about him. She liked keeping him on his toes.

"No sé. Después que termino 'descansando'." She threw his words back at him and stormed out. Of course, she had anxiety about leaving the baby alone. She didn't trust anyone or anything since giving birth. She desperately clung to motherhood for her sanity, and even that barely maintained her. The mere thought of leaving Dena in another room made her sick. But she wasn't going to admit that to Antonio, especially when he seemed so arrogant about knowing better. Maybe it was time he took care of the baby without her around, saw how it really felt to sit there alone. She said all this to herself on her walk, too stubborn to return home and admit defeat.

Gloria hated visiting her parents' house. Her mother constantly gave her unwarranted advice on motherhood, her father told her she should be working, and her sisters wanted to chat about trivial things. What she really wanted more than sipping coffee and spreading rumors was to walk through her old garden alone. Nito started taking better care of it once his farm was cut in half, especially since he refused to be inside with Negra all day. His wife's empty days and aching feet made it impossible to talk to her. All Negra wanted to do was complain. All Nito wanted to do was dig into dirt as he had been doing since he was five when his father handed him a rusty machete and told him to dig because it was the only tool they owned.

Gloria avoided the inside of the house altogether. Her feet carried her to the back wall as if they had a mind of their own. It had been over three years since she lost her first child. She took her shoes off to feel the cold dirt on her heels. She scanned the area, sure she would never find where it happened. Perpetual rainfall had probably flattened the mound, washed her blood away.

But then, she saw it. Her heart began beating faster. She dropped to her knees, unable to stand back up. It was only about four feet tall and no thicker than her big toe. Five branches came off the center stalk and held three dozen oval leaves combined. She rubbed them with her fingertips and a wave of memories flashed through her mind: the day they met, their first kiss, the time they made love in the shade of a similar tree. Startled, she looked around to see if anyone else was there to bear witness to this impossible dream. Somehow, without words or sounds, she could feel his fingers scraping her just as she scraped the leaves. She grazed the smooth center trunk with her right hand. Her body grew warm as if it was cradled in his arms. She indulging in the light spreading through her chest, envisioning herself surrounded by his scent. When she finally let go, she felt ashamed.

What happened to all the fantasies she once imagined? What happened to all their dreams? She had been so intent on creating a perfect life, she ended up in a completely different one altogether. She felt distant from everyone she knew. Even her husband thought she was crazy. He never said it directly, but his words always implied that something was off, that *she* was off. She fought so hard for her own freedom, and now she felt more stuck than ever before, her life merely a whisper of what it once was.

"Regresaré por ti," she promised. To whom? The tree? The child? Marcelo? Herself? She wasn't sure. She felt she owed everyone everything and yet had nothing left to give.

Day Eight

Dena

In the middle of the night, Dena messaged Ariel to pick her up when he was done working. A loyal campesino, he arrived at their spot down the street from Abuela's a quarter past four. She had spent another day successfully ignoring her family and unsuccessfully getting her mind off of Gloria. The entire town was gossiping. She didn't have proof, but she could sense it in the viejitas' eyes at the horas santas.

The comfort she sought was unattainable. Gloria would never give her answers. The only other thing she could think of was to go straight to the source: Marcelo, a man who knew her mother before she started keeping secrets. He would know about a previous child. Or maybe he wouldn't know anything at all. But she had to try.

"¿Cómo tá allá atrás?" Ariel yelled from the front of the motorcycle.

"¿Qué?" She couldn't hear him over the rumbling trucks that passed them.

"¿Que si estás bien?" He asked again, this time turning his head halfway around.

"¡Sí! ¡Mira pa'lante!" She slapped his back and laughed.

"No te preocupes, he manejado por aquí muchas veces," he assured her. As gravity started pulling her down, she found herself hugging him for stability. Her mother had been wrong: riding on the back of a stranger's bike was incredibly fun.

Jarabacoa was the classic Dominican mountainside getaway, filled with cabins, paragliders, and fresh strawberries sold roadside by the pound. The winding road up was cradled by evergreen trees on both sides. The air was cooler and drier than the thick, damp air in the valley below. Dena breathed more deeply and effortlessly as her lungs filled with the scent of fresh pine.

A few minutes after entering town, Ariel pulled over by a shack selling fritura. As he went to buy some food, Dena opened up the GPS on her phone. Though she had visited for two decades of her life, Dena never learned Dominican geography—not her mother's town, the hills in the countryside, nor the creeks that coursed through the land like tears falling down a wrinkled face.

"Falta diez minutos," she said, nervously sliding around the map. He came over and steadied her hands by slipping a kipe into one of them. She bit into it and closed her eyes, savoring the familiar flavors: trigo, ground beef, and a squeeze of lime.

"Pensé que iba a ser más fácil," she sighed, slightly embarrassed by her ambitious plan. Just before she left Tía Rosaly's house the night before, her aunt brought her back to her bedroom and offered the name of a hotel. She heard Marcelo had purchased it years ago. Dena thought she would just show up and talk to him, but as they approached it, she started to feel queasy about the looming confrontation.

"Respira," Ariel encouraged. She closed her eyes and breathed in the semisweet forest air. He kissed her softly as her eyes were closed. When she opened them, she couldn't help but stare at his luminous skin in the golden sunlight.

"Si me dices, tal vez te puedo ayudar," he suggested. She chewed through the kipe and considered this. Her family didn't want to talk. Her girlfriends back home wouldn't understand. She inhaled and, almost uncontrollably, shared all of her discoveries over the last week—everything from her mother's spirit entering Minerva's body to the conversation with Rosaly the previous night. She told him all the information she had gathered, but spared him her conspiracy theories, mainly because she didn't want to admit them out loud. She showed him the notebook, the photo she had taken from the album, and the hotel's address. When she was done, she felt ten pounds lighter.

"¿Y qué le vas a preguntar?" Ariel asked when her presentation was finally over.

"No sé. No tengo ni la menor idea."

"Entiendo." He studied her face, which was numb from overthinking. "Pero es un viejo. Entonces no hay peligro de que él te robe de mí," he flirted to cut the tension. It worked, and she laughed for the first time all day. He tried locking eyes with her to reassure her that everything would be okay, but she swung her hips and walked towards the bike.

"Vamos," she said without turning back.

El Hotel Casa Coralillo was a serene oasis en una loma on the outskirts of town. Tall pine trees bordered the property. Birds and cicadas sang all around. The main building was an L-shaped, taupe edifice surrounded by neatly placed flower bushes. The lobby looked like a cabin complete with large wood decor and warm lighting.

Dena approached reception nervously.

"Buenos días, señorita. ¿Le puedo ayudar con algo?" The

concierge smiled politely. "Tenemos tres habitaciones dispon-
ibles hoy mismo si necesitas."

"Hola. No, solo quería hablar con el dueño. Es un amigo."

The young man nodded and dialed his phone. "Le aviso
ahora, señorita. Se puede sentar allá si quiere." He pointed
towards a chair with a tropical throw pillow that reminded her
of her mother's curtains: tacky, homey.

"Gracias."

Ariel followed her as she went to sit down. He stared at
his palms, sensing her discomfort every time his eyes settled on
her. Meanwhile, Dena's eyes darted around the room, waiting
to see which corner Marcelo might come from. After a few
minutes, she noticed the receptionist talking to a young guy
and pointing to her.

"Buenos días. Me dicen que me buscan." The young guy
walked over and held his hand out.

"Hola." She tilted her head sideways, slightly confused.

"Diego." He held out his hand. His features looked soft in
the light.

"Dena," she said, shaking his hand. "Estaba buscando a
Marcelo Soledad."

"Si, ese soy yo. Marcelo Diego Soledad." He had a warm
and familiar nature to him, like a distant primo.

"No, perdón. Busco a un señor mayor."

"¿A Papí?" He laughed. "Ahora entiendo por qué me
mirabas así. Le digo ahora," he said before promptly sending
his father a voice note on his phone. "Papi, te buscan aquí en
frente. ¿Por dónde andas?" Diego smiled back at them as he
sent it.

"Estoy atrás arreglando algunas flores. Dilen que me
esperen," Marcelo Senior''s voice rang through the phone.
Dena's arms filled with goosebumps at the sound of it. Ariel
reached for her hand. She squeezed his nervously.

"Tá bien. Te esperamos aquí."

"Mejor, ven ayúdame para que termine más rápido," Marcelo Sr. suggested.

"Voy para allá," Diego responded. "Siéntense de nuevo si quieren. Regreso de una vez." He headed to the back of the building. Dena sat down again, wriggling her hands in her lap. She looked around the hotel at the large beams pointing to a wooden ceiling, the massive ceramic pots full of tropical plants, the large windows facing the rainforest. She wondered if her mother had ever visited or even knew about it.

"Hola, ¿a quién esperas?"

Startled, Dena looked back down from the ceiling to find a short, curly haired woman before her.

"A Marcelo."

"¿A mi marido?"

"Sí," Dena forced a small smile and refrained from saying her own name.

"Tal vez le puedo ayudar yo," she offered. The woman had burgundy hair, a plump hourglass figure, and small hands. She slightly resembled her mother—younger Gloria—with dewy skin from lush campo air. The thought made Dena uncomfortable. It was like seeing the life her mother could have had.

"No, gracias. Está bien. Le espero aquí," Dena said. The older woman looked at her warily before walking away. Last night and all morning, Dena had gone over what she would ask Marcelo. She never once imagined having to face his wife or son. She felt small, swallowed up by the heartbreak of her mother's past. She wondered if she could get away with pretending it was all a big mistake, drive off in Ariel's motorcycle, leave all of this digging behind. No.

She stood up abruptly, too anxious to sit any longer, and headed towards the back of the lobby. Ariel followed closely behind. They reached floor-to-ceiling sliding glass doors so clear someone could break a nose mistaking them for air. They were parted slightly at the center, enough to walk through with arms wide open. But Dena stood in the frame, unable to step over the threshold, too afraid of what lay beyond. The view was stunning. A gorgeous wooden deck stretched out towards a vibrant, manicured garden. There were perfectly placed stones, multicolored plants, and butterflies fluttering above. It was what Abuela's house could have been if someone actually maintained it. She could feel the love and devotion in this garden, in the life Marcelo had built for himself—without *her*.

When she saw them, everything in her peripheral vision dimmed, creating a laser focus on the father and son duo. Marcelo stood gracefully beside a hibiscus bush, his black skin contrasting with the bright green leaves, his face framed by delicate pink petals. She could see the highlights and shadows of his profile, his high cheekbones and sharp jawline. He and his son had identical features: button noses, small lips, narrow eyes.

Marcelo Sr. turned towards the lobby so that even from twenty feet away, Dena could see his entire face and eyes—a perfect shade of honey hazel—shimmering in the afternoon light. She knew that color by heart. She memorized it long before she knew what colors were, before she knew what words were. She knew those eyes almost as if they were her own. They were the color of home.

Suddenly, Marcelo pointed to her and Diego nodded. Just as quickly as she had been dragged by the current two days earlier, she felt swept up, in way over her head. Her chest tightened. Oxygen suspended in space in her lungs. She resisted breathing, as if holding her breath would make her disappear. They were walking towards her. Ariel reached for her hand again, but she pulled it across her body, towards her chest instead.

"Vamos," she commanded for the second time in the last hour.

"¿Ya? ¿Tan rápido?" Ariel followed as she stormed back

through the lobby, up the driveway, and onto the motorcycle sitting beneath a prickly pine.

They arrived back in Campesito as the sky turned royal blue. Ariel tried to bring Dena home, but she refused. She couldn't sit through another hora santa or face anyone at home for that matter.

"No, no, no. No quiero ir pa'llá. Vamos a seguir andando," she urged.

He pulled over next to a rice field and turned to look at her.

"¿En qué piensas? Tal vez te puedo ayudar." While that was true earlier in the day, she felt it no longer applied. Everything had changed.

"Tiene que ver con tu mamá, ¿no?" He was trying to solve the mystery, but she didn't want him to. Suddenly, she felt how crazy it had been to involve a total stranger in her family drama.

"Las cosas de familia no se dicen," her mother used to say. She felt sick to her stomach.

"No quiero hablar de eso. Mejor salgamos. Necesito un trago," she said dryly.

He acquiesced and sent his friend a voice note, "¿Qué hacen?"

"Hola, loco. Andamo' rulay aquí en el colmado al lado del play," his friend responded.

At the colmado, the town's baseball team was celebrating their win with the locals. If Antonio were alive, he would have bought everyone a round. Dena thought about him as she ordered a rum on the rocks. She wondered if he knew. It was hard to imagine. Then again, crazier things were true.

She swirled the rum around her tongue so it could reach her bloodstream faster. Leaning on the side of someone's car, she watched Ariel effortlessly navigate the crowd. He seemed so comfortable there saludando his panas one by one. When he described his life on the rooftop, she believed they were the same: outsiders, different from the rest. But she saw now that he was right at home. She was the awkward one getting stares from strangers.

She recognized a few of the colmado patrons. A couple came up to her and offered condolences while grimacing at her presence at such a gathering. She could tell people were acechando, hoping to catch her committing a heinous act like having fun. It was only a matter of time before fulanito por ahí notified one of her family members of her whereabouts. She poured herself a second drink and began to ruminate on her mother. She didn't know her at all. She knew her habits, phrases, favorite shade of lipstick—all the superficial things, nothing that cut deeply. It made sense why the diary pages had been ripped out. And why everyone in her family only had beautiful things to say: they didn't know.

She checked her phone for the first time in hours and saw that Jess had texted her.

"Where are you? Tía Candy's worried and Tía Flaca is ready to lock the doors." She could hear the panic in her sister's words. She was tired of being responsible, making calls, keeping her hair tightly pulled back so it didn't frizz, and dosing herself in bug repellent just to get eaten up anyway.

"Entonce', muchacho, ¿por dónde seguimo' la fiesta?" Yelled one of the players as the colmado's metal gate was sliding shut.

"¡Vamos al Bajo Mundo!" One of the guys said, leading the crowd to the next location.

"¿Tá ready? ¿Quieres ir a tu casa o quieres seguir?" Ariel asked. She could tell he didn't want to sway her decision and yet, his very breath did just that. It was easier to ignore her problems standing next to him, sipping rum, sweating in the midnight air surrounded by campesinos bailando.

"Seguimos," she said, emptying her second refill in one gulp.

"¿Tienes que avisarle a tu familia?" He reached his arm around her as she began to wobble.

"Sí, le mando un mensaje a mi hermana."

"I'm in the underworld," she sent, laughing to herself.

El Bajo Mundo was nothing more than a small patch of dirt above the riverbank. It held Campesito's after-parties when the town bars closed down. Locals congregated beneath dim streetlights to chat, dance, and drink late into the night, sometimes until dawn. There were two makeshift wooden stands that sold liquor, wine coolers, and beer, though most people brought their own bottles. Upon arriving, Dena held her cup out to one of the peloteros, who smirked and poured obediently.

Ariel spotted her refilling. "¿Cómo te sientes?" He asked close enough to her ear that she could hear him over the speaker.

"Perfecta," she smiled, her eyes glossy.

"¿Segura? Quizás deberías irte pa tú casa." He regretted bringing her there. For the last few days, he had indulged her every whim, hoping he could aid in her healing. He recognized the pain in her as he had experienced it himself. But the look on her face now didn't suggest healing. It was defiant. It was the look he used to have when he hurt another man, only Dena seemed intent on hurting herself.

"No. Me quiero quedar."

Gentle droplets of rain began to fall from the sky. Dena cocked her head back and stuck her tongue out to taste. The drops fell down heavier with each passing second until everyone was forced to run and duck for cover under porches, awnings, and thick branches. She and Ariel went into a stranger's marquesina with a handful of other people.

"¿Le diji'te a tu familia dónde estás?" He asked. She nodded in response.

He looked down at her with tender eyes. He knew the pain of losing parents, how it stole the light from someone's eyes and wouldn't let them rest anywhere for too long. He saw how it turned people cold, and he was starting to see it happen to her.

"¿Y respondieron?" He wanted to keep her safe. He knew he could if only she would let him.

She pulled out her phone and found one unopened message. "I'm coming to get you," Jess wrote, twenty minutes prior. Dena looked up and scanned the crowd. The sudden downpour had slowed to a drizzle. She could see the faces more clearly.

"¿Qué paso?" Ariel tried to interpret the emotions flashing on her face: anger, confusion, fear, regret. "¿Estás bien?" He reached for her, but she swatted him away and stumbled out to the darkened lot, muddy from the rain. It seemed sexy and mysterious when she first arrived. Now, she was frustrated by the handful of streetlights that barely lit the crowd. Voices rang in her ears. The music pounded loudly.

She tried calling Jess but the phone went straight to voicemail. Every once in a while, Jess was careless enough to let her phone die. It wasn't usually cause for concern, except Dena remembered leaving the house and spotting her sister's phone plugged into the wall. Was that today? It was unclear which day was which and what drinks she'd had and which story was hers and when and where and why. The last week was a thousand-piece jigsaw puzzle tossed on the ground and stomped on by a hundred dancing feet.

Dena spotted a face she recognized beneath a dim light swarming with bugs. "¿Ha visto a mi hermana?" She asked the random guy without a proper greeting.

"No. Y tú, ¿cómo…"

She was gone before he was done speaking.

"¿Tu hermana vino?" Ariel asked, trailing behind, trying to put the pieces together. She nodded without turning around. She went up to another random group and repeated her question. She didn't recognize them, but she hoped they might recognize her. A woman sipping a wine cooler paused to respond. "Yo no." The rest of the group shook their heads, feigning interest.

"Dena, háblame." Ariel tried to make eye contact, but her eyes darted across the crowd.

"Mi hermana está perdida." She was dizzy from trying to find her sister and drinking with barely any food in her system. She refused to believe Jess wasn't hiding in some shaded corner of the crowd as she often did.

"¿'Perdida'? Pero e'te pueblo e pequeño. Seguro que tá por aquí," he said, now looking around as well.

"No, ella nunca sale sola, especialmente aquí," she said, analyzing all the possibilities in her mind: Manny was with Rubi en la Capital tonight. None of her aunts would have brought her. Jess would have never caught a ride with a stranger. She must have walked. Alone.

"¿Y ella sabe llegar aquí?"

"No sé. Ella no sale sola," she repeated. "Seguro que no vino por la carretera. Es muy peligroso a esta hora," she reasoned. Jess would have been too afraid to walk beside large trucks going 60 miles an hour in the dark, especially after what happened to their father. There was only one other way to get to el Bajo Mundo from Abuela's.

"El otro puente," she said, looking up at Ariel who understood immediately. Together, they pushed past the party towards the river. The water rushed beyond a twenty-foot drop. It was softly lit by the moon and barely audible with the bachata blaring behind them. There wasn't a single soul in sight. Jess should have been there already. It didn't take very long to cross. Unless…Dena didn't want to consider the alternative.

"Jess! Jesssss!!!!!" She yelled her sister's name, instinctively panicking.

Ariel scanned the bank with his phone, but the light didn't reach very far. "Dena, vamos al puente principal," he suggested. From the larger bridge, they would have a much better vantage point of the riverbank.

"¡No! ¡No nos vamos hasta que la encontremos!" She shouted.

"Mira, aquí no vamos a encontrarla. Por lo meno' en el puente de la carretera hay má luz y podemo' ver bien." This time, his suggestion made sense. Without speaking, she held onto his hand and climbed back up towards the party. They got on the back of his motorcycle and went to the main road bridge.

Dena hopped off before Ariel made a complete stop. She raced towards the edge, glanced down, and caught a glimpse of a thin black body dangling off a boulder upstream. Other than the feet, getting brushed by rushing river water, it lay motionless. On it was a twisted white T-shirt, which Jess had been wearing earlier in the day. The realization shook Dena's already unstable bones. She buckled and dropped to her knees on the concrete. Her mouth split open to release a howl from the pit of her belly. Tears streamed down her face, helplessly crying with no control of the sounds she was making.

"¡Mi hermana!" She wailed. Her body shuddered despite the heat.

Ariel approached her slowly. He tried to hold her but even in her weakened state, she pushed him away, looking up at him as if he was a total stranger. He waited, hoping her tears would dissipate but they grew heavier and stronger, pooling beside her, unable to sink into the concrete beneath her feet. If her tears all week were slow and quiet, these were a full body roar. She gasped for air but it was never enough. She bawled for her mother, her father, her sister. For the years of shame and silence that ate at her. For all the fights she had ever had with Gloria. For how she could never be perfect, honest, or tough enough. For all the death. For all the pain. For all the secrets that continued.

"Por dejarla sola," Gloria's voice taunted from within Dena's mind.

"¡Déjame!" She cried out to the voice that had been haunting her for days, weeks, a lifetime. She felt arms holding her down. She looked up and saw a stranger's face.

"¡No!" She released a deep guttural cry like a wounded animal. Someone unfamiliar wiped a damp rag across her forehead. Ariel held her from behind. She didn't want their help. She wanted her sister, La Sombra, who never left her side.

"Nooo!" She screamed louder. Even at this ungodly hour, noisy neighbors were emerging from their shacks, stirred awake by the wailing woman. They whispered about the commotion in the distance like rustling leaves in the wind.

"Why?! How could you?! I can't..." She didn't care that the crowd didn't understand, that her mouth looked twisted en otro idioma. She begged for answers, pushed, pleaded, wept.

"Je...Plea...Yo...Can...No..." The words were falling out of her faster than she could say them. The crowd didn't know her language, but they understood her fingers digging into their skin, her limbs spasming, her hair sticking to the saltwater seeping from her pores. Her body contracted, contorted, communicated what words could not.

"Jeeeeeess!" She saw more footsteps approaching, concealing the view of the river. She wanted to jump out of her body, but the crowd held onto her. Or rather, they held her down, afraid, they would later recount, that she might jump into the river to look for her sister's soul in the shallows.

1998

Gloria

After her fight with Antonio, Gloria started loosening her grip on Dena, allowing other family members to babysit as she ran her errands. Getting out of the house brought a sense of independence and peace she had lost. She reentered her body after months of floating above it. One particular Tuesday, as she stood outside of her doctor's office in La Vega feeling more grounded than she had in a long time, she ran into Marcelo.

"Hola," he said in his beautiful, annoyingly suave voice. "¿Cómo estás?" He spoke as if the previous three years had not happened. As if she were not living a different life that didn't involve him. As if she were not utterly and completely over him.

"Bien. Todo bien," she said calmly. He could tell by her tight smile that she was lying. Gloria never answered any questions with simple one-word answers.

"Entonces, mal." His smile, in contrast, was large, bright. It bothered her that he maintained the same level of confidence and effervescence over time.

"No. Siempre estoy bien." She smacked her lips and raised her eyebrows, challenging his response. Looking him in the eye, she felt sixteen again, aching to see him on a Saturday morning, the sun stroking his back.

In the midst of her silent stare, he grew weak too. Marcelo never knew where he stood with Gloria. She always made herself seem uninterested, annoyed, above it all. But he could tell she was holding her tongue through pressed lips. He hoped that if he managed to crack them open, she might spill the truth. He narrowed the space between them as he spoke the following sentence, "Me haces falta cada sábado."

With just one stroke on her arm, he convinced her to meet him at a motel the next Saturday afternoon. He left feeling victorious, not understanding the depth of his request. Marcelo's smile was a fierce pang of joy in the midst of her postpartum depression. He felt like the light at the end of a dark tunnel, and she had the urge to follow him regardless of the outcome. Perhaps he simply wanted to talk, she suggested to God during her nightly prayer. He did not.

Since then, they met on the second Saturday of every month. Each time, she found a new excuse. She had a doctor's appointment. She needed to file paperwork for their visas. She had to get a dress for Dena's baptism. She began to understand why men kept secrets, hid in the shadows, and wrote corta venas, songs about heartbreak and forbidden love. She managed to drag herself out of the motel room each week, pero no lo pudo dejar. The following month, she would come right back. Aficia'a.

Gloria had never been a sentimental girl and was not a very compassionate woman, but something about his scent made all her cells buzz at once. Her emotions succumbed to body language that spoke only when spoken to. If he pressed just the right spot on her palm, neck, or hips, her body would spasm, a small smirk appearing on her face. He didn't care about her stretch marks or the way her body changed after giving birth. His unwavering affection freed her.

When they were apart, she would close her eyes to replay their encounters. Just imagining his hot breath down her back kept her in bed an hour longer. She learned how to make herself quiver as if his hands were on her. She whispered his name at the peak of her ecstasy, even when he was one hundred miles away.

But a ticking clock hissed in the background of her life. She was leaving. She had to. She was ready to be an independent American woman who raised an independent American woman, if it was the only great thing she ever did. A couple of weeks before her flight, she went to the bus stop, sure of what she had to do.

"¿Gloria? Pa dónde vas?" Johnny was riding past when he saw her in front of the bus stop. He turned around and pulled up beside her.

"Johnny…Tengo que hacer una' diligencia' antes de irme."

"¿Y por dónde? ¿Te llevo?" He offered. Ever since he got his new motorcycle, he wanted to bring everyone everywhere. It made him feel powerful and useful, a rarity in a house full of older siblings.

"En La Vega. Pero no. No te preocupes, queda lejo'."

"No, eso queda ahí mismo." His eyes beamed.

"No, con todo e'te sol, no' quemamo' vivo'." She pointed towards the sky.

"Sí pero nos enfría el viento," he negotiated.

"¿Y tú no vas a jugar en el play ahorita?"

"Eso e más tarde, en una hora. ¡Ven! Olvidate d'eso." He waved her over, confused that she was still resisting his offer.

"No, no, tá bien. Voy a durar mucho. Vete al play. Tú sabe' que Yunior se enoja cuando llegan tarde. No' vemo' de'pué'," she assured him with a half smile.

"Bueno, eso sí. Yunior coge todo demasiado serio." He shook his head and waved goodbye. Johnny was too young and dumb to know what was going on. But seeing him shook her to the core. She started to wonder qué en el nombre de Dios estaba haciendo. It had already been seven months of lies and inner turmoil. Maybe she should not go back at all, leave him without a trace. Then, she wouldn't have to deal with the confrontation.

Desapareciéndose sin explicación was tempting. But she craved to touch him one last time. His presence was grounding. He had seen her through the deep green de la finca and the heavy gray of postpartum. He never judged her bursts of laughter, casual rage, and sudden tears. Yet, the more their skin touched, the less they spoke. They never discussed what happened years ago. They never voiced any of their feelings, except in uncontrollable moans. Their connection existed exclusively in sex and silence, chaos and calm. He caused her anxiety, and he was the only one who could dissolve it.

At the motel, she waited for him beneath the shade of a limoncillo tree.

"¿Cómo estás?" He arrived minutes later, immediately grabbing her waist and pulling her close. He tried to kiss her, but she backed away, paranoid someone might spot them outside.

"¿Qué pasó?" He had waited twenty-eight days to touch her. He couldn't wait any longer.

"Vamos a la habitación primero."

Marcelo paid for a 15-by-20-foot dark, damp room without any air conditioning for exactly one hour. It was all he could afford. The sheets had wide black and white stripes. The walls were mango yellow. The grout between the floor tiles was brown from years of improper cleaning. The single dusty armchair in the corner had an ambiguous stain across the back. It was dingy. It was perfect.

As soon as Gloria stepped into the room, she turned around to drape her arms around him. She kissed him hard before sitting down on the edge of the bed. Then, she pulled him down until she was pinned beneath him. She kissed his lips until his body softened, a trick she learned from him. She had every intention of telling him the truth...eventually.

"Te tengo un regalito," she said, pointing her chin to the fruit beside her bag. "Lo recogí mientras te esperaba." He looked inside, grabbed a small fruit, and snapped it open with his front teeth. He pulled the slippery limoncillo out of its shell, sucked it dry, and spit out the seed. She laughed at the sly grin on his face.

"¿Y de que tú te ries?" He laughed along too.

"No, nada."

"Mejor dejamos los limoncillos para después. Cada vez que comienzo no los quiero dejar." He was still smiling. "Mejor te como a ti." He leaned in and kissed her temple, cheek, and lips. She clenched her jaw.

"¿Qué te pasa?" He whispered in her ear.

"Na. Sigue." She desperately wanted to melt into the sheets beneath her.

"Estás tensa." He read her body like a poem with metaphors only he could decipher.

"No, no, sigue." She insisted. He worked her limbs methodically, ritualistically. They were playing a game of hiding their feelings and seeking ecstasy. He knew exactly what to do to distract her from herself. They pushed and trembled and dug into each other until they finally let go of everything on their minds and chest. She kept her eyes closed as they lay intertwined, synchronizing their breathing.

"¿Qué pasó?" He asked again, turning towards her. He listened as her breaths grew deeper and heavier, knowing that if he gave her enough time, she would fill the silence between them.

"Cuando era una niña, ví a Papá con otra mujer," she nearly whispered.

"Que horrible. ¿Y él supo?"

"Sí. Pero nunca hablamos de eso. A Papá no se le preguntaba nada. Como él decía, así era. Además, yo era tan joven no sé si lo vi bien. Podría haber sido un sueño. Capaz no entendí."

"Pesadilla mejor dicho."

"Lo odié tanto por mentir y por hacerme mentir. Pero después que me casé, me di cuenta que Mamá supo también," Gloria reflected, staring up at the ceiling fan that spun hot air around and around. "Aceptó que así es la vida."

He nodded quietly, knowing many women who had done the same.

"No quiero vivir así."

Marcelo looked back at her, unsure of what she meant. Simply by being in the room, she already was.

"Marcelo, me voy," she said with her eyes closed.

"Yo sé, pero falta mucho para eso."

"No. Me voy en dos semanas."

"¿Qué?" He sat upright on the bed. "¿'En dos semanas'? Pensé que faltaban meses para los papeles."

"Coge mese', sí, pero ya pasaron. Ya tengo mi vuelo, lo' pasaporte' y la maleta preparada," she said, sitting up on the bed now too.

"¿Qué?" He stood and backed away as if her scent repelled him. "¿Y cuando me lo ibas a decir?"

"Te lo e'toy diciendo ahora." Her voice cracked from the tension.

"No, dos semanas antes de tiempo no es aviso. Siempre quieres controlar todo," he spat bitterly.

"No quiero controlar nada. Pero yo sé que si te hubiera dicho antes, te hubieras enojado."

"¿Y ahora no?" His fingers flexed uncontrollably before squeezing into fists.

"Marcelo, te quiero pero me tengo que ir."

"No es eso, Gloria. Es que tenemos meses aquí sin tú decirme nada."

"Sí, y yo con años esperando que me digas …"

"Qué te diga qué?"

"¡Algo! ¡No sé! ¡Cómo te sientes, por ejemplo!"

"¿De qué hablas?" He raised his volume to meet hers.

"No. No. No. No puedo más con e'to." She stood up now, too.

"¿Con qué?"

"¡Con esto!" She pointed back and forth between them. "He durado tanto tiempo amándote que me perdí. Ni me conozco cuando estoy contigo. No sé lo que quiero ni lo que importa." She looked down, ashamed. "Tanto tiempo perdido."

"¿'Perdido'?"

"¡Sí! ¡Te he amado por años!¡ Lo supiste y nunca hiciste nada!"

"¿Y qué estamos haciendo aquí?" He spread his arms, presenting the room and their current predicament. "No, tú me tienes aquí de mojiganga."

"Teniendo sexo, ¿y eso es amor?" She raised her voice again. "No, yo quería ser tu novia. Que llamabas a mi casa. Que cuando me vieras, me dijeras algo. ¡Que me dijeras que me amas, coño!" She looked at him. "Estupida yo que pensé que un día ibas a hacer algo. Pero al final nunca hiciste nada."

"Ay Gloria, no te hagas la víctima. ¡Estás casada! ¡Y sabes que te quiero!"

"¿Cómo iba a saber? Pasamos años viéndonos desde niños antes de casarme y nunca te declaraste. ¿Hasta cuando querías que te esperaba?" In all the times they had lain naked together, this was the most exposed she'd ever felt.

"Nunca me lo pediste tampoco. No me dijiste nada cuando nos veíamos delante de la gente. Estaba estudiando y cuando regresé, estabas con otro." He refused to say the other man's name. All these months, they had hoped the pleasure would drown out the pain. It only served to bury it deeper, growing like weeds neither of them could tear out.

"Pero pudiste luchar por mi. Decirme lo que querías. Ir a mi casa. ¡Algo!"

"¡Tú sabías lo que quería!" He said, wiping the sweat off his face.

"¡No! Ese es el problema, Marcelo, nunca has dicho nada. Solo vienes y me miras y me quitas la ropa y crees que con una mirada ya estamos. Nunca me dices lo que quieres." She lowered her voice, her rage giving way to disappointment.

"¿Qué quieres que te diga? ¿Que te quedes? ¿Que no te vayas? No. No te voy a implorar. Puedes hacer lo que te dé la' gana'." His face went cold and blank.

"Me quiero ir," she restated. "No puedo seguir aquí. No quiero que mi hija crezca aquí, que viva solo para mantener una casa." She shook her head as she spoke. "Quiero ganar mi propio dinero, vivir mi propia vida. No puedo seguir enredada en esto sin idea de lo que puede pasar. Llevo cinco años pensando en ti." She tried to look him in the eye, but he kept his head down. "Ya no. Dejo de pensar que lo que nos falta es un momento perfecto. Nunca iba haber un momento perfecto." She sat back down on the edge of the bed and began putting on her clothes. He did the same.

"Perdóname si nunca te dije. Pensé que era obvio. Sé que no tenemos futuro. Que mi vida es acá trabajando con Papá y la tuya es allá." He sat on the corner chair and lowered his elbows to his knees, too exhausted to keep his back upright. "No voy a ser la persona por la cual te limites." He sighed deeply, knowing her life no longer included him. He grabbed the rest of his belongings and left the room without saying goodbye.

Jess's Week

Jess

In the twenty-five years of Jess's brief life, she had only ever spent ten days apart from her mother. In the last two weeks, that time had doubled. Of everything, her voice was the thing she missed most. It would fill every room she was in, even when she was hoarse and half her syllables were inaudible. Sure, Gloria was rude, but she was also the funniest, most honest person she knew. She gave the best hugs with her full chest and plump arms. And her food was always perfectly seasoned, savory, and sweet. When they first landed, Tía Candy convinced Jess to visit some of the old folks in town to get her mind off of everything. But this only made Gloria feel further away, each room containing a cold silence where her booming laugh should have been. Life lost its sparkle without her mother's light.

Although Jess was born in New York and Dena was born in DR, she always felt more connected to the island, as if part of her was permanently rooted there. She had fond memories of playing with all the kids on Abuela's block. As a child, she was often bullied in the States. A skinny girl with a shy disposition didn't fare well in The Heights. But here, los vecinos embraced her warmly. Maybe it was because she always brought cool toys to play with. She liked to think that it was the energy of Campesito. Everyone was a friend. Everyone was family.

Every day back, she ran into another one of the neighborhood kids, now a full-grown adult with a kid or spouse or both in tow. She was in awe of how much they had changed throughout the years, how different their lives were from hers. In New York, her time revolved around the salon, a handful of friends, her favorite coffee shop, and an occasional art class, although it had been years since she last attended one. She was never as good a student as Dena or as great a hairstylist as Gloria, but the latter provided her with a steady income and, lately, noise for distraction.

In some ways, hairdressing separated her from her problems at home. In other ways, it drew Gloria closer. The salon, which she had been playing in since she was a toddler—the opaque smoky air, the scent of singed hair, the soft piles of split ends sprinkled on the ground like snowfall—was familiar and comforting. While Gloria pulled, stretched, and sprayed hair into different shapes, Jess mastered cutting and styling naturally curly locks. Gloria's clients were mainly older women who left their old countries behind and wanted to morph their hair, life, and past. To transform beyond recognition. Jess's were of a younger generation that sought to reconnect to their natural beauty, dismantling centuries of oppression one strand at a time.

It wasn't the typical art she studied in college, of charcoal nudes and watercolor landscapes, but it granted her the freedom to create with her hands: flow, design, imagine. She found a part of herself in the artistry of her work and, in turn, hoped that her clients would find themselves too. This made her job feel like more than just a job, as her sister often implied. It was one of their never-ending arguments: Dena believed Jess was wasting her talent, Jess thought Dena was condescending.

Ever since she could remember, Jess had been following her sister around. Dena was her warm security blanket, and despite her prickly nature, her presence was comforting. When they were kids, Dena liked being followed. It inflated her ego. As they grew older, she began to resent it. Jess sensed it when her sister hesitated walking into a room she was in. Or how she constantly withheld important information, claiming it was for her own good.

The last two years were especially difficult. Gloria was dying, and Dena couldn't stand to be alone with her for more than a couple of hours. She couldn't stomach seeing Gloria's bodily fluids or hearing her temper tantrums. She was around less often, and when she was around, she frequently grimaced in silence. Even after Gloria passed, Dena felt distant, like an outsider separate from everyone.

At the funeral, Jess's world collapsed in on itself. The older woman channeling her mother shook her to her core. Everyone else shrugged it off, as if watching someone catch un espíritu was normal. At home, the tías had endless rules involving death: no bright-colored clothes, not that she owned any; no loud music or dancing; no sitting alone for too long. She had to chitchat with guests, show them support, be in community. She ached to lock herself in a room like she did back home, close the curtains, and place soundproof headphones over her ears.

During the day, Jess heard her tías whispering about the neighbors, their children, and brothers. At night, the animals outside cooed and cawed loudly. She could hear bats flapping their wings, crickets screaming in the trees. The electricity was inconsistent. The heat was overwhelming. She bit her fingernails down to the quick while she watched her shows. Despite all the interactions at every hora santa, she felt lonelier than ever, like walking around New York during a blizzard, where not a single soul stepped outside.

Before landing, she hoped to reconnect with Dena on the island. But her sister only wanted to talk about bills to pay, things to fix, errands to run. Her beautiful older sister, who was always so composed, gathering information and shining brightly, in one treacherous week, started behaving like her teenage self: reckless, restless, and rude. She was becoming their mother in all the worst ways, pushing everyone away and defying the unspoken rules of mourning.

While Dena was running around with some random campesino, Jess stayed home and placated their aunts who repeatedly cornered her in the kitchen to say things like: "Qué raro se está comportando Dena. ¿Qué es lo que está buscando? Si tu mamá supiera cómo se está portando, le hubiera dado un pecozón."

Jess started worrying the moment Dena asked her to go out drinking. It was one thing to pry into their mother's life. It was another thing to ignore it altogether. That's when she began watching Dena's location more carefully. As a teen, Jess would lie in bed at night and watch Dena ride around the City with her friends like her own personal TV show. Sometimes, when Dena snuck out of the house, their mother would smack the truth out of Jess. Yet she would still triple-check to make sure she was okay. It had been years since she watched her sister's little dot roam the earth for hours. Her behavior warranted it now. She watched as Dena hovered over a nearby house, paced around the backyard, and glided around the island day after day. It comforted her to know Dena wasn't lying about her whereabouts, that she was safe.

Before the eighth hora santa, Jess decided to visit the house Dena went to the day before. She half expected it to be Ariel's house, but when she approached, Minerva's silhouette came into view. Jess shivered, remembering the funeral. Before she could turn around, Minerva lifted her hand to wave hello.

"Buenas tardes. ¿Qué buscas?" Minerva spoke as if she had been expecting her, further creeping her out.

"No sé," Jess said, overtly uncomfortable.

"Si no sabes, no te puedo ayudar," Minerva remained calm.

"¿Mi hermana estuvo aquí?"

"Sí, vino ayer." If Minerva was confused, she didn't let on.

"¿Sabes por qué vino?"

"Ven, entra, que va a llover." Minerva led her inside and pointed for her to take a seat on the couch. "¿Quieres algo de tomar?"

"No, gracias," Jess responded, eager for this to be over. Unlike her sister, Jess always had a deep reverence for spiritual practices. She didn't want to overstep her bounds.

"Hablamo' de varia' cosa'. Parece que lo de tu madre le ha afectado mucho." Minerva always kept her readings private, but she could sense Jess's uneasiness.

"Sí, claro." Jess refrained from asking more direct questions, unsure of what was appropriate or respectful given the circumstances. She didn't want to dig into the spirit world or any other world for that matter. She just wanted to find out what her sister was up to. But Minerva didn't let on. Instead, she offered some advice.

"Yo he perdido a mi madre también. Lo más importante es que ustedes se mantienen unidas y se cuiden." As she spoke, a soft patter came down on her tin roof.

"Me voy antes de que comience a llover más fuerte." Jess left with more questions than answers. What had they discussed? What was Dena looking for? Did she find it?

In the brief time she was out, Dena had left on yet another adventure. Her location indicated that she was moving quickly up the mountains past La Vega. She imagined her sister was running off with her new friend, having an affair in the jungle. But Dena hated clichés and grand romantic gestures. She rarely had boyfriends and didn't trust most men in general.

Then, for the first time all week, Dena didn't go to the hora santa. She was at a bar downtown. When her aunts asked if she'd spoken to her sister, Jess nearly told them. She was terrible at keeping secrets. It was one of the reasons Gloria preferred her: she kept to herself and she kept herself small.

But Minerva's words haunted her. This was bigger than a night out. Dena was falling apart, and she needed her. They needed each other. Jess mustered up all her courage and snuck out of the house to find her sister.

"I'm coming to get you," she texted Dena after successfully convincing her aunts she was going to bed. Her GPS suggested a route that looked far too long and possibly dangerous at this time of night. Her arms sprouted with goosebumps, remembering her father's tragic end. The only other option was to cross the pipe bridge down the street from Abuela's. It looked sketchy, but she had seen enough people cross it successfully to consider it safe.

As she stepped onto the pipe, she reached her arm out to hold onto a metal beam. She kept her phone in her other hand, lighting the path ahead of her. She managed to stabilize herself and walk forward step by step, staying in the center of the pipe, avoiding the rounded sides. Halfway across, she looked up, proud of her progress.

Then, like the crack of a whip, the sky opened up and started to cry. She was used to sudden bursts of rain in Campesito, including earlier in the day at Minvera's house. But her precarious situation was unnerving. It felt like a cruel joke from the universe, reminding her exactly why she never went out alone at night in the middle of the campo.

Rain pounded loudly on the bridge's metal beams and began falling into her eyes, blurring her vision. She needed a free hand to wipe it away. She managed to slip her phone into her pocket. But without the flashlight, the rounded pipe was much more daunting. She moved awkwardly, hesitantly. As she took a small, measured step, her phone slid out. She instinctively reached for it, attempting to break its fall. But gravity moved faster. She watched it fall and plop into the darkened river.

"Nooo." Jess lost her footing in the rain, slipped, and landed on her belly. Before she could even comprehend what was happening, she was sliding off the side of the pipe. Her fingertips clung to big screws on the top, their jagged edges jolted her nervous system awake.

"¡Ayudaaa!" She shouted, aware no one would be out during the downpour.

"¡Ayudaaa!" She could hear faint music across the water, but they could not possibly hear her over the rain. She attempted to swing a leg up, but failed to get enough momentum. Unlike Dena, Jess wasn't athletic. She was skinny, frail. She spent her days lying around at home or slumped over someone else's scalp.

"¡Ayudaaa!" Her stomach churned in fear. The current rushed below, taunting her. She wouldn't be able to hold on for much longer. She had two options: hold on and hope someone found her, or let go while she still had enough energy to swim. She thought about her sister. When something needed to get done, Dena gritted her teeth and did it.

The river was deep enough that she barely scraped the bottom rocks as she plummeted down. But the water was fast and choppy, immediately thrashing her forward, smacking her limbs. She rushed to the top, gasped for air, and accidentally swallowed ice-cold foggy water. Coughing, gurgling, breathing—barely. The clouds started to part. The moon's halo peeked out. Its light pulled her like a tide.

Jess pushed away from the center current towards the river's edge where a tree's roots were covered in mud. They were impossibly tall, curved, and exposed to the elements. She tethered herself around them as soon as they were close enough to touch. Her body whipped back and forth onto the rocky bank. She managed to launch herself just out of reach of the roaring river, its mouth foaming at the chance to pull her back in. Then, she collapsed onto a boulder, exhaling every ache in her body.

As everything faded into darkness, Jess thought about every member of her family, dead and alive. She thought she heard her name faintly in the distance. Maybe somewhere out there, someone was waiting for her, in this world or the other.

1998

Gloria

Gloria wore bright red, skin-tight pants and a matching top for her first day en Nueva York. Negra spent weeks saving, sewing, and assembling the outfit. She made Dena a little dress too. It was all she could afford as a parting gift for her fiery daughter. Although Negra was tough on her kids, the thought of another one leaving made her more tender than usual.

"Para romper cuellos allá," she winked at Gloria playfully. Negra knew all of her kids inside out, every obsession—every tick. She knew her daughter spent years dreaming of this day, and she wanted her to go in style. "Te vas pero siempre tendrás tu ombligo sembrado acá. Siempre tendrás tu casa y tu familia," Negra said, squeezing her tightly goodbye. Gloria took in her mother's familiar scent of starchy, sticky fruit. It was the exact moment that she realized she would miss su vieja querida que jodía tanto. No one else knew Gloria as deeply, not even el pobre Antonio, who could barely keep up with her thoughts and mood swings.

Gloria, of course, made Antonio wear a matching red shirt on the flight. She wanted to make sure they landed en los

Estados Unidos with coordinating outfits that set the right tone. She insisted que esto iba a ser la mejor época de sus vidas.

They landed in JFK and waited for Julia outside. In her daydreams and nightmares, Gloria imagined that the best part of New York would be the views and the worst would be the cold. As it turned out, the cool air suited her. She was tired of sweating through every good outfit she put on. Meanwhile, JFK was horrendously gray and gloomy. She couldn't believe it was the arrival port to the greatest city in the world. The drive was similarly depressing, with traffic worse than la Capital because people in New York waited respectfully behind each other and moved demasiado lento. The City itself looked good from a distance: tall skyscrapers glistening in the afternoon light, reflecting the perfectly blue sky. But up close, it was filthy, dirtier than la finca but no open field in sight. She looked over at Julia a couple of times, double-checking that it wasn't a mistake and that this was, in fact, the magical place she had heard all about. But Julia was too obsessed with the baby to notice.

"¡Llegamos!" Julia pointed to the building as the driver slowed down.

Gloria did everything she could not to look disappointed. Her sister had been working for nearly two years to get them green cards. This was her destiny. She would never go back to pounding batches of dulce into shape.

She stepped out of the car cautiously. The concrete was uneven and unfamiliar. The street was full of people determined to get somewhere. She looked at Antonio's watch and wondered where everyone could be rushing to at six in the afternoon. This was the time everyone back home was descansando en una mecedora. She took Dena out of the car while Antonio grabbed their maletas. Julia paid and thanked the taxi driver.

"Me avisas si necesitas algo," he said from the driver's seat. Julia nodded and waved goodbye.

"¿Se parece buena gente, no?" Julia asked her younger sister.

"¿Por qué? ¿Te gusta? ¿No e un poco viejo?"

"Salí con su hijo hace una semana y creo que lo voy a ver otra vez." Julia was strangely giddy. The only things that made her that happy were organizing and ordering people around.

"¿'Su hijo'?"

"Sí, cuando lo llamé hace dos semanas y le dije que te tenía que recoger, el me mencionó su hijo. Ya van como tres veces que lo hace. Me dijo que pudiéramos hacer algo tranquilos… e'to y lo otro." Julia had been waiting the entire car ride to spill. He was Tía Estefany's go-to driver, a fellow Dominican York from the neighborhood. Julia had only used him a couple of times, but it was enough for him to mention his young, hardworking son, Hernando. "Entonces, le dije que sí, está bien. Salí con él a ver una película sobre animales. 'Yuro'…'Yurassin'… Algo así. Dique en la selva. ¿Te imaginas?" She looked at Gloria, who was more confused than before. They were still outside, and Julia was going on and on.

"Sí. Mira, hablamos de todo eso pero primero, ábreme la puerta que esta niña pesa," Gloria said, looking at the door. Julia frowned. She was desperate to have someone around to gossip with, help her cook, and pass the time. It was harder making friends in America than she imagined. For all the people who passed her on the street, almost none actually spoke to her. Usually, it was only older women or kids or guys making slick remarks. Tía's kids offered to take her out, but she hated their loud friends who only wanted to complain about the very city she desperately clung to.

"Entramos entonces." Julia pulled out two sets of keys and gave one to her younger sister.

"Estas son las tuyas. Te las voy a enseñar a usar." She walked up to the front door of the building and pulled out the largest key in the bunch. "Esta es para la puerta de afuera." Gloria and Antonio watched as she turned the key.

"¿Ven estos botones? El de nosotros es el 4B. Si alguien viene, ellos le tocan aquí para llamar para allá arriba. Te enseño arriba como funciona." She pressed the button and Gloria jumped at the sound of the buzzer.

"Que sonido má fuerte."

"Acostúmbrate."

The walls inside were covered with thick beige paint. Only one frosted glass window leaked light into the lobby, and it faced a solid brick wall. The floor was covered with thousands of dirty one-inch tiles, mostly white with black ones bordering the walls. A large chandelier, which looked more dusty than luxurious, hung from the center of the ceiling.

"Esta llave es para el correo." Julia held up the smallest key and pointed towards the wall on the right that held two rows of twenty chrome-colored mailboxes. She inserted the key into the 4B slot, opening it to reveal a narrow, empty box.

"Vamos para arriba," Julia pointed to a dark gray elevator.

"Pero no cabemos. ¿No hay otro?" Gloria asked.

"No, tal vez cuando somos ricas compramos uno." Apparently, America taught Julia sarcasm. They pushed the suitcases towards the elevator walls and squeezed inside, shoulder to shoulder. It made a horrible screeching sound as it jolted. Upstairs, Julia pulled the keys out again.

"Esta es la llave de esta puerta."

"Julia, pero yo sé cómo usar una llave," Gloria said finally.

"Aha, ¿pero quieres que entremos o no? Porque si quieres entrar, la tengo que usar." Julia gave her sister a dirty look. It had been almost two years since they last saw each other, and Gloria was just as impatient.

"Y esto es la casa." She opened the door to reveal a white, boxy apartment that smelled like cheap vanilla air freshener masking sazón.

"¿Cocinaste?" Gloria asked, officially impressed.

"Sí, claro. Ahora, les enseño la casa."

Gloria passed the baby, who was just waking up from her car nap, to Antonio and followed her sister. He remained quiet, taking everything in with wide eyes and a bright smile.

Julia had only been in America for four years. She sent most of her paychecks back home and saved any spare change in glass jars. It was a miracle she could save up enough money to leave Tía Estefany's house. She only risked it because her boss promised Gloria and Antonio jobs at the supermarket upon landing. She was proud of the small home she was able to secure for them. Julia was nothing if not an older sister eager to provide.

"Esto es la sala." She spread her arms out wide and nearly touched the walls on either side of her.

"Por aquí es la cocina." She walked over to the left, where a tiny kitchen held a fridge, an electric stove, and enough counter space for exactly three plates side by side.

"¿Y eso es una estufa?" Gloria had never seen someone cook without fire.

"Sí, te la enseño a usar ahorita." Julia was out of the room before Gloria could ask another question. "Por aquí…" Julia's voice faded as she went down the elongated hallway. "…está la primera habitación. Esta es la mía, como es más pequeña." She swung the door open. Gloria poked her head inside. It was smaller than her room back home.

"Aquí está el baño." She opened the next doorway. "Esto es el closet." She pointed to the third door down the hall. "Es para las toallas, sabanas y cosas de la casa." Gloria looked inside and saw that every shelf was empty except one, which held a set of sheets and three towels.

"Y por aquí está la habitación de ustedes." The last doorway sat at the end of the hallway. Julia let Antonio, who had moved himself ahead on the tour, open it up. He seemed pleased with the queen-size bed and single window.

"¿Te gusta, bebé?" Antonio asked Dena as he bounced her in his arms. "Aquí vas a vivir ahora. ¡En Nueva York!" He shouted triumphantly. Antonio had been waiting a long time for this day. His marriage to Gloria had been strained over the last year. He watched her transform drastically after giving birth. No longer carefree, she was protective, easily irritated, tense. She hated living with his family but refused to return to her family's house. This was different. Here, they could build their own life together. Antonio believed New York could grant Gloria the freedom she sought, offer them fabulous adventures, fix everything wrong between them. They just needed time.

Gloria stepped into the room and saw that the firescape she had seen downstairs was just outside her window. The room was brightly lit. The bed was pushed up against a corner, leaving a large empty area in the center of the room. It was surprisingly spacious.

"Empuje la cama a la pared porque así tienen espacio para una cuna para la bebé. Le he preguntado a varias personas por aquí a ver si alguien puede regalar una usada o venderla más barato," Julia said, excitedly. "Este closet es para la ropa. Por ahora, no tienen un bureau o gavetas pero creo que lo que tienen puede caber." Again, Gloria looked inside to find an empty closet. "Pero el espacio da." Julia looked back at them, waiting for their nod of approval. She knew Gloria was picky and stubborn. She hoped America would cast a spell on her, charm her. She also believed that New York could make everything better in time.

"Está perfecto. Muchas gracias, Julia. Yo sé que trabajaste mucho para todo esto," Antonio said, smiling giddily along with Dena.

"Sí... ¿Y no lleva llave el closet?" Gloria asked.

"No, aquí no se usan llaves para los closets. Además, no hay tanto para robar tampoco," Julia laughed awkwardly. Gloria was grateful that she had left her old journal hidden in her parents' home. There was no room for secrets in this apartment except the one that kept gnawing at her from the pit of her belly.

"Gracias, Julia. Todo se ve muy bien," Gloria reassured her, hoping they could let go of all their formalities and finally relax. "Entonces...¿la comida?"

"Sí, vengan." In the kitchen, Julia opened up two large tupperware containers full of rice and chicken. "De verdad, Tía cocinó. Casi no tengo tiempo con el trabajo y ella cocina mejor que yo."

"¡Lo sabía!" Gloria laughed and smacked Julia's arm. "¿No tienes guineo o aguacate?" She looked around the cabinets. They were almost as empty as the closets.

"No, pero si quieres, te doy dinero y puedes bajar a comprarlo'. Me quedo aquí a calentar esto, que se enfrió." She went to get her wallet from the purse in the living room.

"¿Abajo?" Gloria, in her fire-red outfit, looked more nervous than Julia had ever seen her.

"Pero eso queda ahí mismo." She couldn't believe a mundane task like buying fruit would overwhelm Gloria.

"¿Y hablan español?" Gloria was also taken aback by her sudden anxiety. The dark shadows cast from the buildings mixed with the unfamiliar scents in the street made her uncomfortable. She didn't like being sent out alone on her first day, but she would not admit it either.

"Casi todo el mundo en este barrio habla español. Hasta los letreros están en español. Si no sabes algo, le puedes preguntar a cualquiera," Julia said, pouring food into a large pan to heat it up. "Cuando salgas, vas a tomar una izquierda. Ahí en la esquina hay un colmado. Aquí se dice 'bodega'. El señor que trabaja ahí se llama Pipo. Dile que eres mi hermana. Él te ayuda." She placed three dollars in Gloria's hand and pushed her gently towards the door.

Gloria repeated the instructions over and over again in her head: down the stairs, take a left, head to the colmado, and if there's a problem, talk to Pipo.

The bodega looked like a colmado back home, except most things were on her side of the counter and had English labels.

She lingered in the aisles perusing the foreign products. She did not intend to buy anything extra, as she learned early on to never do anything more or less than what Julia instructed. In the back, she found a pile of mangos stacked in a crate, begging to be cut into. She grabbed one, hoping Julia would accept it as her own "welcome-to-America-I-know-you-miss-home" gift to herself. At the front, she looked up to find a young guy about her age manning the register.

"¿Pipo?" She asked, placing her items on the counter.

"No, Pipo es el dueño. Soy Juan." He smiled at her.

"¡Tengo un hermano que se llama así!" She said more excited than even she expected. Maybe this was a Dominican barrio after all.

"¿De dónde eres?" He looked at her curiously, ringing up the items slower than he needed to.

"De la República Dominicana. ¿Y tú? ¿Eres de allá también?" She was uncontrollably flirtatious, though her pants did most of the talking.

"No, de Puerto Rico." His smile matched the white undershirt peeking out from under his oversized jersey. "¿Nunca has ido?"

"No, todavía no."

"Bueno, señorita, eso será $3.55. Debes ir a ver mi tierra. Es hermoso."

"El mío también." She smirked and pulled out the money Julia gave her. "Coño…solo tengo tres." She looked at the three items and couldn't believe they cost so much. Back home, she could get a dozen of each for less.

"¿Sabes qué? Te regalo el mango. Algo dulce de bienvenida." He smiled at her again and handed her a white plastic bag with red letters on the front.

" 'Tank ju,' " she tried to read the bag out loud. He laughed at her attempts.

"De nada." He winked.

Upstairs, Julia begrudgingly accepted the fact that Gloria had spent all the money she had given her. They ate Tía Estefany's food with the sounds of the city echoing in the background. Julia didn't have a TV yet, not even a radio. Their only source of entertainment was screaming sirens and bickering neighbors. After they ate, Gloria went into the kitchen and picked up the mango, squeezing it all around.

"Vamos a ver si en dos o tre' día' estará para comer."

"Nunca va a estar," Julia explained. "Algunas cosas aquí no valen la pena. Tienes que poner atención a lo que es necesario y lo que no vale," she said. Gloria couldn't tell if she was cautioning her from careless budgeting, dreadful food, or something else. "Cuando vienes a ver, gastas un cheque entero en comida que a veces ni sale buena. Mira ese mango," she pointed to Gloria's newly purchased fruit. She held it vertically on a cutting board and slid a knife across the front. Gloria picked up the fallen piece, hoping to suck on it just as she did back home, but the fruit was pale and dry. She nearly spit it out after taking a bite. It was the least juicy mango she had ever tasted.

"¿Tú ves?" Julia sighed. "Un peso por eso. Mejor no como mango," she shook her head, mostly disappointed by a wasted dollar.

Gloria felt her stomach cramp up as she attempted to eat another bite of the mango. Again, that sinking feeling. "Me voy a acostarme." She went to the bedroom to lie down. She faked being asleep so her sister and Antonio would grant her a moment of solitude. Lying on the thin, foreign mattress, staring out at the fire escape that looked more like a cage from her angle on the bed, she daydreamed of being back at la finca. She couldn't help herself. The images flickered in her mind like a lullaby. She pictured the creek teasing her toes as it raced by, Marcelo holding her hand as she led him upstream, dried leaves gently falling all around them, sunlight trickling in from the canopy of cohoba above.

Sunset filled the room with a tangerine light. She turned away from the open window and placed her hands on her belly. She felt a lump in her throat along with a small thump beneath her fingertips. She wasn't sure who was responsible for this new life, but it didn't matter. She had made her choice.

Day Nine

Dena

Tía Julia, a light sleeper, opened the door first. Somehow, the crowd on the bridge managed to put Dena in a car and take her home against her howling protests.

"Jess...Mami...Papi..." Dena collapsed into a corner of the living room and mumbled to herself as tears streamed down her face. "Jess...Mami...Papi..." She repeated as if at any moment, they would burst into the room and remind her she was not alone. Her aunts tried one by one to dry Dena's cheeks, rub her back, and carry her shame, but none of them pudo lograr nada. She was inconsolable, squeezing all the tears from her eyes like a ripe limón. She heaved until the air wheezing through her was only a whisper. Her aunts, however, remained steadfast, unwilling to fold or cry until they had definitive answers.

Julia called an old friend, the chief of police, to get further information on Jess. Sol called a couple of the guys from around town to find out what Dena had been up to, since she was incoherent. Candy called Rosaly. Flaca called Manny. Within thirty minutes, the house had a dozen people, both family and friends, reporting everything they knew.

247

Across town, Ariel led a group of four men down to the river to rescue Jess. Their path was lit by flashlights, cell phone lights, and slick boulders reflecting moonlight. They found her tucked between the exposed roots of a massive ceiba tree, as if she were taking a brief nap from this world. Despite her condition: wet, scratched up, and unconscious, they found a pulse steadily beating beneath the tender skin on her neck. They carried her out carefully, so as to not tumble back into the roaring river, then delivered her to the small medical center in town.

Ariel called Julia first, la jefa de la casa Vega. She declared it "un milagro de la gloria de Dios." Candy believed it was Jess's guardian angels watching over her. Flaca, a more practical sister, said the water had been deep enough after the rain to catch her fall. Sol kept her thoughts to herself and brewed more coffee. And for the first time all week, Dena became still.

Hours later, surrounded by cheap hospital cords and wrapped in low-count thread sheets, Jess muttered her first word of the day. "Dena."

She caught a glimpse of a dark blur in the midst of a glaring white light and hoped it was her. Dena had been slumped over the side of a hard plastic chair since three o'clock in the morning. The previous highs and lows of horror and relief eventually steadied into a neutral numbness. She waited for hours, hoping to hear any sound from her sister. As soon as she heard her name out loud, she threw herself on top of her, eyes welling with tears.

"Are you crying?" Jess croaked.

"Are you kidding?" Dena wiped her eyes with the back of her hand.

"What happened?" Sombra was suddenly aware of all the tubes around her. "I went out...then..."

"You don't remember?" Dena stood up, arms hugging her own body.

"The bridge...I think...But the water..." She closed her eyes, trying to remember. "I couldn't see..."

"You fell...or you..." Dena couldn't bring herself to suggest the other thing...the thing that had been eating away at her since the moment she saw her sister's white T-shirt from thirty feet above.

"I fell," she confirmed. They looked at each other. There were some things they didn't dare say out loud, but could communicate in silence.

"You fell," Dena finally went to touch her sister's arm. Jess looked down and saw the scars. She trembled at the sight of them. The roots of the tree cut into her as she grabbed them to climb out of the water.

"Mami would have come back to life and killed me if something happened to you," Dena joked. Jess tried to laugh, but her voice was too hoarse. Choking on the Camú waters made her more ronca than Flaca had been all week. Dena passed her a cup of water.

"Yeah. And the tías?"

"Don't worry. They're outside. You should have seen them! I swear they've been through this before because I've never seen them so organized." If there was one thing they could agree on, it was how synchronized their aunts were. "I have to tell you something," Dena thought about this moment carefully all night. She considered keeping it to herself, sparing Jess more agony after her accident. But she didn't want to keep secrets, remain guarded, hold back. If she were getting another chance with her sister, then she would tell her the truth.

"I know this is a horrible day, and you literally almost... you know..." She inhaled deeply before going on. "But yesterday, I went out to Jarabacoa with Ariel."

"Yeah, I saw."

"And I…" Dena couldn't get herself to look Jess in the eye. Suddenly, she was angry at her mother all over again. Here she was, delivering the most challenging news of her life to the most precious person in it.

"I know what it is," Jess whispered, barely audible through the beeping heart monitor.

"No, you don't." Dena's eyes swelled with tears again. Now that the waterworks started, she couldn't switch them off.

"I do." Jess nervously scrunched the sheets in her palms for comfort.

"What? No. How?"

"Mami," Jess said, her eyes full of tears as well. "She told me…sort of."

"What do you mean?" Dena said louder this time. "That's impossible. That would be crazy." Dena sat down, unwilling to accept her sister's revelation. Jess took another sip of water before going on.

"You know, she was in a bad place before she went." Jess wiped a tear slipping down her face. "Her emotions were all over the place. One moment she was laughing, then cursing, then telling me she loved me, then yelling at me. It was like she knew it was happening, but she didn't want to admit it."

"Yeah, I remember."

"One night, when we were alone, she just said 'Perdóname. Hay cosas en la vida que uno hace para proteger a los niños'."

"That's it?"

"That was the first time. Then…" More tears streamed down Jess's face. "The second time she said, 'Lo debes saber. Lo debes conocer…' I told her, 'Mami, está bien. No tienes que decirme nada'. She was crying, and you know she never ever cried. I said whatever I could to get her to stop. She handed me a paper with an address, and I had this sinking feeling when she placed it in my palm. Like she was confessing something big." Jess took a napkin off the bedside stand and wiped her face before continuing. "It took a few days before I considered that the 'lo' in 'lo debes conocer' meant I should know *him* not *it*. But I never brought it up again. She got mad if I asked her what she wanted for dinner. There was no way I was going to ask about this." She gulped more water to coax her scratchy throat.

"I always felt something was off, but I told myself it was just me. I was the weird one in the family. My hair didn't curl like yours, I wasn't as light-skinned as Papi, my body didn't curve like Mami's. Dominican families are like that: all different shapes and sizes, right? That's what I told myself. I didn't want to think about it. Not *really*. Because then, everything would change. And everything had been hard enough as is..." Jess's voice got quieter the more she spoke. Dena took measured breaths, trying to follow along without freaking out. It was the most her sister had spoken aloud all week.

"I kept the address in my wallet. When we got here, you started asking a ton of questions and going out every day. I don't know if you realized, but I've been tracking your location for days." She looked up at her sister. Dena figured Jess would have looked, but not every day. Before she could defend herself, Jess spoke again. "You went to that address. I finally looked up the hotel, and I saw his face on the front page of the website. It was like a mirror staring back at me. My hazel eyes, thin face, brown skin—all *his*." She shivered.

"You're so calm right now. When I saw him, I thought I was going to throw up," Dena said, both hands on her face as if she needed help holding up her own head.

"I knew you figured it out when you didn't come home. You never missed an hora santa before," Jess said, shaking her head. "You don't have to protect me from this, you know."

"Mami's done some crazy things, but this..."

"Trust me, I get it. I'm angry. I feel like she had so many chances to tell me the truth. I mean, I deserved to know my father..." Jess took a deep breath in. "That we're not full sisters..."

"No. Don't say that. We *are* full sisters." She went to hold her sister's hand.

"She lied to me, to you, to Papí..." Jess said, wiping her eyes. "But at the same time, I could tell she was destroyed from keeping it to herself. You should have seen her face when she cried that day. It was like she hated herself."

"Wait...Is that why you've been so quiet and distant this past week?" Dena's mind started spinning, putting the pieces together. "This is so much worse than I imagined." She was mostly upset that she didn't see the signs sooner, didn't act faster, that she failed Jess. And what did this mean for them? "So now what? You forgive her? Just like that?" She slumped back down on the chair, unable to both pace the room and process all this new information.

"Nah. Calm down. I didn't say all that. But you act like everything she did was horrible, and it wasn't. She got married at nineteen and then went to a new country at twenty-one pregnant with a toddler. She moved away from her entire family. Think about how you were at that age. I'm not saying Mamí's perfect, she made a lot of mistakes, and I will definitely need therapy because of it. But this is my thing to work through, not yours." Jess was starting to get dizzy from all the emotions.

"So...Are you okay?"

"I don't know."

"Do you want to meet him?"

"I don't know," Jess repeated.

"Well, how can I help you?"

"Honestly, stop trying to help. Everything is not your problem to fix. Just take a seat."

"I am sitting." Dena pointed down to the chair beneath her.

"Seriously, Dena. Let it go. Whatever you're holding onto, all that resentment and rage, you gotta let that shit go, or it's gonna eat you alive." Jess paused to see if her sister was really listening. "You don't want to be Mami, literally sick to death but too prideful to say it. This is your chance to be happy. Like, actually happy."

"You mean with a guy?"

"Oh my God." Jess sighed and rubbed her temples with her fingertips. "No. I mean with your life."

"So, you almost died, and now you're the wisest one in the family?" Dena tried to lighten the mood.

"It's not hard. There aren't that many of us left," Jess momentarily played along. "Are you listening?"

"Yes. Yes, I'm listening," Dena sighed in equal measure. Their entire lives, they had been running from one tragedy to the next. In that quiet moment, they both wondered when they could finally catch their breath.

"I want to go home, man," Dena admitted.

"Same. But there's only one day left."

"Are you crazy?"

"You want to stay here for longer?"

"We can't leave. Look at where you are." Dena spread her arms as her eyes darted around the room. "The doctors said you'll be in here for at least another day. I already moved our flights and extended my time off work til next week. Actual time off." She went up to hold her sister's arm. Before Jess could respond, the door swung open, and the tías walked in unannounced.

"¡Ay, mija! Que Dios me perdone!" Flaca came in first. She spread her arms wide around Jess, slightly tugging at the IV.

"¡Ay, mija!! Que milagro de Dios!!" Julia followed, her glasses nearly falling off her face, rosary beads tightly coiled around her right hand, her left hand pressed to her heart.

"¡Dios mío!" Candy came in last, holding several Tupperware containers full of food. "Traje esto, porque la comida aquí no sirve." She put her index finger over her lips, indicating this secret stayed between them.

"Pero Candy, deja eso y ven hablar con la niña," Flaca swatted her sister towards her. The three tías crowded around Jess, kissing her hands, brushing her hair, tucking her into her sheets.

"Tía, estoy bien," Jess spoke to the group as if they were one person.

"¡Y ese assusto que no' di'te!" Flaca sounded a tinge more irritated than relieved.

"No, no, gracias a Dios que estás bien." Julia pointed towards the ceiling with open palms.

"Sí, mi hija. Gracias a Dios." Candy went to fill a plate of food for her niece to hide the tears falling from her face. Group hugs were not common in la familia Vega, but just standing in the hospital room felt as if they were in one. They all looked around at each other, tears in their eyes. If Gloria had been present—and it almost felt as if she was—she would have broken the silence with a joke to relieve the tension.

"Gracias por ayudar y hacer todo esta semana," Dena said, looking around at her aunts, admiring their sense of calm.

"Ay, mija, eso es lo de menos. Tu mamá hubiera hecho lo mismo," Tía Julia said, extending her arm towards Dena.

"Yo sé, Tía. Pero también sé que no era fácil."

They smiled back at her for about ten seconds before listing everything they had to do for the day. For the next hour, they buzzed around the room with an anxious energy that reminded Dena of her mother. On any given Sunday, when the rest of the world was resting or praising, her mother was finding reasons to bounce off the walls.

"Déjame llamar allá abajo a ver si tiene el pedido de la comida hecha ya," Flaca reached for her phone.

"Sí, dile que te lo repite dos veces para que no nos haga lo que le hizo al vecino los otros día' que se le olvidó la mitad del pedido," declared no-nonsense Julia.

"Buena idea. Esa mujer se le tá olvidando todo última-mente." Flaca started dialing.

"Voy a mandarle un mensaje a Sol a ver si los muchachos trajeron todas las sillas del otro día," said Candy, swiping through her phone.

"Y tú…vete a descansar que nosotras hacemos todo," Julia ordered Dena. The tías walked out united by their shared sense of purpose. If there was work to be done, they would do it together.

The earth does not judge in any language, yet Dena felt emba-rrassed in two. She spent the morning nervous to face everyone attending the last hora santa. She thought about the bridge, how exposed she had been, an open wound on the open road. She was sure the crowd would mock her agony, which seemed exaggerated and unnecessary now that Jess was alive. But those were her biases, not theirs. The same faces from earlier looked at her with warmth. For the first time since arriving, she began paying attention to what they were saying.

"Te entiendo. También perdí a mi mamá."

"Nunca se siente igual."

"Diablo. Todo esto cansa."

"Debes descansar."

"Tantas lágrimas. Hace falta reír un poco."

Everywhere she turned, someone was picking up an empty cup, passing around a plate, splitting a dulce, telling a story while pantomiming the essential details like only Dominicans can. She could barely remember half their names, but she grew to enjoy the murmur of all their voices talking at once, the way their subtle chaos lit up the room, the irreplaceable solace of talking to people who knew her mother.

Since it was the last hora santa, more guests came than any day before—notably, a lot more men. Dena was relieved to see

255

Ariel walk in beside his tía, dressed in black slacks and a white polo. She blushed when he hugged her.

"¿Cómo estás?" She wasn't exactly sure what to say.

"Bien. Te traje algo. No sé si te lo doy ahora o después."

"Ahora." She followed him as he walked out past the front gate. He pointed down to a skinny, three-foot-tall plant. Its tangled roots were covered in soil and wrapped in a thick plastic bag.

"Es una mata de la Gloria."

It was a dark green plant with pointy leaves. Little buds and royal purple flowers bloomed from its stems. She had never heard of it before, but she knew her mother would have loved it.

"Wow. Es hermosa."

"Te mando instrucciones para sembrarla, si quieres," he offered when she let go.

"Gracias." She fiddled with her hands as she spoke. "Mira, lo de anoche…"

"Olvídate de eso," he tried to ease the awkward tension.

"Me querías ayudar…y te empujé…y lloré…y…"

"Dena, no tienes que pedir perdón por llorar," he said simply.

"Yo sé, pero no es eso. Te quería decir gracias por todo lo que has hecho. Sé que te pedí mucho y me ayudaste tanto."

"Bueno, fue divertido también." His eyes glistened. He wanted to grab her hands and steady them, but he knew to keep a healthy distance from her. If he learned anything about her, it was that she was a private woman. And the whole town was an arm's length away.

"Claro, ¿divertido cuando casi me ahogué?"

"Deja eso, muchacha. No tiene' que tener vergüenza. A todos no' ha pasado eso," he assured her.

"¿Te has ahogado?"

"En agua, no. Pero en la vida, sí." His words were heavy, but he maintained a flirtatious smile.

"En serio. Gracias por todo. Me has ayudado más de lo que sabes."

"Entonces me debes," he teased.

"¿Y qué pasó con 'a la orden' y 'no te preocupes'?'"

"Mira, lo único que te pido…" For the first time, he was asking for something instead of the other way around. "es que regreses." His body language was calm, but his eyes pleaded with her. She nodded before tucking herself back into his arms, not caring who saw.

"Bueno, me tengo que ir. Pero nos vemos, Dena," he said, letting her go.

When all the guests had finally departed, Dena found her aunts in the marquesina.

"Ponte las pilas y vamos a comenzar a limpiar," Julia ordered Flaca. Below Julia's shorts, her varicose veins painted a map of hard work on her legs, outlining decades of dedicated labor all in the name of love. They marked her exhausted, and yet she wanted to do more.

"¡Anda la porra! Tú si jodes. Me duelen las rodillas y dice mi doctor que cada año tengo que cogerlo más suave," Flaca declared, elevating her feet on another chair. Her voice was barely audible now after the final hora santa. She struggled to string together her syllables, tighten her chest, make herself heard. Yet she went on, "mira, e'ta muchacha aquí tiene casi do' semana' andando pa'rriba y pa'bajo. Ella quiere limpiar. ¿No e verdad?" Flaca grinned at Dena.

"Sí, claro." Dena took the hint and got up to clean, leaving her aunts to rest in their rocking chairs. When she was done, she walked around the house, deciding where to plant the Gloria bush. A week ago, she thought they yard was run-down and messy. Now, she understood that every dead organism fueled the living and every plant was intentionally placed there by someone in her family. It was in her blood to get her hands dirty and sow fruit she might never enjoy.

She walked until she came face to face with the old, wide mamey tree she had plucked dry just a couple of days earlier. She considered placing the plant there, since she knew her mother loved it. But the Gloria plant needed full sunlight. It belonged in the front yard, where everyone who passed by could see its bright flowers in bloom.

Dena held out her palm and ran it across the trunk of the tree, poking the bits of fruit she had smashed into the tree two nights before, which had hardened and faded. She picked a new fruit, this time feeling around to make sure it was ripe. She yanked it off and poked her index finger inside the peel. The flesh was a bright red-orange.

She sank her teeth in slowly. Suddenly, she envisioned her mother playing by a creek, following a skinny morenito, whose eyes looked just like her sister's. She could hear her mother's laugh echo as the boy nearly tripped back into a tree. She could hear splashing as they dipped their toes in the water. She took a larger bite and saw Gloria working all day, sticky juice clogging her pores. Her eyes were tired, her body weak, her hands dirty. Another bite, and she saw her mother crying, bleeding, and falling on a dark night. Loss after loss, Dena's body ached in all the same places, as if the memory had been stored in her own body. She feared taking another bite. Just as reading the diary, the visions began to feel intrusive.

She dropped the fruit and placed her palm on the tree's trunk—feeling the ridges as they rose and fell beneath her fingertips—knowing it held memories her mother could not withstand to hold alone.

One Week Later

Dena

La finca de la familia Vega was three miles from Abuela's house. It was sprawled out in the open valley, with clear views of the surrounding mountains. The bordering land that had been purchased during Antonio and Gloria's union. It was still owned by Antonio's parents, who lived in Pennsylvania now. Theirs was the side that bordered the creek.

A couple of days after Jess had been discharged, she and Dena decided to invite their family there to eat and swim. The Vega siblings had not set foot on that part of the land in the three decades since it had been sold. The conquistadors left every Dominican jaded for generations to come. No one went on land that wasn't theirs, not without asking and not without good reason. The girls finally offered them a reason.

They packed their cars and drove down the grassy slope towards the creek. Everyone carried what they could from the car to the edge of the water. Manny held onto the massive olla of pollo guisado. Dena carried trays of cooked rice and sides, fearful a tía would lose her balance crossing the slippery rocks. By the water, Tío Johnny set up the fire, Tía Candy got to work on cooking, and Tía Julia chased everyone around with a bottle

259

of SPF 50 sunscreen, even though the dense forest foliage kept them mostly hidden from the sun. Jess watched them all, taking photos to paint when she returned home.

"Prima, ¿pero para qué quieres fotos del río? ¿Qué va' a hacer con eso?" Manny asked, taking off his shoes and getting ready to jump in. "Mejor métete en la agua." He tossed his phone to the side and hopped into the water.

Jess put her camera down to sit on the rocky bank and dip her feet in the water. When they were kids, Dena always recruited her to beg their parents to go to the beach. But Jess wanted to go to the river. She loved the colors, tones, dark forests, and shallow edges. She loved that they constantly expanded and carried tiny particles of land everywhere they went. Even after her accident, the rushing water tickling her toes made her feel at peace. Rivers were ferocious, but they were forgiving, loving, and playful too.

"Tírate!" Dena said, sitting down beside her.

"¡Tírate tú!" Jess pushed her sister's shoulder towards the water. "I'm enjoying this."

"What? Doing nothing?"

"Yeah. Exactly. You should try it sometime. You always gotta run around and do something." She quipped. Dena rolled her eyes in response. "There's something I've been meaning to tell you," Jess lowered her voice so no one else could hear.

"What is it? I can't handle more surprises. I'm at capacity for this trip."

"I'm gonna stay here longer."

"In DR?"

"Yeah. Before you say that's crazy and I shouldn't..."

"I think that's a great idea."

"You do? I thought you said we should start traveling to new places, stop spending time here, explore..."

"Yeah...I was wrong." Dena paused for added dramatic effect. "I really liked seeing new places while I was here. And I think you will too. You just have to get out of your head and go outside." Dena tapped her sister's temple with her index finger. Jess swatted her away like a bug.

"Okay, okay. I get it." Jess grew quiet again.

"What are you thinking about?"

"The girls at the salon said they can take over my regulars until I'm back. Tía Candy said she would check up on the apartment and water the plants. Tía Julia told me I can stay in Abuela's house as long as I want."

"I'm not hearing the problem, girl."

Jess hesitated saying her next sentence. "I think I want to try to meet him."

"Oh my god…Okay…" Dena was at a loss for words.

"I know…But I feel like if I don't try now, I'll keep ignoring it. I'll go home, get back to my life, and pretend like none of this happened. And who knows for how long. Look at Mami, she spent twenty-five years ignoring it."

"Do you want me to stay?"

"No, you can't. You have work to get back to. I gotta do this myself." Jess dipped her fingertips in the water and played with the droplets, using her senses to stay grounded. "I don't know… Maybe this is absolutely insane. I might change my mind. But I should try… I want to try." She wasn't sure if she was trying to convince Dena or herself.

"I'm happy for you, seriously. Whatever you need, I'm just a call away." Dena hugged her extra tightly. When she pulled away, she wiped an eminent tear off the corner of Jess's hazel eye. "Enough tears. Let's get in!" Dena pulled off her dress and hopped across a couple of rocks. She thought about her mother every time they went to the river. Gloria always dunked her whole body in one leap. She counted down from three and did the same. The water swooshed all around her. It was refreshing on the hot summer day. She imagined her mother splashing around with a boy she liked. Then, just a couple of years later, having to carry two screaming toddlers up and down subway stairs, her entire world turned on its head. How challenging it must have been for Gloria, a heartbroken kid who left her glorious homeland behind in search of something better. This land held the buried dreams of her potential lives.

Dena crouched down on a flat rock and ran her fingers across the top of the water. The speckled sunlight sparkled on her skin. The air smelled like spring water, hibiscus, and smoke. She knew this was what her mother craved: carefree afternoons outside.

It was the first day of the whole trip that Dena wasn't chasing after someone—not Minerva, not Marcelo, not even Ariel. She looked around at her family scattered across the jungle. Tía Candy was cooking food over the fire. Sol and Flaca were sipping cervezas and gossiping beneath the shade of swaying branches. Julia had her glasses folded in her lap, her eyes peacefully closed. Tía Rosaly was washing Tío Johnny's hair in the water, her fingers rubbed against his scalp. Manny was splashing around, looking for freshwater crabs upstream.

She thought of her mother twisting the branches that lit the fire en el fogón, laughing loudly as she sipped her drink, jumping into the river like she was born from it. Gloria was all around her: the emerald green leaves, the echoes of chirping birds, the mist expelled from the waterfall, the mud that dried between her toes.

Acknowledgements

The idea to write this novel came to me when my abuelo was diagnosed with cancer eleven years ago. Watching him take his last breath was both humbling and transformative.

I lost many family members in the years I spent working on this novel. They inspired some of the characters, and exuded the kind of wisdom, strength, and effortless joy that comes from a lifetime spent on our sunny little island. RIP Patecuca, Tío Martin, Doña Rosa, Tía Patria, Tío Golo y Tío Jorge.

Thank you to the rest of my 100+ family members, who have filled my life with vivid technicolor and provided many quotes & phrases. This book would not exist without you.

Special shout out to my cousin Milka, who was the first person to ever read this story and spent countless hours with me discussing ideas, Dominicanisms, and nuanced character subplots. Thank you for your honesty and brilliance.

Massive thank you to my incredibly talented editor, Amanda M. Ortiz, who understood my vision from the beginning and worked meticulously for months. I am a better writer because of your suggestions and expertise.

Thank you to the Dominican Writers Association for the resources, events, and community. The 2023 DWA Writers Retreat changed me as a writer and this story.

Thank you to my beta readers Diany, Marilyn, Yamberlie, Arlenys, and my friend Amanda. I hope you enjoy how the book has evolved after your invaluable feedback.

Thank you to Jenn for gifting me an office space to work.

Thank you to Olumide for talking me down after I burst into tears, nervous about releasing this into the world.

Thank you to my parents, who (unknowingly) provided a lot of information for this book.

Thank you to my sisters, who respected my privacy as I locked myself in my room for days/weeks/months to write. Thank you for keeping me grounded and letting me use your cars.

Thank you to the lovely city of Buenos Aires, where I wrote the first and second drafts, and all the friends I made there.

Thank you to la República Dominicana y los Dominicanos, who inspire me every day.

Thank you to the hummingbirds.

About the Author

Anny Caba is a Dominican American writer, graphic designer y aventurera based in New Jersey. On her blog, *Anny Abroad*, she shares tips, guides, and her misadventures on the road. Her work has been featured on *Spanglish Voces, Business Insider,* and *Trails Magazine*. Her goal is to empower others—especially women—to step outside of their comfort zones and discover new places. *Mamey* is her debut novel.

Learn more on **AnnyCaba.com** & **@Anny.Abroad**